I0749249

SON OF POWER

WILL LEVINGTON COMFORT
and ZAMIN KI DOST

Son of Power

Will Levington Comfort and Zamin Ki Dost

PO Box 2211
Fairfield, IA 52556
www.1stworldlibrary.com
First Edition

LCCN: 2007920706

Softcover ISBN: 978-1-4218-4019-2
Hardcover ISBN: 978-1-4218-3919-6
eBook ISBN: 978-1-4218-4119-9

1st World Library Literary Society

Giving Back to the World

"If you want to work on the core problem, it's early school literacy."

- James Barksdale, former CEO of Netscape

"No skill is more crucial to the future of a child, or to a democratic and prosperous society, than literacy."

- Los Angeles Times

Literacy... means far more than learning how to read and write... The aim is to transmit... knowledge and promote social participation."

- UNESCO

"Literacy is not a luxury, it is a right and a responsibility. If our world is to meet the challenges of the twenty-first century we must harness the energy and creativity of all our citizens."

- President Bill Clinton

"Parents should be encouraged to read to their children, and teachers should be equipped with all available techniques for teaching literacy, so the varying needs and capacities of individual kids can be taken into account."

- Hugh Mackay

PUBLISHER'S NOTE

Zamin Ki Dost is a title given to one who lived in India many years—from the time when she was little more than a child. The tale of tales would be her own story. Her name is WILLIMINA L. ARMSTRONG

CONTENTS

CHAPTER I

THE GOOD GREY NERVE

His name was Sanford Hantee, but you will hear that only occasionally, for the boys of the back streets called him Skag, which "got" him somewhere at once. That was in Chicago. He was eleven years old, when he wandered quite alone to Lincoln Park Zoo, and the madness took him.

A silent madness. It flooded over him like a river. If any one had noticed, it would have appeared that Skag's eyes changed. Always he quite contained himself, but his lips stirred to speech even less after that. He didn't pretend to go to school the next day; in fact, the spell wasn't broken until nearly a week afterward, when the keeper of the Monkey House pointed Skag out to a policeman, saying the boy had been on the grounds the full seven open hours for four straight days that he knew of.

Skag wasn't a liar. He had never "skipped" school before, but the Zoo had him utterly. He was powerless against himself. Some bigger force, represented by a truant officer, was necessary to keep him away from those cages. His father got down to business and gave him a beating—much against that good man's heart. (Skag's father was a Northern European who kept a fruit-store down on Waspen street—a mildly-flavoured man and rotund. His mother was a Mediterranean woman, who loved and clung.)

But Skag went back to the Zoo. For three days more he went, remained from opening to closing time. He seemed to fall into deep absorptions—before tigers and monkeys especially. He didn't hear what went on around him. He did not appear to miss his lunch. You had to touch his shoulder to get his attention. The truant officer did this. It all led dismally to the Reform School from which Skag ran away.

He was gone three weeks and wouldn't have come back then, except his heart hurt about his mother. He felt the truth—that she was slowly dying without him. After that for awhile he kept away from the animals, because his mother loved and clung and cried, when he grew silently cold with revolt against a life not at all for him, or hot with hatred against the Reform School. Those were ragged months in which a less rubbery spirit might have been maimed, but the mother died before that actually happened. Skag was free—free the same night.

The father's real relation to him had ended with the beating. It was too bad, for there might have been a decent memory to build on. The fruit-dealer, however, had been badly frightened by the truant-officer (in the uniform of a patrolman), and he was just civilised enough to be a little ashamed that his boy could so far forget the world and all refined and mild-flavoured things, as to stare through bars at animals for seven hours a day. In the process of that beating, hell had opened for Skag. It was associated with the raw smell of blood and a thin red steam, a little hotter than blood-heat. It always came when he remembered his father. . . . But his mother meant lilacs. The top drawer of her dresser had been faintly magic of her. The smell came when he remembered her. It was like the first rains in the Lake Country.

But that was all put back. Skag was out in the world now, making it exactly to suit himself. He was in charge of himself in many ways. A glass of water and a sandwich would do for a long time, if necessary. . . . The West pulled him. Awhile in the mountains, he lived with a prospector; there was a period in the desert when he came to know lizards; then there were years of the circus, when he was out with the Cloud Brothers, animal men of the commercial type. Ten queer, hard years for the boy—as hard almost as for the animals.

Back in Chicago the caged creatures had been kept better—as well as beasts belonging to the outdoors could be imprisoned, but the Cloud Brothers didn't have fine senses like their charges. They tried to make wild animals live in a place ventilated for men. There was a bad death-percentage and none of the big cats were in show form, until the Clouds began to take Skag's word for the main thing wrong. It wasn't the hard life, nor the coops, nor the travel, but the steady day in and day out lack of fresh air. Skag knew what the animals suffered, because it all but murdered him on hot nights. Of course, there are tainted-flesh things like hyenas that live best on foul air, foul everything, but "white" animals of jungle and forest are high and cleanly beasts. When well and in their prime, even their coats are incapable of most kinds of dirt, because of a natural oily gloss.

At nineteen, Skag was in charge of the packing, moving and feeding of all the big cats, including pumas, panthers, leopards. He was in and out of the cages possibly more than was necessary. He learned that there are two ways to manage a wild animal—the "rough-neck" way with a club, and the fancy way with your own equilibrium; all of which comes in more to the point later.

He was interested at the time, but not really acquainted with the camels and elephants. He often chatted with Prussak, the Arab, who loathed camels to the shallow depths of his soul, but got as much out of them as most men could. Skag dreamed of a better way still, even with camels. Often on train-trips, at first, he talked with old Alec Binz, whose characteristic task was to chain and unchain the hind leg of the old "gunmetal" elephant, Phedra, who bossed her sire and the little Cloud herd, as much with the flap of an ear as anything else. . . .

No, old Alec must not be forgotten, nor his sandalwood chest with its little rose-jar in the corner, making everything smell so strangely sweet that it hurt. A girl of India had given Alec the jar twenty years before. The spirit of a real rose-jar never dies; and something of the girl's spirit was around it, too, as Alec talked softly. All this was unreservedly good to Skag—thrilling as certain few books and the top drawer that had been his mother's. . . . But something way back of that, utterly his own deep heart-business, was connected with the rose-jar. It was breathless like opening a telegram—its first scent after days or weeks. If you find any meaning to the way Skag expressed it, you are welcome:

"It makes you think of things you don't know—"

"But you will," Alec had once answered.

The more you knew, the more you favoured that old man of the circus company,—little gold ring in his ear and such tales of India!

It was Alec who led Skag into the fancy way of dealing with animals, but of course the boy was peculiar, inasmuch as he believed it all at once. Skag never ceased to think of it until it was his; he actually put it into practice. Alec might have told a dozen American trainers and have gotten no more than a yawp for his pains. This is one of the things Alec said:

"If you can get on top of the menagerie in your own insides, Skagee—the tigers and apes, the serpents and monkeys, in your own insides—you'll never get in bad with the Cloud Brothers wild animal show."

There wasn't a day or night for years that Skag didn't think of that saying. It was his secret theme. So far as he could see, it worked out. Of course, he found out many things for himself—one of which was that there is a smell about a man who is afraid, that the animals get it and become afraid, too. Alec agreed to this, but added that there is a smell about most men, when they are not afraid.

For hours they talked together about India—tiger hunts and the big Grass Jungle country in the Bund el Khand, until Skag couldn't wait any longer. He had to go to India. He told Alec, who wanted to go along, but couldn't leave old Phedra.

"I've been with her too long," he said. "She's delicate, Skagee. I'm young, but she couldn't stand it for me to go. Times are hard for her on the road, and the little herd needs her as she needs me. . . ."

Skag understood that. In fact, he loved it well. It belonged to his world—to be straight with the animals. Gradually as the distance increased between them, the memory of old Alec began to smell as sweet as the sandal-wood chest in Skag's nostrils—the chest and the rose-jar that never could die and the old friend became one identity. . . .

India didn't excite Skag, who was twenty-five by this time. In fact, some aspects of India were more natural to him than his own country. Many people did a lot of walking and they lived while they walked, instead of pushing forward in a tension to get somewhere. Skag approved emphatically of the Now. The present moving point was the best he had at any given time. He thought a man should forget himself in the Now like the animals.

Besides they didn't regulate dress in India; in fact, they dressed in so many different ways that a man could wear what he pleased without being stared at. Skag hated to be stared at above all things. You are beginning to get a picture of him now—unobtrusive, silent, strong in understanding, swift, actually in pain as the point of many eyes, altogether interested in his own unheard-of things.

Alec told him how to reach the jungle of all jungles, ever old, ever new, ever innocent on the outside, ever deadly within—the Grass Jungle country around Hattah and Bigawar—the Bund el Khand. The Cloud Brothers had paid him well for his years; there was still script in his clothes for travel, but Skag had a queer relation to money, only using it when the law required. Not a tight-wad, far from that, though he preferred to work for a meal than pay for it; much preferred to walk or ride than to purchase other people's energy, having much of his own.

He came at last to a village called Butthighur, near Makrai, north of the Mahadeo Mountains in the Central Provinces. On the first day, on the main road near the rest-house, there passed him on the street, a slim, slightly-stooped and spectacled young white man. The face under the huge cork helmet, Skag looked at twice, not knowing why altogether; then he followed leisurely to a bungalow, walked up the path to the steps and knocked. The stranger himself answered, before the servant could come. He looked Skag over, through spectacles that made his eyes appear insane, at times, and sometimes merely absurd. Finally he questioned with soft cheer:

"And what sort of a highbinder are you?"

Skag answered that he was an American, acquainted with wild animals in captivity, and that he had come to this place to know wild animals in the open.

"But why to me?" the white man asked.

"It seemed well. I have looked into many faces without asking anyone. There is no chance of working for the native people here. They are too many, and too poor."

"You do not talk like an American—"

"I do not like to talk."

The white man was puzzled by Skag's careful and exact statements and remarked presently:

"An American asking for work would say that he knew about

everything, instead of just animals in captivity."

"I have not asked for work before. I can do without it. I like it here near the forests."

"You mean the jungles—"

"I thought jungles were wet."

"In the wet season."

"Thank you—"

The slim one suddenly laughed aloud though not off-key:

"But I haven't any wild animals in captivity for you—"

Skag did not mind the mirth. He appreciated the smell of the house. It was like a hot earthen tea-pot that had been well-used.

"I will come again?" he asked tentatively.

"Just do that—at the rest-house. I drop in there after dinner—about nine."

That afternoon Skag went into the edge of the jungle. It was a breath of promised land to him. He was almost frightened with the joy of it—the deep leaf-etched shadows, the separate, almost reverent bird-notes; all spaciousness and age and dignity; leaves strange, dry paths, scents new to his nostrils, but having to do with joys and fears and restlessness his brain didn't know. Skag was glad deep. He took off his boots and then strode in deeper and deeper past the maze of paths. He stayed there until the yellow light was out of the sky. At the clearing again, he laughed—looked down at the turf and laughed. He had come out to the paths again at the exact point of his entry. This was his first deep breath of the jungle—something his soul had been waiting for.

At dinner in the village, Skag inquired about the white man. The native was serving him a curry with drift-white rice on plantain leaves. After that there was a sweetmeat made of curds of cream and honey, with the flavour and perfume of some altogether delectable flower. In good time the native replied that the white man's name was Cadman: that he was an American traveller and writer and artist, said to be almost illustrious; that he had been out recently with a party of English sportsmen, but found tiger-hunting dull after his many wars and adventures. Also, it was said, that Cadman Sahib had the coldest-blooded courage a man ever took into the jungle, almost like a *bhakti yogin* who had altogether conquered fear. Skag bowed in satisfaction. Had he not looked twice at the face under the helmet—and followed without words?

"How far do they go into the jungle for tigers?" he asked.

"An hour's journey, or a day, as it happens. Tigers are everywhere in season."

"Within an hour's walk?" Skag asked quietly. The other repeated his words in a voice that made Skag think of a grey old man, instead of the fat brown one before him.

"Within an hour's walk? Ha, Ji! They come to the edge of the village and slay the goats for food—and the sound cattle—and the children!"

Skag laughed inwardly, thinking how good it had been in the deep places. However, it was now plain that these native folk were afraid of tigers—afraid as of a sickness. He walked out into the street. Though dark, it was still hot, and the breeze brought the dry green of the jungle to him and life was altogether quite right.

That night he met Cadman Sahib. They talked until dawn. Skag was helpless before the other who made him tell all he knew, and much that had been nicely forgotten. Sometimes in the midst of one story, the great traveller would snap over a question about one Skag had already told. Then before he was answered fully, he would say briefly:

"That's all right—go on!"

". . . Behold a phenomenon!" he said at last. "Here is one not a liar, and smells have meanings for him, and he has come, beyond peradventure, to travel with me to the Monkey Forest and the Coldwater Ruins!"

It had been an altogether wonderful night for Skag. Talking made him very tired, as if part of him had gone forth; as if, having spoken, he would be called upon to make good in deeds. But he had not done all the talking and Cadman Sahib was no less before his eyes in the morning light—which is much to say for any man.

These two white men set out alone, facing one of the most dangerous of all known jungles. The few natives who understood, bade them good-bye for this earth.

Many stories about Cadman had come to Skag in the three or four days of preparation—altogether astonishing adventures of his quest for death, but there was no record of Cadman's choosing a friend, as he had done for this expedition. Skag never ceased to marvel at the sudden softenings, so singularly attractive, in Cadman's look when he really began to talk. Sometimes it was like a sudden drop into summer after protracted frost, and the lines of the thin weathered face revealed the whole secret of yearning, something altogether chaste. And that was only the beginning. It was all unexpected; that was the charm of the whole relation. Skag found that Cadman had a real love for India; that he saw things from a nature full of delicate inner surfaces; that his whole difficulty was an inability to express himself unless he found just the receiving-end to suit. Indian affairs, town and field, an infinite variety, Cadman discussed penetratingly, but as one who looked on from the outside.

"She is like my old Zoo book to me," he said, speaking of India their first night out. "A bit of a lad, I used to sit in my room with the great book opened out on a marble table that was cold the year round. There were many pictures. Many, many pictures of all beasts—wood-cuts and copies of paintings and ink-sketchings—ante-camera days, you know. All those pictures are still here—"

Cadman blew a thin diffusion of smoke from his lungs, and touched the third button down from the throat of his grey-green shirt.

"One above all," he added. "It was the frontispiece. All the story of creation on one page. Man, beautiful Man in the centre, all the tree-animals on branches around him, the deeps drained off at his feet, many monsters visible or intimated, the air alive with wings—finches up to condors. That picture sank deep, Skag, so deep that in absent-minded moments I half expected to find India like that—"

There were no better hours of life, than these when Cadman Sahib let himself speak.

"I haven't found the animals and birds and monsters all packed on one page," he added, "but highlights here and there in India, so that I always come back. I have often caught myself asking what the pull is about, you know, as I catch myself taking ship for Bombay again. Oh, I say, my son, and you never got over to the lotus lakes?"

"Not yet," Skag said softly.

"There's a night wind there and a tree—I could find it again. I've lain on peacock feathers on a margin there—unwilling to sleep lest I miss the perfume from over the pools. . . . And the roses of Kashmir, where men of one family must serve forty generations before they get the secrets; where they press out a ton of petals for a pound of essential oil! And that's where the big mountains stand by—High Himalaya herself—incredible colours and vistas—get it for yourself, son."

It was always the elusive thing that Cadman didn't say, that left Skag's mind free to build his own pictures. Meanwhile Cadman as a companion was showing up flawlessly day by day.

At the end of a long march, after many days out, they smelled the night cooking-fires from a village. A moment later they passed tiger tracks, and the print of native feet.

The twilight was thick between them as they hastened on. Cadman Sahib stepped back suddenly, lifting his hand to grasp the other, but not quite soon enough. That instant Skag was flicked out of sight, taken into the folds of mother-earth and covered—the bleat of a kid presently identifying the whole mystery.

Skag fell about twelve feet into the black earth coolness. He was unhurt, and knew roughly what had happened before he landed. His rush of thoughts: shame for his own carelessness, gladness that Cadman Sahib was safe above, the meaning of the kid's cry and the tracks they had seen; this rush was broken by another deluge of earth that all but drowned the laugh of Cadman. Skag had jerked back against the wall of earth to avoid being struck by the body of his companion who coughed and laughed again faintly, for his wind was very low.

"You couldn't ask more of a friend than that, son. I couldn't get you up to me, so I came down with you—"

Of course, it was an accident. Cadman presently explained that he had set down his dunnage and crept close on his knees to look into the pit when the dry earth caved. Doubtless it was intended to do so, since this was a native tiger-trap baited with live meat. But Cadman had not considered fully in time. . . . Dust of the dry brown earth settled upon them now; the grey twilight darkened swiftly. The chamber was about nine by fifteen feet, hollowed wider at the bottom than the top, and covered with a thin frame of bamboo poles, upon which was spread a layer of leaves and sod. The kid had been tethered to escape the stroke if possible.

"It's all night for us," Cadman remarked. "They won't look at the trap until morning. My packs are above—rifle and blanket—"

"I have the camera," Skag chuckled.

Cadman's thin hand came out gropingly.

"The cigarettes are in the tea-pot," he said in a voice dulled with pain.

"I have the pistol," Skag added dreamily. Something of the situation had touched him with joy. If he spoke at such times, it was very dryly.

"Doubtless you have our bathing-suits," Cadman suggested.

"And my cigarette-case has—" Skag felt in the dark, "has one—two—three—"

"Go on," the other said tensely.

"Three," said Skag.

"Let's smoke 'em now. They're calling me already."

Skag passed him the case, saying; "I'm not ready. I do not care just now."

The other puffed dismally.

"I don't always quite get you, son," he said. "But it's all right when I do—"

Skag mused over this. He was hungry and he put the thought away. He was athirst and he put that thought away also. The wants came back, but he dealt with them more firmly. The two men talked of appetites in general, and Skag explained that he handled his, just as he had handled the wild animals in the circus, being straight with them and gaining their friendliness.

"Don't fight them," he said. "Get them on your side and they will pull for you in a pinch."

"You talk like a Hindu holy man—"

"Do they talk like that?" Skag asked quickly. . . . "It was my old friend with the circus—who taught me these things. He taught me to make friends with my own wild animals. It is true that he was many years in India. . . ."

"He was the one that had the ring in his left ear?"

"Right ear."

The other laughed. "It's such a novelty to find you are not a liar—with all you know and have been through. I'll stop that nasty business of testing you. Hear me, from now on, I'm done!"

Hours passed; it was after midnight. The waning moon was rising. They could tell the light through the trees. Cadman had smoked again, but Skag still expressed an unwillingness.

"It doesn't want to, now," he said.

"Oh, it doesn't—"

"I have persuaded it to think of other things. It is working for me."

Cadman swore softly, genially. "I never forget anything, son," he whispered. "Never anything like that."

"Old Alec said I should never let a day pass without doing something I didn't want to—or without something I wanted. He said it was better than developing muscle."

"Some brand of calisthenics—that. And he was the old one with the rose-jar?"

Skag's hand lifted toward the other and Cadman's met his.

There was a wet, meaty growl, indescribably low-pitched—but no chance even to shout—only to huddle back together to the farthest corner. The beast had stalked faultlessly and pounced, landing upon the thin cross pieces of bamboo, but short of the bait. Down the twelve feet he came with a tearing hiss of fright and rage. Something like a muffled crash of pottery, it was, mixed with dull choking explosions. The air of the pit seemed charged with furious power that whipped the leaves to shreds.

"The pistol, Skag—"

They were free, so far, from the rending claws. The younger man's brain was full of light. Cadman Sahib's voice had never been more calm.

Skag drew a match, not the gun. He scratched the match and held it high in front. They saw the great cowering creature like a fallen pony in size—but untellably more vivid in line—the chest not more than seven feet from them, the head held far back, the near front paw lifted against them as if to parry a blow.

Skag changed the match from his right hand to his left. When the flame burned low, he tossed it on the ground, half way between them and the tiger. There was a forward movement of the beast's spine—a little lower and forward. The lifted paw curved in, but did not touch the ground. The last light of the match, as it turned red, seemed bright in the beast's bared mouth. In it all there was the dramatic reality of a dream that questions not.

"He's badly frightened," Skag said.

No sound from Cadman Sahib.

"It's too big for him," Skag went on calmly. "He thinks we put over the whole thing on him. It's too big for him to tackle. Wonder if he's got a mate?"

One big green eye burned now in the pit—steady as a beacon and turned to them, enfolding them. Cadman Sahib cleared his throat.

"All right to talk?" he asked huskily.

"Sure. It will help—"

He cleared his throat again and inquired in an enticing tone: "You actually don't mean to use the pistol?"

"I'm not a crack-shot," Skag said queerly.

"You might pass it to me. I'm supposed to be—"

"It is bad light."

"And then again, you might not," Cadman laughed softly. "I've got you, son—"

"I will do as you say," Skag said steadily.

Cadman hiccoughed. "The eye moved," he explained. "There—it did it again. I got a feeling as if an elevator dropped a flight. What were you saying?"

"That I am here to take orders."

"I'm taking orders to-night, son. I wouldn't risk your good opinion by shooting your guest—"

"He is perfect—not more than four or five years—got his full range, but not his weight."

Skag stopped abruptly, until the other nudged him.

"Go on—it's like a bench-show—"

"We called them Bengalis—but that is just the trade-name—"

"You intimated he might have a lady-friend—do they hunt in couples?"

The boy didn't answer that. "You've never been in a tiger's cage?" he asked suddenly.

"I'm telling you not, so you'll excuse my apprehensions about our lodging—in case Herself appears. The fact is, there isn't room—"

"She won't come near, if we keep up the voices—"

"It becomes instantly a bore to talk," Cadman answered.

Sometime passed before they spoke again. The tiger didn't seem to settle any; from time to time, they heard the tense concussion, the hissing escape of his snarl. The kid had either escaped or strangled to death.

"Will he stand for it until morning?" Cadman asked abruptly.

"He may move a little to rest his legs."

"And won't he try for the top?"

"I think not. He has already measured that. He sees in the dark. He knows there's no good in making a jump."

"Nothing to jump at—with us here?"

"We have put it over on him. You have helped greatly."

"How's all that?"

"You don't smell afraid—"

"Ah, thanks."

Long afterward Cadman's hand came over to Skag's brow and touched it lightly.

"I was just wondering, son, if you sweat hot or cold."

There was a pause, before he added:

"You see, I want to get you, young man. You really like this sort of night?"

"It is India," said Skag.

Every little while through the dragging hours, Cadman would laugh softly; and if there had been silence for long, the warning snarl would come back. The breath of it shook the air and the thresh of the tail kept the dust astir in the pit.

"There is only one more thing I can think of," Cadman said at last.

The waning moon was now in meridian and blent with daylight. The beast was still crouched against the wall.

"Yes?" said Skag.

"That you should walk over and stroke his head."

"Oh, no, he is cornered. He would fight."

"There's really a kind of law about all this—?"

"Very much a law."

After an interval Cadman breathed: "I like it. Oh, yes," he added wearily, "I like it all."

It was soon after that they heard the voices of natives and a face, looking grey in the dawn, peered down. Cadman spoke in a language the native understood:

"Look in the tea-pot and toss down my cigarettes—"

At this instant the tiger protested a second time. The native vanished with the squeak of a fat puppy that falls off a chair on its back. For moments afterward, they heard him calling and telling others the tale of all his born days. Three quarters of an hour elapsed before the long pole, thick as a man's arm, was carefully lowered. Skag guided the butt to the base of the pit, and fixed it there as far as possible from the tiger. This was delicate. His every movement was maddeningly deliberate, the danger, of course, being to put the tiger into a fighting panic.

"Now you climb," Skag said.

"No—"

"It is better so. I am old at these things. He will not leap at you while I am here—"

"You mean he might leap, as you start to shin up the pole—alone?"

"No, that will be the second time. It will not infuriate him—the second one to climb."

"I'll gamble with you—who goes first."

"You said that you were taking orders," Skag said coldly.

"That's a fact. But this isn't to my relish, son—"

"We do not need more words."

Cadman Sahib had reached safety. The natives were around him, feeling his arms and limbs, stuttering questions. He bade them be silent, caught up his rifle and covered the tiger, while Skag made the tilted pole, beckoning the rifle back.

"It's been a hard night for him," he said.

The two men stood together in the morning light. Cadman's face was deeply shaded by the big helmet again, but his eyes bored into the young one's as he offered his cigarette-case. Skag took one, lit it carelessly. Cadman was watching his hands.

"You've got it, son," he said.

"Got what?"

"The good grey nerve. . . . Not a flicker in your hand. I wanted to know. . . . Say, cheer up—"

Skag was looking toward the tiger trap.

"Ah, I see," said Cadman Sahib.

"The circus is a hard life," Skag said.

That was a kind of a feast day. . . . At noon the natives had the tiger up in sunlight, caged in bamboo. Skag presently came into a startling kind of joy to hear his friend make an offer to buy the beast. Negotiations moved slowly, but the thing was done. That afternoon the journey toward Coldwater Ruins was continued with eight carriers, the tiger swung between them. Skag was mystified. What could Cadman mean? What could he do with a tiger at the Ruins or in the Monkey Forest? The natives apparently had not been told the destination, but they must know soon. It was all strange. Skag liked it better alone with his friend. Halt was called that afternoon, the sun still in the sky. The two white men walked apart.

"You get the drift, my son?"

Skag shook his head.

"Of course, the natives won't like it; they won't understand. But we're sure he isn't a man-eater—"

Skag's chest heaved.

"I never knew a more decent tiger—" Cadman went on. "Besides, he's a friend of yours, and not too expensive—"

"You bought him to—"

"I bought him for you, son—a tribute to the nerviest white man I ever stepped with—"

That evening a great whine went up from the bearers. It appears that while some were cutting wood, others preparing supper and others gathering dry grass for beds, the younger white man, who had made magic with the tiger in the pit, suddenly failed in his powers. The natives were sure it was not their fault that the cover had not been securely fastened. The bearers repeated they were all at work and could find no fault with themselves. They were used to dealing with white men who did not permit bungling. Their wailing was very loud. . . . To lose such a tiger was worth more than many natives, some white men would say. . . . But Cadman Sahib was rich. He fumed but little; being of all white men most miraculously compassionate. . . . Also it was true the beast, though full grown, was not a man-eater. . . .

"And to-morrow we shall go on alone—it is much pleasanter," said Skag, after all was still and they lay down together.

CHAPTER II

SON OF POWER

His Indian name was given to Skag in the great Grass Jungle; but he did not know the meaning of the words when they first fell upon his ear. There India herself first opened for him the magic gates that seal her mystery. But he did not know it was her glamour that made him utterly forget outside things, in the unbelievable loveliness of Grass Jungle days; did not know it was just as much her spell that made him forget his own birthright, in the paralysis of perfect fear.

A part of her mystery is this forgetting—while she reveals canvas after canvas of life—uncovers layer beneath layer of her deeper marvels. Skag was involved with his animals—and interests peculiarly personal—till it all came to seem like a dream. Yet underneath his surface consciousness it was working in him, as the glamour of India always does, to colour his entire future—as the magic of India always will.

After their night in the tiger pit-trap, Cadman and Skag had wandered southeast-ward—still searching for the Monkey Forest and the Coldwater Ruins—and had become lost to the world and the ways of civilisation in the mazes of the Mahadeo mountains. They had found a dozen jungles full of monkeys, but none of them looked to Cadman like his dream. The monkeys were all so melted-in to everything else; and there was so much too much of everything else.

As for Ruins, the thing they found was too old. It was like an exposure of the sins of first men—alive with bats and smaller vermin. The monkeys there had preserved from age to age the germs of all depravity. Without words the two Americans turned away from that spot, to forget it.

Skag was learning that his training in the circus had been but a mere beginning in the study of wild animals. It seemed impossible that there could be a jungle anywhere with more beasts or greater variety, than they heard at night.

It was as hard to come in good view of any wild creature—excepting monkeys—as it had been hard at first to sleep, on account of the voices of all creation after sundown. To approach undiscovered, and to lie out and watch undiscovered, taxed and developed all their faculties; the fascination and excitement of it stretched their powers; and their successes enriched them both for a life-time.

After the first eagerness to get twenty different positions of a tigress playing with her kittens, Cadman had become a miser of material and an adept in noiseless movement. Finding that he was in danger of going short on sketching paper, he used it more and more as if it were fine gold, till his outlines were not larger than miniatures. Also, he learned to glance for the flash of approval in Skag's eye.

The two men had grown into a rare comradeship. This time of year, sleeping in the open was luxury. They had not suffered for food, excepting in the memory of such things as had once been most common. Well above fever-line, no ailment had touched them. So, eating simply, sleeping deeply and working hard, they toughened in body and keened in mind—the days all full of quickening interests, every next minute due to develop surprise.

It was by a little headlong mountain stream, that the revelation came. Skag was looking to see which was the business-end of his tooth-brush that morning when Cadman broke his sheath knife. The accident was a calamity, because Skag's was already worn out cutting step-way to climb out of khuds, and this was all they had left to serve such a purpose.

"That settles it, we must go," said Cadman, looking ruefully at the stump of his old blade. "Our nearest kin wouldn't know us, but we are still recognisable to each other, and I'm not exactly ready to quit—are you?"

"No," Skag answered absently—unwilling to realise the necessity.

Cadman studied the crestfallen face—they had loved this life together and equally.

"But do you realise, my son," he asked, "that others will have to see us, before we can ever again be clothed and groomed properly?"

Now Skag looked at his friend with seeing eyes and blushed.

"It's not the clothes, so much as—" Skag stopped.

Cadman focused on Skag's face through his queer spectacles, then he laughed as only Cadman could laugh.

So they climbed down and took train for Bombay. Like fugitives they dodged the sight of correctly dressed Englishmen all the way; stopping over more than seven hours at Kullian—so as to reach the great city at night.

Next morning two clean-faced and very much alive Americans arrived at the Polo Club for late breakfast. Indeed they were good to look at, being in the finest kind of health and full of initiative. That breakfast was royal in every flavour; they felt like young spendthrifts squandering their patrimony. Just as they were finishing, a distinguished looking Englishman came across the room and greeted Cadman:

"Now this is my own proverbial good luck! Come away up to the house and give account of yourself. Where are the pictures? We'll take 'em along."

Cadman presented Skag to Doctor Murdock of the University, explained that it was imperative for them to do some general outfitting, but promised to bring his friend in the afternoon.

"Doctor Murdock is an extraordinary man, Skag," said Cadman, as the Englishman hurried away. "Beside his chair in the University, he is said to be top surgeon of Bombay. Barring none, he has more of different kinds of knowledge than any man I know; becomes master of whatever he takes up—authority, past question."

"I wondered why you promised to take me along," Skag put in.

"You'll be glad to have met him. He'll be interested in you," Cadman answered. "He's quite likely to take us to see some of the Indian nautch-girls. They're one of his fads—for their beauty. He has specialties in art as well as in science; but he's clean stuff—nothing rotten in him."

They forgot time in the Bombay bazaars; first looking for bags, to be easily carried on their own persons; and then giving themselves to quality and workmanship in things designed for their special uses. There was no hurry. All life stretched before them, in widening vistas.

Doctor Murdock's house was high on Malabar Hill. Their hired carriage came in behind his trim little brougham, as it turned on the driveway into his compound.

"My fortune again!" the Doctor called. "I've been detained by a case and properly sweating for fear you'd reach my den first."

Tea was served on a verandah entirely foreign and tropical and strange looking to Skag. A field of palm-tops stretched away from their feet to the sea. They told him the city of Bombay was hidden under those fronds.

"And now you understand, Cadman," the Doctor was saying, "there's your own room and one next for your friend Hantee. Your traps will be up before you sleep, which may not be early, for I've a tamasha on for you this night—you remember, I enjoy dinner in the morning?"

That tamasha was a maze of strange colour, strange motion and stranger perfume to Skag; not penetrating his conscious nature at all—feeling unreal to him.

"I've been watching you without shame this night, young man," the Doctor said to him, as they finished the after-midnight meal. "My entertainment fell dead with you. Sir. You've been 'way off somewhere else. I'm simply consumed to know what you have found in life, to make your eyes blind and your ears deaf to the lure of human beauty. You're not to be distressed by my impudence—it's innocent."

"If I may answer for my friend, I belive [Transcriber's note: believe?] I can tell you, Doctor." Cadman saw consent in Skag's eye and went on: "He has found the lure of creatures. He has entered into the spell of a young tigress playing with her kittens, in her own place. He has watched another tigress fight her mate to a finish, defending her little ones from their sire. He has listened to the symphonies of night and seen the drama of the wild. He lives in the clean glamour of the primeval jungle."

The Doctor's eyes widened for seconds; then they gloomed as he spoke:

"Between you, you challenge modern manhood. We have not conceived that 'clean glamour' since men were young—forgotten ages past. No, there was no human beauty to-night to make a man forget those tigresses. . . . She was not there. I am one of many who miss her, but I would give—" The

Doctor broke off, searching their faces before he spoke again: "There is no hope you will know the depth of the calamity; the bitterness of the loss. Speaking of clean things—"

"Who was she?" Cadman asked.

"She was the most beautiful thing on earth. She was indeed the most marvellous thing on earth, being a Bombay singing nautch-girl—undefamed. There has been no one else, these ages."

The Doctor sat smoking, apparently oblivious of his guests.

"The Spartan Helen?" Cadman suggested.

"Hah! The Spartan Helen was not invincible!"

"The Noor Mahal?"

"The Noor Mahal was always in seclusion."

"Her name?" Skag questioned.

"She had no name," the Doctor answered, "but she was called 'Dhoop Ki Dhil'—Heart-of-the-Sun; possibly on account of her voice. There has been none like it. The master-mahouts of High Himalaya, their voices pass those of all other men for splendour; but I tell you there was none other in the world, beside hers. Rich men in Bombay would give fortunes to anyone who would find her."

"Then she is not dead?" Skag spoke startled.

"We do not know that she is dead," the Doctor answered. "We would suppose so, but for a curious happening four days before she disappeared. Down in the silk-market a dealer was buying silk from an up-country native—a man from the Grass Jungle. The native was exceptionally good to look upon. Dhoop Ki Dhil came into the place to make some purchase.

Her eye fell on the jungle man and she stood back. She was a valuable customer, so the silk-merchant made haste to signal her forward. But she shook her head and moved further back."

The Doctor stopped to smoke.

"After a while Dhoop Ki Dhil came forward, moving like one in a trance, and said to the jungle man, 'Are you a god?' and the jungle man answered her with shame, 'No, I am a common man.'

"Now that silk-merchant will tell no more. One doesn't blame him. The natives are not patient with such a tale of her. To hear that any man had taken her eye, maddened them. She had passed the snares of desire—immune. She had turned away from fabulous wealth. She had denied princes and kings. She smiled on all men alike—with that smile mothers have for little children."

"She was a mother-thing," murmured Cadman.

The Doctor turned, questioning:

"A mother-thing? Yes, probably. But she led the singing women like a super-being incarnate. She led the dancing women like a living flame. They sing and dance yet, but the fire of life is gone out!"

"Where is the Grass Jungle?" Cadman asked.

"Nobody seems to know. As for me, I never heard of it—till this. The silk-merchants say that once in several years some strange man—one or another—in strange garments, comes down with a peculiar kind of silk, to exchange for cotton cloth. He won't take money for it and he's easily cheated. He won't talk—only that he's from the great Grass Jungle. He usually calls it 'great.'"

"It must be possible to find," said Cadman, glancing at Skag.

"What do you say?"

"I'm with you," Skag answered.

"Now am I gone quite mad, or do I understand you?" the Doctor enquired.

"I think you understand us," Cadman answered.

The Doctor sprang up, exclaiming:

"I've often told you, Cadman, you Americans develop most extraordinary surprises. Most remarkable men on earth for—for developing at the—at the very moment, you understand!"

"Do you know anyone who might give us something on the locality?" Skag asked Cadman.

"That's the point. I think I do," Cadman nodded. "But we'll have to go and find out."

"My resources are at your disposal," the Doctor put in.

"Your resources have accomplished the first half," smiled Cadman. "It's fair that the rest of it should be ours."

"Then what's to do?" the Doctor questioned.

"A few things to purchase first, easily done to-day," Cadman answered, glancing out at the faint dawn. "Then, I know Dickson of the grain-foods department, at Hurda—Central Provinces. He ought to be familiar with the topography of all the inside country. We'll risk nothing by going to him."

"Then away with you to bed and get one good sleep. The boy will bring you a substantial choti-hazri when you're out of your bath at six. I have a couple of small elephant-skin bags—you'll not find the like in shops—they're made for the interior medical service."

So Cadman and Skag went up from Bombay that night on the Calcutta-bound train, facing the far interior of India. The boy in Skag found joy in every detail of his outfit; especially the elephant-skin bag, stocked with necessary personal requirements and nothing more. But somewhere, far out before him, lost in this mystery-land—was a woman. That woman must be found.

"What's the secret about the Doctor?" he asked Cadman, after they had been rolling through the night some hours.

"Nobody knows, unless it's a woman he didn't get," Cadman answered.

"What's the grip this wonder-woman has on him?"

"Beauty and music and life, in the superlative degree; when it all happens together, in one woman—she grips."

After that they both dreamed vague man-dreams of Dhoop Ki Dhil.

"There stands Dickson Sahib himself!" Cadman exclaimed, at Hurda station; and Skag saw the two meet, perceiving at once that it was a friendship between men of very different type.

Then Dickson Sahib promptly gathered them both into that Anglo-Indian hospitality which is never forgotten by those who have found it. Skag was made to feel as much at home as the evidently much-loved Cadman; not by word or gesture, but by a kindly atmosphere about everything. He met a slender lad of twelve years, presented to him by Dickson Sahib as "My son Horace," whose clear grey eyes attracted him much.

After dinner Cadman told the story of Dhoop Ki Dhil. There was perfect silence for minutes when he finished. Skag was groping on and on—his quest already begun. Dickson was smoking hard, till he startled them both:

"Of course, it's altogether right; I'd like to be with you."

"Then will you direct us?" Cadman asked.

"As an officer in a land-department, you understand—" Dickson answered slowly, "I'm not supposed to send men into a place like that, to their death. But I want you to know that my responsibility has nothing whatever to do with my concern. Because I value your lives as men—I want to be careful. You must let me think it out loud. It's a maze. I may place you, as I get on."

"We appreciate your care," Cadman said earnestly.

"The 'great' Grass Jungle is the proper name for vast territory—not all in one piece," Dickson Sahib began. "It comes in rifts between parallel rivers among the mountains. Seepage back and forth between the streams, gives the moisture necessary for such growth—year round.

"When white men come to the edge of one of those rifts, they turn back. It's pestilential with wild beasts. Natives call it the Place-of-Fear. White men don't challenge it—they go round. Government has named one part of it—over toward the eastern end of the Vindhas—the Bund el Khand, the closed country; that name tells its own story."

Dickson Sahib stopped, frowning.

"The native with silks to exchange goes down to Bombay?" he went on. "That means, not Calcutta-way. It also means, not anywhere in the Deccan—which clears us away from large tracts. Yet he usually calls it 'great'—that should mean, the Bund el Khand. No one knows how far in; but you'll best approach it from this side. I'm not dissuading you; I'd like to be along. I'm offering you choice of my assortment of firing-pieces. I'll work you out some running lines—they'll be ready by late-breakfast time. But I'm certain your best place to leave the tracks will be Sehora."

Dickson Sahib was worrying with a match, his face troubled, as he muttered:

"Now if Hand-of-a-God—"

"What is that?" Skag asked quietly, of Cadman.

"That," smiled Dickson Sahib, "is a Scotchman. This civil station of Hurda is famous because he lives here. He is an absolutely perfect shot. Years ago he took all the medals and cups at the great shooting tournaments. He took 'em all, till for shame's sake he withdrew from contesting. He goes to the tournaments just the same—the crackshotmen wouldn't be without him—but he doesn't enter for the trophies any more."

"He is called the avenger of the people, Skag," Cadman put in, "because he goes out and gets the man-eaters; never sights for anything but the eye or the heart, and never misses."

"As I was saying," Dickson Sahib went on, "if Hand-of-a-God were here, he'd go without asking. Or even if the Rose-pearl's brother Ian were here, he's quick enough. But he plays with situations, rather."

"Don't let this situation trouble you, Dickson," said Cadman.

There fell a moment of curious silence. Cadman was a bit pale, but Skag's face looked serene, as he questioned innocently:

"Rose-pearl?"

"Yes," Dickson Sahib began absently, "she's here when she's not visiting one of her numerous brothers; just now it's Billium in Bombay. Her degree is from London University and the medical service recognises her work among the people. She's a holy thing to them; indeed, she never rests when there's much sickness among them. But one wouldn't ask a favour of one of her brothers."

"Hold on, Dickson, I protest!" Cadman interrupted laughingly. "I'm not such a bad shot myself, you know!"

"The Grass Jungle is crowded—I say crowded—with the worst kinds of blood-eaters. You may want an extra good shot; at the very top notch of practice, what's more."

As Dickson Sahib came out with it, he noticed Skag's surprise, and challenged him:

"Bless your soul, man, I believe it's your grip that grips us!"

Skag's serene face got warm, but Cadman assented.

"Skag dwells in the fundamentals," he explained; "most of us never touch 'em. He's practically incapable of fear; and the idea of failure never occurs to him."

Early next morning Cadman got a telegram calling him to Calcutta; and afterward to England.

"We'll take time to do this big thing first, though," he said, putting the wire into Skag's hand. "They want me sooner—as you see; but they'll get me later. Come away and I'll send word to that effect."

Skag was realising what it would have meant to him, if Cadman had failed; so he asked—vaguely—something about the Rose-pearl.

"Don't let yourself get interested in her, son. That family is like a secret sanctuary; and she is the holy thing behind the altar. She's unattainable."

CHAPTER III

SON OF POWER (CONTINUED)

They left the train at Sehora and struck out through rough country, following Dickson Sahib's directions. They camped in full jungle—wild beast voices ringing through the night.

Next day they came into a valley like Eden, nourished by a small river. On its banks—near a mud-walled, grass-thatched village—Cadman discovered a devout man of great learning, who rested on the path of a long pilgrimage. The devout man was approachable and spoke perfect English; so they asked him about the land ahead.

"The Grass Jungle, sons? It is the place of secret ways. Only the very innocent of men-things dwell there; those not soiled by the wisdom of evil. To the wise of the world, it is the place of plague and pestilence and fear; and swift death by heat—and the shedding of blood. Past all else—to such—it is the place of the shedding of blood."

He stopped a moment, musing; then in softer tones went on:

"The days are all still there. The creature-multitude sleeps in hidden lairs—black and gold and brown and grey—all veiled in golden gloom. The little men-things go their ways, on their own man-paths, which they only know; remember this—they only know.

"When you go in, they will send boys with you from one village to the next; but only in the early hours, or in the late hours of day. See that you do not persuade them otherwise. The full-day heat is called 'blight' because it robs men of their wits."

Skag scarcely breathed, till the Learned spoke again.

"At night—I speak who know—at night the earth rises up to the heavens on the voices of the wild and the ears of the gods are offended. Creatures go out on their own paths—as the men-things go on theirs by day. They rend and contend, they kill and are killed; but they do not cease till dawn."

The devout man's head sank low upon his breast and he was very still.

"It's romance, Skag," whispered Cadman, "but that's not saying it's our romance. The man's off again in his abstractions; but I'm going to try once more."

Skag nodded.

Touching the wise man's foot with reverence and speaking in the form of utmost respect, Cadman asked:

"Is it well that we go in? We search for one who sings as the super-human sing; we search for the sake of sick hearts—her heart and others. Is it well?"

The eyes that lifted were not abstract; they were very deep and keen. Both the Americans felt winnowed before he spoke again.

"Ignorance is not good, but innocence is the supreme defence. If it is the will of the beneficent gods that you find the unmothered woman of great beauty in time, then it shall be so. But be patient. Move slowly through the little peoples, forgetting your search—I say forgetting your search, as you go.

Be kind; haste will not delay the sacrifice—kindness may. The way lies before you. Peace."

Cadman rose at once. They had been dismissed with a benediction; nothing further could be obtained. Otherwise Skag would have been a question-mark before that poor old man till morning.

"But he knows!"

The words seemed wrung out of Skag, as they sat apart.

"He does; there's no gamble about that. But if we challenge him, the chances are—he'll revoke that benediction!" Cadman speculated whimsically. "Then we'll have all the people against us—which is to say, every prospect of success would go glimmering. No, there's nothing for it but to go ahead, as fast as we can—slowly."

"But what do you suppose he meant by 'forgetting'?" Skag asked. "That we mustn't let the natives know we're looking for her?"

"I believe you've got it!" Cadman assented.

"Then I've forgotten!" Skag said with decision.

"I will have forgotten, by morning," Cadman answered.

They were on their way as soon as it was light enough to see their compass. They slept at two villages; and early the third day came out of sketchy mountains into full view of the great Grass Jungle itself. In long low waves, it billowed away from them to the dim rugged line of Vindha against the sky. It looked like massed plumes of feathers—all golden-green.

That day they walked down toward it with few words. To Skag it was perfectly natural enchantment—veiling the mystery of Dhoop Ki Dhil. He never thought of it as a death-trap for himself.

Under the late afternoon sun, the rolling waves of golden-green took on an aspect of measureless distance; clean reaches, absolutely unbroken by anything save their own majestic undulations. The most innocent landscape on earth, more enticing than the sand-desert—its softer mystery breathed forth the faint searching perfume of growing things. Its undertone was well-being. Its overtone was peace.

"Do you suppose they're doing any harm to her, in there?" Cadman asked.

"No," Skag answered, but his face was grim as he spoke.

When they came into it, they found not grass but bamboo, twelve to sixteen feet high, standing root to root. They camped at a village in its edge; and before they slept, twenty lads were ready to lead them in the man-paths, next morning.

The villages had not been visible from the mountain-side, being solidly double-thatched with bamboo. Garden and fruit-stuffs were underneath; and animals for milk and butter.

The people were semi-primitive. Physical degeneration was not found. Indeed their bodily perfection was extraordinary. In mind, they were like children; happy and friendly, joyful to teach all they knew—joyful to show all they had. The days rang with clean, childish laughter; but there was no philosophy. There was no deep concern, no lasting grief, no hate.

"Skag, my son," said Cadman solemnly, "if a man really wants to depart from sin—this is the place to come!"

By this time they had passed through several villages, camping under double-thatch and inside heavy stockade guards. Being unable to release himself from the thrall of his life-quest, even while every element of his manhood was deep in the thrall of a "singing nautch-girl—undefamed—" Skag's trained ears had been extending his education in what was the cult of cults to him. He had listened longer than Cadman at night, to those voices of the wild by which the ears of the gods are offended.

Surely his secret consciousness—during those night-watches—had grappled with the unknown ahead, reaching impatient fingers to find and save Dhoop Ki Dhil in time. But he let no flicker of that thought colour his answer.

"I don't know," he said dubiously, "if I'm not mistaken, I've heard some sinful language at night."

As they got further in, two names attracted their attention—spoken together like one word—Dhoop Kichari-lal and Koob Soonder. Of course Koob Soonder—Utterly Beautiful—they first thought could mean none other than the Bombay nautch-girl whom they sought—yet later they were to learn the truth. But the last part of the first name—Kichari-lal—they did not know. Yet no one would interpret it to them; the innocent people looked frightened when they asked.

Still, the name recurred; and like following golden threads through meshes of green—all this life was gold and green—they became fascinated by the tracing of it.

Then they heard of a man who "knew everything and was able to tell it." They found him strangely clothed in soft brown, surrounded by youngsters; and asked for all he knew about Dhoop Kichari-lal and Koob Soonder. (Their request would have been made in different form, if they had recognised his order at first glance.) He eyed them keenly, before speaking:

"Dhoop Kichari-lal? That is the name of a colour which the woman from far wears; she whom Jiwan Kawi loved and would have wed. And Koob Soonder—small sister of Jiwan Kawi—our strong young man who went away; she whose mother was taken by Fear when she was a babe, she who was stricken by the blight when she began to run—she who was named for her perfect beauty, before the Grass Jungle had seen beauty more perfect—"

"Do you know all the story?" Cadman interrupted, with dry lips.

"All," said the man. "Am I not here to teach the little people with the telling of tales? Jiwan Kawi was sent on the great adventure, to change our silks for cotton cloths—which the people consider more desirable." (There was the hint of a tender smile on his lips, as he said the last words.) "Jiwan Kawi was the most strong, the most beautiful of all our young men when these same leaves were small, in the spring." He paused, seeming to forget them—his eyes on the leaves.

Then his manner changed, taking on a quality of austere impressiveness, as he continued:

"Jiwan Kawi returned from the great adventure; but a woman came after him—sunrise to sunset behind. She had followed him from the place of the multitudes, where all the people dwell together. He had seen her there; he had loved her there; he had fled in fear from her beauty; he had fled in distraction away back to his own place. Now—his joy showed, past telling. But she had come without a mother to give her in marriage; and marriage cannot be, otherwise.

"If it had not been for her so great beauty! Surely our women are beautiful—as the gods know how to make common women. But when they saw her—they went back into their houses and covered their faces from the light of her eyes.

"That was the calamity; for a woman must be given in marriage by the heart of a woman—sincere and unafraid. And there was not one without fear. Jiwan Kawi went out into the jungle that night; and he never came back. Fear may have taken him."

The man looked away toward the horizon.

"Then she put on her body the one garment of hindu-widowhood, unadorned; but without marriage. She said, 'I will mourn for the children that have not been—that are not—that cannot be.' The women heard the voice of her mourning; and they forgot her too-great beauty, to serve her too-great pain—when it was late.

"They gave her the little Koob Soonder, to mother. Now it is that the child, who has no wit and little reason, goes out into the place of sacrifice to find Fear; and the woman in a widow's garment goes after, to fetch her back. Then the woman who mourns for unborn children, goes out into the night-paths—as Jiwan Kawi went—and the little Koob Soonder follows, to fetch her back.

"So they are going, always going out into the place of sacrifice—where Fear lives. Some day or some night—Fear will take them."

"What kind of fear?" Cadman asked, with a dry throat.

"Fear is name enough. There is none other."

The man's reply was spoken in conclusive tones. He sat as if oblivious, for several minutes. Then searching them both earnestly with haggard eyes, he spoke direct:

"Have you looked on Dhoop Ki Dhil, for whom you come so far? Have you heard her voice?"

Both the Americans shook their heads.

"Will you look on her in the paths of my understanding? Will you render yourselves to know her in the currents of my blood?"

"We will," Cadman answered tensely.

The man lifted his face toward the night-sky, becoming

perfectly still before he spoke:

"She is the breath of the early spring-time, when the pulse of the earth awakes. She is the midnight moon of all summers, in all lands. The rose of daybreak is in her smile; the flames of sunset in her face. Lightnings of the monsoon break from her eyes; and she mothers the mothers of men with their tenderness. Her body moves like flowing water; and she is the joy of all joy and the sorrow of all sorrow, in motion."

The man lifted his hand, as if to interrupt himself.

"The majesties of High Himalaya are in her voice; and distances of star-lit night."

He stopped, seeming to listen to something they could not hear.

"The tides of the seasons flow through the blood of common men," he went on; "they carry the gold of delight away; and the rock-stuff of strength. Then men are old. It is not so with her. Bitter waters of grief have drenched her, they have covered her as the deep covers the lands below; but her ascending flames of life consume them all. She rises like a creature made of jewels, to enlighten men against the snares of that same deep from which she has come up—wearing splendours of loveliness for garmenture.

"The people weep their tears for her pain; but she heals their hurts with a look. She restores their dead memories of youth to old men—their memories of dead loves. She restores the eyes of girlhood to the elder women, who have long been weary with yearning after dead little ones—after dead men. She has taught the little people who cannot think—the child-hearted people—that Love-the-transcendent can never die!

"Dhoop Ki Dhil? She is youth, eternal! She is motherhood—the divine lotus of the world!"

Turning to face Cadman and Skag, the man said gently:

"The way lies before you. Go swiftly now. Peace."

And rising softly in the dead hush, he moved away.

Cadman sat long meditating, before he spoke at all; then it was like thinking aloud:

"A mystic brother of the Vindhas—one with the old man outside; not leaving these little semi-primitives alone—identifies himself with them—that's good business!"

"Let's get on!" breathed Skag.

They made the utmost speed possible, till they came to the village that startled them. The childlike care-freedom was gone. Light-heartedness was quenched. Apprehension took its place; low tones, no laughter—a look of helpless suffering like the large-eyed wonder in the face of a grieved child.

They asked about the next village.

"Fear lives there," they were told.

"What fear?" Cadman asked.

"Do you know the king of all serpents—he who comes over any wall, he who goes through any thatch? He dwells there. He feeds upon the children of men and upon their creatures. He comes only to the edge, but he eats!"

The boy who told them this was so different from other boys they had seen, that Cadman asked him direct:

"Who are you?"

"I am here under a master, doing a certain work in my novitiate," the boy said simply.

"Will you take us there in the morning?" Cadman asked.

The boy looked at them intently, before he answered:

"It is just inside the nesting-place of all the serpents in the world; but Fear is their king. We who are here to serve, have no weapons; and we cannot overcome malignant things with kindness. If you will deliver the people from that serpent-king, by destroying his evil life, all the snakes will go further back into the jungle. For many generations—if the gods will, for always—the innocent people will be safe. I will take you there, if you will kill him."

"We will try," Cadman said, not even turning to look at Skag.

They found the village in total paralysis of all natural activities. It was like a deadly pall. This was no new terror; it was old devastation—bred into the bone of consciousness.

A little girl came near to watch Cadman, who was getting out his gun. She had never seen one before. He whispered to her—it seemed not right to speak aloud in this place—and asked her where was Dhoop Ki Dhil. The child shook her head, but answered him:

"Wherever you will see the sun-melted red."

"What is that?" he wondered.

"That? That is the long-long, wide-wide cloth that covers all her body. It is made of so-thick silk" (she showed him six fingers), "that many times as thick as we know how to make."

"What is the name of the boy who led us here?" he asked next.

"We call him *Dhanah* and many other names; but he is not a small boy, he is a man—very wise and sad."

At that moment they heard a voice like golden 'cellos and

golden clarions and golden viols—calling "Koob Soon-n-der, Koob Soon-n-der!" and the boy came past, running hard.

"Soon!" he shouted.

But Skag was at his heels and Cadman followed close, the short firing-piece in his hands.

The paths were narrow, the bamboo dense; the boy leaped into a curve and was lost. They raced after him, till the path broadened at the top of an elevation. Pausing an instant to listen, they saw—directly in front of them a little way distant—a tall post; a dark post, seven or eight feet above the bamboo tops, stiff and straight.

It held their eyes by its strange sheen. It began to lean stiffly toward one side—as if falling. It straightened and leaned the other way. Then undulation crept into it, till the top-end followed the outline of a double loop—like a figure-of-eight.

The snake had chained them this long. Skag recovered with an inward revulsion that rent him. He plunged down the path, his faculties surging—thought, feeling, realisation, volition—tearing him.

He met Dhanah carrying an utterly limp girl in his arms—the boy's face gone grey.

As Skag fled on past Dhanah, the whole story of Dhoop Ki Dhil was eating in his brain like fire. She was somewhere in there ahead of him—somewhere near that monster snake.

The weaving of the serpent's head, looping in long reaches above the bamboo tops—looking over them, looking down into them, looking for its prey—had frozen him to the marrow of his bones.

Dhoop Ki Dhil had come out into this blind maze to find and save the heat-blighted child from—that death. He knew what that death was like—he had seen a big snake kill a goat once, in the circus, for food. . . . The frost in his bones bit deeper, because this was Dhoop Ki Dhil—the wonder-woman—who was in there, somewhere close to that snake. He heard the Bombay Doctor's tones again, as he ran; and the words of the brown-robed mystic went like flame and acid through his blood.

. . . Why couldn't he hear Cadman? Cadman had the gun. But if he himself could only reach her before the snake—if he could only— And a soft blur of sun-melted red loomed ahead of him.

Dhoop Ki Dhil did not walk, she did not run; but her glide was almost as swift as Dhanah's flight.

When Skag met her face to face, he shivered with a shock of realisation—her ineffable beauty glowed like coals in a trance of some unearthly devotion. Her human mind was not there—an incomparable calm reigned in its stead.

"Come!" he urged strangely.

She moved with him, tilting her beautiful head to indicate something behind.

He looked—the snake was coming through the long narrow path, coming on; huge undulations, touching the ground but coming through the air, without any look of haste. The path was plenty wide for it, there was plenty time for it—it was overtaking them as if they stood still.

Then, for one eternal moment, Skag knew fear. It was cold—long—metallic. It was invincible—without pity. He heard human voices and the sound of running water—in a dream. Near by, he heard a low sweet laugh. The eyes of fathomless splendour beside him were not looking into his, but they were full of that love which transcends fear. And the birthright of Sanford Hantee rose up in him.

"That's right, come on!" he cried to her.

She looked up; and he followed her glance—one great undulation swayed above them—surging in oozy motion—curving down; just higher than their faces—a broad flat head—thin lateral lips—stark lidless eyes.

Skag ran with his arm about Dhoop Ki Dhil's shoulders. He ran as fast as he could—and still look up. He dared not loosen his eyes from those eyes of evil—he must hold them with what strength he had.

They were utterly patient—those eyes of unveiled malice; as if there had never been strength in the universe but that of sin—as if sin looked down for the first time on something different.

Skag was perfectly definite in his intention; he meant to hold the snake if he could. Some of his training had been in the use of his eyes to control animals under stress.

So he ran with his arm about Dhoop Ki Dhil's shoulders, the flame of his volitional power burning straight up into those pitiless, lidless eyes—till he came into a sentiency that had no cognisance of time.

. . . The raw curse of wickedness and the bitter length of hate, beat down upon him—out of the great snake's naked eyes. The deadly stench of old corruption, poured down upon him—in the great snake's breath.

It challenged the manhood and womanhood of his humankind, with all the crimes of violence they had ever done. Skag met it wistfully at first, with knowledges of loving-kindness; then a rising force that almost choked him, of confidence in ultimate good.

. . . Cadman had found the right path at last. What he saw blotted everything else out. Calling his reserves of control, he sighted with the utmost care. His big-game bullet shattered the serpent's head. It launched backward and Skag heard a heavy stroke on the ground, almost before he realised that the lidless eyes of ancient evil had disappeared from so near his face.

A mighty shout went up from the people, as the monster coils began to thresh living bamboo into pulp. No one saw the hands of the two Americans grip.

Then the majesties of High Himalaya and the distances of star-lit night, poured forth from Dhoop Ki Dhil's lifted lips.

Cadman and Skag followed her among the people going back to the village. Once she whirled with an inimitable movement, flinging her fingers toward Skag, in a gesture that seemed to focus the eyes of the whole world upon him. (And in that instant, the American men could not have spoken a word—for the richness of her in their hearts.)

The light of intelligence flooded her face; her mind had returned to her, unmarred—a radiant scintillance.

"She is naming you 'Rana Jai' for the generations to come," Cadman interpreted. "She says no mortal man ever held the king of all serpents from his stroke—ever delayed him from his chosen prey—this thing they have seen you do. It is your tradition for the future.

"She says I am your guardian, sent by the gods, to destroy the serpent—for your sake—so saving the people." Cadman finished huskily.

"But I didn't reach him, Cadman," Skag protested. "I didn't touch him—inside!"

As they all came into the village enclosure, Dhoop Ki Dhil slipped into a house near by, saying that Dhanah thought the child slept too deeply—she would care for her.

The people were beside themselves with joy. But presently

Dhoop Ki Dhil came out, looking straight up. Her hands were palm to palm, reaching slowly upward from her breast to their full stretch; there she gently opened them apart. A perfect hush fell on all.

"The child is gone," Cadman said, in an undertone.

Then the people began a low chant. It was not mourning. It was as if a great multitude sang a great lullaby together.

"Boy, boy! This is a hard knock at our civilisation!"

Cadman was not aware that he had spoken. Skag shook his head.

"God! how I love it!" burst from him; and he had no shame of that love.

Little Koob Soonder's body—in heavy silks of gleaming blue—was laid on a bamboo pyre. Dhoop Ki Dhil tenderly sprinkled flower-petals and incense-oils over all, and lighted the four corners for the motherless one, herself. Cadman and Skag watched the clean flames, till only silver ashes were on the ground. And all the while the people sang their great soft lullaby, without tears or any sign of mourning.

Hours later, the voice of Dhoop Ki Dhil rose on the night—far away. It seemed to compass the planet with its golden power and to descend from the empyrean of sound; further and further—transcending the voices of the wild—the very heart of love, the very soul of light. But they saw no more of her; and the people next morning made no reply to Cadman's natural enquiry; no one would tell what had happened to Dhoop Ki Dhil.

All the way to the edge of the great Grass Jungle, where they had come in, a multitude went before and after—establishing the tradition of their deliverance. Finally Cadman asked the people why they spoke no word of Dhoop Ki Dhil, excepting as to things finished. The people bowed their heads and one answered for them all:

"It is finished. When we of the Grass Jungle mourn, we do not use words."

As they walked slowly into the open, listening to the voices of the child-people, the name "Rana Jai" recurred often.

"I haven't heard what that word means yet," Skag said.

"Rana Jai?" Cadman repeated. "The exact translation is Prince of Victory; but Dhoop Ki Dhil made her meaning clear—Son of Power; a great deal more."

After that, they had little to say. Certainly Cadman would never forget the length of time he had seen the looming head—less than two feet from Skag's face—the incredible power that flamed up out of the young man's eyes. Certainly Skag was full of content as to the safety of the people. But all realisations were lost in a gnawing depression about Dhoop Ki Dhil.

When they came to Sehora, the station-man held out a letter in quaintly written English; it read:

From the wayside Dhoop Ki Dhil sends greetings to Son of Power, most exalted; and to his guardian, most devoted.

She pays votive offerings from this day, at sunrise and at sunset, for those men—incense and oils and seed—to safety from all evil, and fulfillment of their so-great destiny.

The gods, all-beneficent, have preserved him—Jiwan Kawi, the man of men! He met her in the night-paths; and he goes now with her—to her own people. Jiwan Kawi, the man of men!

The Grass Jungles are in her heart, like dead rose-leaves; their perfume in her blood, is forever before the gods—remembering Son of Power and his guardian.

Dhoop Ki Dhil touches their holy feet.

The two Americans looked into each other's eyes, without words—the Calcutta-bound train was alongside.

"Remember, I'm responsible for you from now on, son!" Cadman said, as he loosed Skag's hand.

CHAPTER IV

THE MONKEY GLEN

Skag and Cadman were back in Hurda where Dickson Sahib lived, and the younger man was disconsolate at the thought of Cadman's leaving for England. During those few last days they were much together in the open jungle around the ancient unwalled city; and once as they walked, two strange silent native men passed them going in toward the wilderness.

"The priests of Hanuman," Cadman whispered.

Skag enquired. He had a new and enlarged place in his mind for everything about these men. Cadman explained that these priests serve the monkey people: to this purpose they are a separate priesthood. Abandoning possessions and loves and hates of their kind, they live lives of austerity, mingling with the monkey people in their own jungles; eating, drinking with them; sleeping near; playing and mourning with them—in every possible way giving expression to good-will. All this they do very seriously, very earnestly, with reverence mingled with pity.

"The masses here think these men worship the monkeys," Cadman added. "It's not true. Most Europeans dismiss them as fanatics—equally absurd. I've been out with them."

Skag had actually seen the faces of the two men just passed. The impression had not left his mind. They were dark clean faces, grooved by much patient endurance, strong with self-mastery and those fainter lines that have light in them and only come from years of service for others.

Cadman certainly had no scorn for these men. He had passed days and nights with their kind in one of the down-country districts. His tone was slow and gentle when he spoke of that period. It wasn't that Cadman actually spoke words of pathos and endearment. Indeed, he might have said more, except that two white men are cruelly repressed from each other in fear of being sentimental. They are almost as willing to show fear as an emotion of delicacy or tenderness.

"The more you know, the more you appreciate these forest men," Cadman capitulated and laughed softly at the sudden interest in Skag's face as he added: "I understand, my son. You want to go into the jungle with these masters of the monkey craft. You want to read their lives—far in, deep in yonder. Maybe they'll let you. They were singularly good to me. . . . It may be they will see that thing in your face which knocks upon their souls."

"What is that?"

Cadman laughed again.

"In the West they know little of these things; but the fact is, it's quite as you've been taught: the more a man overcomes himself, the more powers he puts on for outside work. And when a man is in charge of himself all through, he has a look in his eye that commands—yes, even finds fellowship with the priests of Hanuman."

"Would these priests see such a look?"

"Of course!"

"But why?"

"Because they have it themselves. It's evident as sun-tan, to the seers, who are what they are because they rule themselves. Your old Alec Binz had it right. You handle wild animals in cages or afield just in proportion as you handle yourself. Those who command themselves see self-command when it lives in the eye of another. . . . They called me—those priests did—years ago. I almost wanted to live with them for a while; but it was too hard."

"How was that?"

"They said I must forsake all other things in life to serve the monkey people—that I must stay years with them, winning their faith, before I would be of value—that all life in the world must be forgotten."

Cadman laughed wistfully. "I wasn't big enough," he added, "or mad enough, as you like. Perhaps they'll know you at once, or it might take labour and patience to convince them you have not an unkind thought toward any of their monkey friends and no scorn of them because they serve in such service."

The out and out staring fact of the whole matter, Skag realised, was that these priests believed the monkeys to be a race of men who have been far gone in degeneration. They gave their lives to help the return progress. The order of Hanuman had already endured for many generations. The value of their work was hardly appreciable from any standpoint outside; they counted little the years of a man's life; they were trained in patience to a degree hardly conceivable to a Western mind.

". . . Of course they work in the dark," Cadman said. "The natives try to obey in these matters, but do not understand; and one young European with a rifle can undo a whole lot of their devoted labour among the tree-people. You see, the priests work with care and kindness, following, ministering, accustoming the monkeys to them, never betraying them in the slightest—"

Skag nodded, keenly attentive. He knew well from his experience as a show trainer what it means to get the confidence of the big cats; and how months of careful work could be ruined in a moment by an ignorant hand. Deep, steady, inextinguishable *kindness* was the thing.

"Yes, to be kind and square," Cadman resumed. "And one of the strangest and most remarkable things that ever came to me in the shape of a sentence was from one of these priests. He was an old man, grey pallor stealing in under the weathered brown of his face. He had that look in his eye that has nothing to do with years, but means that a man is so sufficient unto himself that he can forget himself utterly. . . . He spoke of the condition of the tree-folk, of the incommunicable sorrow of them—as if it were his own destiny. The one sentence of his, hard to forget—in English would be like this:

"*'After a man has lived with these monkey people for a long time, and always been kind, one of them may come and stand before him and let tears roll down his hairy face. And this is all the confession of sorrow he can make!'*"

Skag caught the deep thing that had stirred Cadman. The latter added with a touch of scorn:

"Once I told this thing, as I have told you, to a group of Europeans in a steamer's smoking room. And two of them laughed—thought I was telling a funny story. . . . These priests are apt to be very bitter toward one who wrongs one of their free-friends. They believe that it is a just and good thing to make a man pay with his life, for taking the life of a monkey; because it impedes his coming up and embitters the others. One way to look at it?"

Skag was in and out of the jungle most of the days after Cadman left for Bombay to sail. Closer and closer he drew to the deep, sweet earthiness and the mysteries carried on outside the ken of most men. One dawn, from a distance he watched a sambhur buck pause on the brow of a hill. The creature shook his mane and lifted up his nose and sniffed the dawn of day.

Skag knew that it was good to him, knew how the sensitive grey nostrils quivered wide, drinking deep draughts of cool moist air. The grasses were rested; the trees seemed enamoured of the deep shadows of night. The river gurgled musically from the jagged rocks of her mid-current to the overleaning vines and branches of her borders.

This was a side stream of the Nerbudda. Already Skag shared with the natives the attitude of devotion to the great Nerbudda. She was sacred to the people, and to every creature good, for her gift was like the gift of mothers. When all the world was parched and full of deep cracks, yawning beneath a heaven white and cloudless, and rain forsook the land, and every leaf hung heavy and dust-laden; when heat and thirst and famine all increased, till creatures crept forth from their hot lairs at evening and moved in company—who had been enemies, but for sore suffering—then would she yield up her pure tides to satisfy their utmost craving. . . .

Skag lived deep through that morning. The rose and amber radiance of dawn fell into all the hearts of all the birds; and wordless songs came pulsing up from roots of growing things. The sambhur lifted high his head again and spread the fan of one ear toward the wind, while one breathed twice. Then there fell a sudden rustling on the branches; and swift along the river's brim, the sharp, plaintive cry of monkeys, beating down through all the startled stillness with their wailing voices. These turned, hurrying away in one direction, with fearless leaps and clinging hands and ceaseless chattering. Their cries at intervals, bringing answers, until the air was a-din with monkeys, leaping along the highways of the trees.

Women of the villages, children tending goats, labourers among the driftings of the hills and on the open slopes, holy men and those who toiled at any craft—heard the shrill calls along the margins of the jungle and knew that some evil had fallen on a leader of his kind among the monkey people.

Then Skag saw two priests of Hanuman rising up from the denser shadows where the river was lost in the jungle. Quickly girding themselves, they followed the multitudes. Skag did not miss their stern faces, nor the instant pause as they dipped their brown feet with prayers into the river. He dared to follow. The priests turned upon him, silent, frowning; but he was not sent back.

Skag recalled Cadman's words, but also that he was known among the natives as one white man not an animal-killer. His name Son of Power had followed him to Hurda; word about him had travelled with mysterious rapidity. To his amazement Skag found that the people of Hurda knew something of the story of the tiger-pit and his part in delivering the Grass Jungle people from the toils and tributes of the great snake. . . . He was not sent back.

For a long time, until the forenoon was half spent, the three marched silently. One halted at length to pick up from the leaves a white silk kerchief, bearing in one corner two English letters wrought in needle-work. This was lifted by the elder of the priests and folded in the thick windings of his loin-cloth. Deeper and deeper into the jungle they travelled, never far from the river.

Suddenly the branches parted, the path ceased; a smooth, perfect carpet of tender, green grass spread out before them and reached and clung to the lip of a deep, clear pool—beaten out through the ages, by the weight of the stream falling on a lower ledge of rock from the brow of a massive boulder. The mighty trees of the forest stretched their huge arms over this spot, as if to keep it secret, so that even the fierce sunshine was mellowed before it touched the earth.

In the midst of rich grasses, in the shadow of an overleaning rock, a wounded monkey lay stretched upon fresh leaves. The two priests went near him, softly, while the tree-branches filled in and swayed—under weight of monkeys finding places. Here and there a local chattering broke the stillness for a moment, where some dry branch snapped, refusing to bear its burden.

For minutes the two hesitated, considering the wounded one; then the elder priest drew out the kerchief. Skag did not understand all the words spoken, but he made out that this kerchief was a token that should find the hand that caused the wound "*and seal it unto torment.*" The second priest's lips moved, repeating the same covenant. The elder then turned back toward the city, signifying that Skag might follow.

After they had walked some time, the old priest halted and drew forth the kerchief again. He examined the monogram woven with a fine needle into the corner. To him the shape of the first English letter was like a ploughshare, and the second was like the form in which certain large birds fly in company over the heights of the hill country. The priest looked long, then hid the kerchief once more, and they hurried on.

Near the unwalled city, the priest sat down before the pandit, Ratna Ram, whose seat was under the kadamba tree by the temple of Maha Dev. Ratna Ram was learned in the signs of different languages and could write them with a reed, so that those who had knowledge could decipher his writing, even after many days and at a great distance: Ratna Ram, to whom the gods had given that greatest of all kinds of wisdom, whereby he could hold secretly any knowledge and not speak of it till the thing should be accomplished. (The pandit was well known to Skag who studied Hindi before him for an hour or more, on certain days.)

Taking the reed from Ratna Ram, the old priest carefully reproduced the letters he had memorised—A. V.—explained that he had found a kerchief, doubtless fallen from some foreigner as he walked in the jungle. . . . Did the pandit know the man whose name was written so? . . . Now the priest spoke rapidly in his own tongue, repeating the covenant Skag had heard him pronounce in the monkey glen.

For a while Ratna Ram sat silent. The priest waited patiently, knowing that the pandit's wisdom was working in him and that he was considering the matter.

Then Ratna Ram spoke to the priest:

"Oh, Covenanted, you are learned in many things and I am ignorant. But knowledge of some things has pierced to my understanding like a sharp sword. Consider, oh, Covenanted, Indian Government, who is lord over all this land, over the Mussulman and over us also, over our lands and over all our possessions, in whose hand is the protection of our lives and the safety of our cattle. The foreigner has no honour to the life of any creature of the jungle, neither in his heart, nor in his understanding, nor in his laws. But know this and understand it; to Government the life of one human is heavier to hold in the hand than all the lives of all the tribes of the people of Hanuman. This is a good and wise thing to remember at this time, for there is no safe place to hide from Government in all this land; no, not even in the rocks, if he be searching for those who have taken one of his lives; and there is no force to bring before him to meet his force; and there is no holding the life from him, that he will take in punishment; and if many lives have taken his one life, he will have them all. Consider these sayings."

When Ratna Ram had ceased speaking, the priest sat without answering for a short space; then he inquired:

"Has Government force enough to put between, that we should not accomplish to take the slayer alive?"

"No. His armies are not here; but it would not be many days before they would reach this place."

"Not before our purpose could be fulfilled?"

"It may be, not *before*. But soon after."

"That is well. We fear not death. Shall we not surely die? What matters it? Our covenant stands."

Ratna Ram begged the priest to rest a little under the kadamba tree. Rising up, he gathered his utensils of writing and put them in a cotton-bag; and with a glance at Skag to follow, left the place walking toward the city. Skag knew by this time, that his teacher, the pandit, considered the matter of serious import. They reached the verandah steps of an English bungalow and Skag would have retired, but Ratna Ram would not hear, wishing him to keep a record of this affair.

"The priest of Hanuman trusts *you*," he said, "and my righteousness to him, as well as to Government, must have witness."

He knocked. A girl came to the door. All life was changed for Skag. . . . The girl, seeing the shadowed face of the pandit, inquired if he sorrowed with any sorrow.

"Only the sorrow that over-shadows thy house, Gul Moti-ji."

Ratna Ram explained that he had come in warning, but also in equal service for the priests of Hanuman who wanted the life of her cousin—A. V.—the young stranger from England. The fact that the young man was away from Hurda this day was well for him, because he had shot and wounded a great monkey, the king of his people.

In the next few minutes Skag missed nothing, though his surface faculties were merely winding spools, compared to the activity of a great machine within. He grasped that A. V. stood for Alfred Vernon, the girl's cousin, a young man recently from England. . . . Yes, A. V. had occasionally gone into the jungle with a light rifle. Sometimes he had brought in a wild duck, or a grey *marhatta* hare; once a black-horned gazelle, but usually a parrot, a peacock or a jay. . . . Yes, sometimes he had been gone for hours. . . . Yes, she had told him about the evil and also the danger of shooting monkeys.

Skag now recalled the young man with the rifle—a well-fed,

well-groomed, well-educated young Englishman, thoroughly qualified sometime, to make a successful civil engineer and a career and fortune for himself in India.

The girl apparently had not seen Skag so far. The pandit had called her Gul Moti-ji. So this was the Rose Pearl—the unattainable! . . . And now the pandit informed her that though the cousin might be scornful, it would only be because he was foolish with the foolishness of the ignorant.

"But I am not scornful. I understand—" the girl said. "I am only considering swiftly what can be done."

"They are waiting the death of the great monkey—"

The girl's eyes were filled with shadows and great energies also.

"If his life could be saved?"

"Then his life could be saved, Gul Moti-ji," the pandit replied briefly, but Skag knew he meant the life of the cousin.

"Is it far?"

"Yes, two hours' walk."

Someone within the door of the bungalow now spoke, saying: "Carlin, dear, I may be a bit late—you must not be troubled about me."

The girl answered the voice within. . . . So her name was also Carlin. She had many names surely, but Skag liked this last one best. She turned to the pandit now, speaking slowly:

"Did one of the priests of Hanuman come to you with this story—just now?"

"Yes, Gul Moti-ji."

"Is he waiting?"

"Yes."

"Will he take me—to the place of the wounded one?"

The pandit considered. Skag felt very sure that the priest would do this.

"I will ask him. I can do no more. If the monkey still lives—your cousin's only hope will be in your healing power, Hakima."

"Wait—I will go with you, now."

Skag released his breath deeply when she had re-entered. Apparently she had not seen him so far.

The old priest arose as the three approached the kadamba tree.

"Peace, Brother," the girl said to him.

"Unto thee also, peace," he replied.

Skag marvelled at the inflections of her voice—low trailing words that awoke at intervals into short staccato utterances. It was all awake and alive with feeling. She did not ignore a fact the English often miss, that there are certain unwritten laws of these elder people which are as potent and unswerving as any mind-polished tablets that have come down to England from Greece and Rome.

It was an hour of marvelling to Skag. He saw something that he had not seen so far in India. To her face the darker Indian blood was but a redolence. Doubtless it was because of this—some ancient wonder and depth of lineage—that Skag had looked twice. He had never looked upon a woman this way before. No array of terms can convey the innocence of his concept. . . . She was tall for a girl—almost eye to eye with him.

He didn't quite follow her words of Hindi, but his mind was running deep and true to hers, in meanings. She told the priest that she had come to save her cousin, who never could be made to understand what he had done, even though he lost his life in forfeit. She said the monkey people would be devastated, if he paid his life; that the priests of Hanuman would be driven deeper and deeper into the jungles; that her heart was with them in soundness of understanding, for she was of India who hears and understands. She held up a little basket saying she had brought bandages, stimulants, nourishments, and had come asking permission to go with the priests now, to the wounded one, to care for him with her own strength. . . .

Skag saw that her scorn for the ignorance that had caused the wound was a true thing; that she felt something of the mystery of pity for the monkey people; that she could be very terrible in her rage if she let it loose, but that she loved this stupid cousin also. All Skag's faculties were playing at once, for he perceived at the same time this girl would see many things of life in terms of humour and it would be good to travel the roads with her because of this. . . . Apparently she had not seen him, Sanford Hantee, to this moment.

The priest weighed her words and spoke coldly, saying that his order did not consider consequences to men, when they took life. A monkey king had been shot. The wound was eating him to death. It was unwritten law which may never be broken, for the life of one who kills a monkey to be taken by the priests of Hanuman. Up through the ages this law had not served to destroy the monkey people, but to protect them.

The girl said gently: "Let me go to him. Do you not see that I am indeed of this land, with its blood in my veins?"

Ratna Ram had taken his seat once more under the kadamba tree. It was early afternoon and the three were travelling through the jungle. The girl Carlin was always looking ahead—one thing only upon her mind—time and distance and words, as clearly obstructions to her, as the occasional branches across the path. Once when Skag fixed a big stone for her to pass dry across a shallow ford, she turned to thank him, but her eyes did not actually fill with any image of himself. He missed nothing—neither the standpoint of the priest, nor of the English, nor the vantage of this girl who stood between.

It was a queer breathless day for him, altogether to his liking, but more intense than he understood. The girl's lithe power, the tirelessness of her stride, the quick grace, low voice and steady-shaded eyes full of, full of—

Skag hadn't the word at hand. Cadman Sahib would know. . . That look of the eyes seldom went with young faces, Skag reflected; in fact, he had only found it before in old mothers and old nurses and old physicians. Certainly it had to do with forgetting oneself in service. . . .

The priest began to talk or chant as he strode along. It was neither speech nor song. It did not bring the younger two closer together, though they saw that monkeys were following, up in their tree-lanes. At times when Skag dropped behind, he wondered why the girl did not see the things that delighted him—a sparkling pool, the gleam of damp rocks, the velvet moss with restless etchings of sunbeam. Yet he knew that it was only to-day she looked past these things; that these really were her things; that she belonged to the jungle, not to the house. . . . She must greatly love this stupid cousin. . . . Skag never tired watching the firm light tread of her—like the step of one who starts out to win a race. . . . There was jubilant music of a waterfall—the priest reverently stopped his chanting.

Then they came to the great rock and the second priest arose, his eye glancing past Skag and Carlin to the eye of his fellow of the order of Hanuman.

For an instant the silence was of an intensity that hurt.

"Is he—?" Carlin began.

The priest who had brought them answered, though there had been no words:

"No, the king yet lives."

Under the shadow of the overleaning rock, stretched on fresh wet leaves, the monkey king was lying. His eyes were bright, but the haze of fever was over them; thin grey lips parted and parched; a strained look about the mouth. He breathed in quick, panting breaths—too far gone to be afraid, as Carlin leaned over; but there was a forward movement in the over-hanging branches, a swift breathless shifting of the monkeys.

She opened the little basket. Skag watched her face as she first laid her hand on the monkey's head. He saw the thrill of horror and understood it well, for this was alien flesh her hand touched—not like the flesh of horse or dog or cow which is all animal. She struggled with a second revulsion, but put it away. She found the wound in the shoulder and asked for hot water, which a priest quickly prepared and brought in an earthen jar. She bathed the wound, and put some liquid on his dry lips. The tree man was too full of alien suffering to be cognisant, as yet; but the great test was now, when under her hands appeared a little instrument of jointed steel. . . . She was talking to him softly as to a sick child. He drew a quick breath—his eyes wide as a low cry came from him, and the whole forest seemed to quiver with a suffocating interest, monkeys ever pressing nearer. Skag saw one little brown hand stretch (twisting as if to bury its thumb) and lay hold of Carlin's dress. . . . Then he sighed, like a whip of air when a spring is released and Skag saw the bullet in the instrument.

It was held before him. She dropped it into Skag's hand thinking it was the priest's. . . . Then she dressed the wound, giving medicine and nourishment until the tree king slept.

The afternoon was spent.

CHAPTER V

THE MONKEY GLEN (CONTINUED)

In the lull Carlin appeared to have no thought of going back to Hurda. The younger priest made her comfortable with dry leaves. Skag brought a log for her to lean against. For the first time she appeared to notice that he was not one of the priests of Hanuman. . . . She did not speak. Dusk was falling. At intervals she would look into his face. The priests brought fruit and chapattis. Delicate sounds of a wide stillness began to steal through the shadows. Creatures of the forest crept out from their lairs and called, one to another. Down towards the river a tiger coughed; and there was a shiver along the branches where the monkeys sat. The priests had merely glanced at each other. Carlin had not seemed to hear.

Three torches were kept blazing through the night, and by their light the girl gave medicine and nourishment to the wounded one from time to time. She did not speak to Skag, who often sat before her for an interval, but she would occasionally look into his face, her eyes dwelling with a curious calm upon him.

In the morning the wounded one was conscious. That day the suffering wore upon him, and they brought wet leaves as the sun rose higher and kept them changed beneath him, for coolness. . . . The fever left him after the heat of noon. Not until then, did Carlin look upon Skag and speak at the same time.

"Have I seen you before? . . . Who are you?"

When Skag heard himself answer, he realised his voice had something in it he had never known before.

. . . That afternoon Carlin went back to Hurda, but came again for an hour late in the afternoon. The next morning early, she came once more and Skag was there. That afternoon, the elder priest said:

"He will live."

"Yes," Carlin repeated softly.

"But you don't seem glad," Skag said.

She was looking back toward the city.

"I was wondering if I could make them see what it means to spend the afternoon in the jungle with a rifle."

"Couldn't they understand that this work of yours has delivered your cousin from death?"

"Oh, no, they would laugh at that. They would remind me that I have always been strange. Even if my cousin lost his life, they would not learn. The priests would be called fanatics and would be made to suffer and all the monkey-peoples—"

Skag could see that.

"Why do you not leave them?"

"Oh, I do not hate my people. I have many brothers, real men; and then you must know English Government does wonderful things."

They were starting back toward the city leaving the two priests. Most strangely, as no one Skag had ever met, Carlin could see the native and the English side of things. He felt that Cadman would say this of her, too. He wanted sanction on such things, because he felt that already his judgment was not cold—on matters that concerned her. Everything about her was more than one expected. She seemed to have an open consciousness, which saw two or all sides of a question before speech.

A great weakness had come upon Skag. It was in his limbs and in his voice and in his mind. It had not been so when the priests were near, nor when there was work to do. Now they were alone; the jungle was vast with a new vastness. The girl was taller and more powerful—her sayings veritable, equitable. There were golden flashes among the rich shadows of her mind, like the cathedral dimness of the jungle on their right hand as they walked, slanting shafts of sunlight raining through.

They walked slowly. Skag reflected that since his first sight of the sambhur, he had watched and done nothing. All his life had been like that. Yet this girl watched and worked, too. She loved the English and the natives, too. She had skilled hands, a trained body, a cultured mind—certainly a wonderful mind, as full of wonder as this jungle, with a sacred river flowing through.

Moreover, she could ask questions like Cadman—the spirit of things. He told her of his mother, of his running away from school when he first saw the animals at Lincoln Park Zoo, how they enveloped him, so that he thought nothing but of them, lived only for animals later as a circus trainer, and had come to India to see the life of the wild creatures outside of cages. . . . His tongue fumbled in the telling.

"But I do not see yet, why the priests of Hanuman let you go with them—"

"Nor I," said Skag.

"But they know you are not an animal-killer—"

They walked rather slowly. . . . Night was upon them when they reached the edge of the jungle and heard voices. The back of Skag's hand nearest Carlin was swiftly touched and she whispered breathlessly:

"My people. They are coming for me—good-bye—"

The last few words had been just for him; the tone might have come up from the centre of himself.

Skag was alone, but he did not hurry into the city. There was more in the solitude than ever before, more mystery in the jungle, more in the dusty scent of the open road. Greater than all, in spite of all doubting and realisation of insignificance, there was unquestionably more in himself.

Early the next morning, Skag was abroad in the city and saw the two priests of Hanuman approach Ratna Ram. They raised their hands in silent greeting as he came near and immediately arose and turned toward Carlin's bungalow. Skag was glad to follow, when they signified he might, for the thing at hand was his own deep concern. There was a catch in his throat as Carlin appeared on the verandah. Her eyes met Skag's before she spoke to the priests.

"Is he worse?"

The elder spoke for both, as is the custom:

"Peace be on thee, thou of gentle voice and skillful hands. We greet thee in the name of Hanuman; and are come, to render up to thee the forfeit life, even according to our covenant; for thou hast saved the wounded king, and he will not die. Behold the cloth with the shape of the foreigner's sign in it; this we held for a token that the foreigner's life was ours: this we render now to thee. His life is thine and not ours."

The old man laid the silk kerchief at Carlin's feet.

Skag had thought the danger over yesterday, but he saw that the young Englishman's life held in ransom, had only just now been returned to the girl. . . . That forenoon was the time to Skag of the great tension. Carlin had stood for a moment longer than necessary on the verandah, after the priests had turned away. It was as if she would speak—but that might signify anything or nothing. It was just a point that made the hours more breathless now, like the sentence of quick low tones last night, when the voices of her people were heard at the edge of the jungle. Were these everything or nothing—glamour or life-lock? Often he remembered that her eyes had sought his to-day, even before looking to the priests for news.

He stood at the edge of the jungle at high noon. The city was filmed in heat. Faint sounds seemed to come out of the sky. Skag was watching one certain road. The trance of stillness was not broken. He turned back into the green shade. . . . He would not delay in Hurda. He would not linger. His friend Cadman had been gone for some days. Yet about going there was a new and intolerable pain.

Skag forced himself back from the clearing. He felt less than himself with his eyes fixed upon that certain road; a man always does when he wants something terribly. Still he did not enter the deep jungle. At last he heard a step. He turned very slowly, not at all like a man to whom the greatest thing of all has happened. . . . Carlin had come and was saying:

". . . I heard voices in the house this morning when you came. Someone was listening, so I could not speak. . . . Something keeps growing—something about our work in the jungle. I want to go to the monkey glen again—now."

It was like unimaginable riches. There were moments in which he had counterpart thoughts for hers in his own mind; as if she spoke from another lobe of his own brain. Her words expressed himself.

"I thought you would be here," she told him presently. "I

wanted to see you again."

She was flushed from crossing the broad area tranced in noon heat; and now the green cool of the jungle was sweet to her, and they were close together, but walking not so slowly as last night. . . . Loneliness came to them when they reached the empty place where the wounded one had lain in the shelter of the rock. They felt strangely excluded from something that had belonged to them. All the wide branches above were empty. Still that was only one breath of chill. Tides of life brimmed high between them; they had vast mercies to spare for outer sorrows.

"He may not have done so well after being moved," she whispered.

Skag was thinking of the cough he had heard. The monkeys had understood that. . . . Just now the younger of the two priests of Hanuman appeared magically. There was quiet friendliness deep in his calm, desireless eyes.

"All is well," he told them. "They have carried their king to a yet more secret place, where we may not—"

He did not finish that sentence but added: "Only we who serve them may go there. All is well. They would not have moved him, had they not been sure that life was established in him."

The priest did not linger. Then Carlin wanted to know everything—how India had called Skag at the very first. . . . Was it all jungle and animal interest; or was he called a little to the holy men? Did he not yearn to help in the great famine and fever districts; long to enter the deep depravities of the lower cities with healing?

Skag had listened in a kind of passion. Wonderful unfoldment in regard to these things had come to him from Cadman Sahib, but as Carlin touched upon them, they loomed up in his mind like the slow approach to cities from a desert. Carlin's eyes, turned often to his, were like all the shadows of the jungle gathered to two points of essential dark, and pinned by a star veiled in its own light.

"I thought it was only the wild animals that called to me, but now I know better," he said. "And my friend Cadman, who has gone, opened so much to me. He often spoke of the holy men, until one had to be interested—"

Carlin halted and drew back looking at him with a kind of still strength all her own.

"You do not know that the natives think *you* are something of the kind?"

"I—a holy man?"

"I heard them speak of you last night. You see they have heard of your deliverance of the Grass Jungle people."

Skag was learning how wonderfully news travels in India.

"Of course, it was all easy to believe, after what I saw—"

"What did you see?" he asked.

"That the two priests of Hanuman permitted you to follow them here—"

Then Carlin verified what Cadman had said, that the priests make no mistakes in these things. . . . Presently Skag was listening to accounts of Carlin's life. He was insatiable to hear all. In some moments of the telling, it was like a phantom part of himself that he was questing for, through her words. Her story ran from the Vindhas to the Western Ghat mountains, touching plain and height and shore (but not yet High Himalaya), touching tree jungle, civil station, railway station and cantonments; stories including a succession of marvelous names of cities and men; intimations that many great servants of India and England were of her name; that she had seven living brothers, all older; all at work over India. Finally Skag heard that Carlin had spent eight years in England studying medicine and surgery, and again that the natives called her the *Gul Moti*, which means the Rose Pearl; or *Hakima*, which means physician. But her own name was Carlin!

When they came back to the edge of the jungle again, it was the hour of afterglow. Its colours entered into him and were always afterward identified with her. Carlin left him, laughingly, abruptly; and Skag was so full of the wonder of all the world, that he had not thought to ask if he should ever see her again.

As night came on, Skag thought more and more of the parting; and that there had been no words about Carlin's coming again. He felt himself living breathlessly towards the thought of seeing her; and it was not long before this fervour itself awoke within him a counter resistance. Manifestly this pain and yearning and tension—was not the way to the full secret. As carefully stated before, Skag approved emphatically of the Now. The present moving point was the best he had at any given time. He thought a man should forget himself in the Now—like the animals.

Yet the hours tortured. That night had little sleep for him, and the marvels of Carlin—face and voice, laugh, heart, hand—grew upon him contrary to all precedent. This was a battle against all the wild animals rolled into one; most terribly, a battle because there seemed such a beauty about the yearning which the girl awoke in him.

He was abroad early next day. The thought had come, that she might find him in the jungle at noon or soon afterward as yesterday. As the dragging forenoon wore on, Skag was in tightening tension. He hated himself for this, but the fact stubbornly remained that all he cared for in the world was the meeting again. It seemed greater than he—this agony of separation. It brought all fears and self-diminishing. It told him that Carlin would run from him, if she knew he wanted her presence so. He knew her kind of woman loves self-conquest—the man who can powerfully wait and not be victimised by his own emotions. . . .

So it was that Skag fled from himself, when there was still a half hour before noon. He could not meet her, longing like this.

There was sweat on Skag's forehead as his limbs quickened away from the place of meeting yesterday. The more he left it behind, the more sure he became that Carlin would come. It seemed he was casting away the one dear and holy thing he had ever known—yet it resolved to this: that he dared not stand before her with his heart beating as if he had run for miles and his chest suffocating with emotions—the very features of his face uncertain, his voice unreliable. . . . If a man entered the cage of a strange tiger, as little master of himself as this—it would be taking his life in his own silly hands. Skag couldn't get past this point, and he had a romantic adjustment in his mind about Carlin and the tiger—one all his own.

Deeper and deeper into the jungle he went, along the little river, but all paths appeared to lead him to the monkey glen; and there he sat down at last and remembered all that Alec Binz had told him about handling himself in relation to handling animals, and all that Cadman Sahib had told him from the lips of wise men of India . . . but all that Skag could find was pain—rising, thickening clouds of pain.

He kept seeing her continually as she entered the jungle (walking so silently and swift, her face flushed from crossing the open space this side of the city in the terrible heat of noon)—and then not finding him there. Something about this hurt like degrading a sacred thing, but he didn't mean to. He repeated that he didn't mean to hurt her. . . . Then suddenly it occurred to him that it was all his own thinking about her coming at noon. There had been no word about it. She might not have thought of coming again. This was like a cold breath through the jungle. It was as intolerable as the other thought of her disappointment.

. . . There was an almost indistinguishable *slithering* of soft pads in the branches. Skag looked up suddenly and the air seemed jerked with a concussion of his start. The monkeys were back. They had been watching, the branches filling. When he looked up, the whole company stirred nervously.

Skag laughed. It was good. There was but one formulated thought—that Carlin would be glad to hear this; she would appreciate this. The return of the monkeys had a deep significance to Skag, because he had really first seen the wonder of Carlin just here—working over the wounded one. The immediate tree-lanes were filled with watchers in suffocating tension then. It was curiosity now—nothing covered, but playful. Skag wished he could chant like the priests, for the monkey-folk. He wished he had many baskets of chapattis to spread out upon the grasses for them. . . . As he sat, face-lifted, he heard that tiger-cough again.

The monkeys huddled a second—it was panic—then they melted from sight. It was like the swift blowing away one by one, of the top papers of a deep pile on a desk.

Skag was now essentially absorbed. It couldn't be a mistake. The monkeys knew. He himself knew from days and nights with the big cats. There was no cough just like that. It was in a different direction from before, back toward the city this time, but as before, muffled and close down to the riverbed. . . . Nothing of the cub left in that cough; neither was there hurry or hunger or any particular rage or fear. A big beast finishing a sleep, down in some sandy niche by the river; a solitary beast full of years, a bit drowsy just this moment, and in no particular hurry to take up the hunt. Such was the picture that came to Skag with a keen kind of enjoyment. The thrill had lifted his misery for a minute. This was something to cope with. It took away the heart-breaking sense of inadequacy.

It wasn't the thrill of a hunt that animated Skag. The fact is, he hadn't even a six-shooter along. This was the closeness of the real thing again—the deep joy, perhaps, of testing outside of cages once more, the power that had never failed. And just now along the river and beyond the place where the cough came from—Carlin was coming!

The last of the monkeys had flicked away. Skag arose and held his hand high, palm toward her. She beckoned, but still came forward. Skag moved without haste, but rapidly. All the beauty and wonder of Carlin was the same; it lived in his heart, integrate and unparalleled as ever, but some power had come to him from the cough of the tiger. Around all the fear, even for her life, was the one splendid thing—that she had followed him into the monkey glen.

She was nearing the place where the cough had come from, yet Skag did not run. A second time he held up his hand, palm outward, but she still came forward laughing.

"You ran from me?"

"I did not think of you coming so far—to-day."

Skag had stepped between her and the river, turning her toward the city, but Carlin drew back.

"I have come so far. I want to go to our—to the monkey glen!"

She was watching him strangely. Skag understood something that moment: that he might know of Carlin's delight through her eyes, of all joy and good that he might bring, but that he should never know from her eyes if he brought hurt. Skag put this back into the deep place of his mind.

"All right. We'll go back," he said. "They were here—the whole troupe. Just a minute ago, they swung away—"

He saw for an instant her wonderment that he had come

alone. She would have been very glad to see the monkey people again; she could not quite see why she should have missed this; she did not understand his words—that he had not expected her to follow into the glen.

She was sitting down on her own log, but he stood. Skag was driven to speak. The need had now to do with one of his favourite words. It was a matter of *equity* that he speak. The words came in a slow ordered tone:

"I was waiting for you there—back at the edge of the jungle—but it came to me that I was not ready."

Carlin had been looking away into the three-lanes. Her eyes came up to his.

"Not ready?" she said.

"All night I could only remember one thing—"

"What thing?"

"That you had not told me you would come again."

Carlin's shoulders lifted a little. She cleared her throat, saying:

"I thought of it."

"This morning the idea occurred that you might come to the jungle at noon—like yesterday, but the hours wouldn't pass after that. I met something different that would not be quiet—"

"Where?"

"I mean in myself."

Carlin's eyes widened a little, but she only said:

"Oh!"

"It would not rest. I could not wait in calm. I was afraid you wouldn't come—yet I was afraid of your coming. My face worked of its own accord, and my words would not say what I knew—"

"When was that?"

"It was worse when I reached the jungle a little before noon and began to watch for you."

"And—you ran away?"

"I was not good to look upon."

"But you are not like that now—quite controlled—like blue ice—"

Skag turned his eyes slowly back the path by the river where the cough had come from.

"I am better now," he said.

"I wonder if anyone ever thought of running away like that?"

"It is not a good feeling to be at the mercy of oneself," Skag said.

Carlin caught a quick breath. There was a steadiness in his eyes. It was steadier than anything she knew. The light of it was so high and keen that it seemed *still.*

"Nothing like this has happened before," he said quietly.

Carlin arose. Their eyes met level.

"Everything is changed," he went on. "It was like a grief that you were not here—when the monkeys came in. . . . I'm not right. I did not know before that a girl was part of me. It was all animals before. I'm not ready—but I will be! You are good to listen, but really you had to—"

Carlin let her lids fall a second.

"I mean I couldn't stop when it started."

There was silence before he finished: "I know everything better. I know all the creatures better—all the cries they make. And yet I'm less—I'm only half—"

It was then her hand came out to him.

"Does it mean anything to you?" he asked.

"Yes—"

"*Does it mean everything to you—too?*"

Her voice trailed. It was closer. It was everywhere. It was like a voice coming up from his own heart:

"Yes, everything—especially because you could run away. . . . But I—came!"

They were walking toward Hurda among the shadows, Skag closer to the river. . . . The night was coming with a richness they had never seen—tinted shadows of purple, orange and rose—almost a living gleam to the colours; the evening air cool and sweet.

Carlin told him that her family must understand and be considered and give approval. . . . There was an eldest brother in Poona who must be seen. . . . All arrangements must be made with him. Skag said he would go to Poona at once. . . .

They were lingering now at the edge of the jungle; its spices upon them in the dry air.

". . . And I will wait here in Hurda," Carlin was saying. "You may be gone many days. You may not find him at once, and you will have to wait at Poona, but I shall know when you come. The train coming *up* is before noon. Listen! You will not find me at the bungalow. No, that would not be the way for us. . . . This will be perfect. I will be waiting for you—our place—back in the monkey glen."

"It is the perfect thought, but you must not go back there alone," he said. "I had not meant to tell you now, but it was that—made me steady—a tiger back there. He gave me nerve for your coming—a good turn it was, the most needful turn! . . Yes, a tiger lying down on the river margin, as we talked—do not go in deeper, when I am away. . . . And on the day I come, meet *me here* at the edge of the jungle and we will go in there to our place—together."

CHAPTER VI

JUNGLE LAUGHTER

It was while Skag was waiting near Poona, for Carlin's eldest brother Roderick Deal, that he became toiled in the snare of his own interest in jungle laughter. It is a strange tale; lying over against the mud wall of the English caste system in India. It is to be understood that a civil officer of high rank in that country is a man whose word is law. His least suggestion is imperative. The usages of his household may not be questioned by a thought, if one is wise.

Police Commissioner Hichens was such a man. He was stationed in Bombay and there is nothing better in appointment in all India. His responsibilities were heavy like those of an empire. Personally he was austere—entirely unapproachable. Of his home life no one knew anything whatever, outside the very few of equal rank. It was understood that the mother of his two small children had died more than a year ago. Some indiscreet person had mooted that she was not sent Home in time. Still, European women do not live long in that climate anyway; and it is common knowledge that to maintain a family requires several successive mothers.

The present Mrs. Hichens was but recently a bride; a mere girl and lovely; but within a few weeks of her landing, Bombay fever had begun to destroy the more tangible qualities of her beauty—which could not be permitted.

It does not take long for the most exalted official to discover that Bombay fever resembles the Supreme Being in that it is no respecter of persons. Yet it was not even so nearly convenient to send this Mrs. Hichens Home, as it had been to send that Mrs. Hichens Home; and that had been quite out of the question. But the Western Ghat mountains furnish a very good barricade against Bombay fever. (Devoutly inclined persons have even intimated that they were specially placed there for the convenience of men who are much attached to their homes.)

Extending a thousand miles parallel with the coast, from five to forty miles inland, built mostly of pinnacles and peaks rising a few hundred or a few thousand feet from near sea level, more rugged than any mountains of their size in the world, the Western Ghats are like a section of Himalaya in miniature. The railway line up has a reversing-station proclaimed far and wide to be the most splendid piece of railway engineering on earth. (That there are several more splendid in the Rocky Mountains is unimportant.)

Just over the top, about seventy miles from Bombay, is Khandalla and Lanowli and further on, Poona. Poona is a military station, sometimes too far. Lanowli is a railway station—which means that no one lives there who is fit to associate with a police commissioner's wife. But Khandalla is no station at all, being only a small mountain village with three or four abandoned bungalows far apart from each other. Heaven knows who built them in the beginning, but whoever it was, they must have done it too late, because there is a neglected grave or two near each one.

The native agents got in every good argument for the bungalows, but Police Commissioner Hichens was not persuaded. He seemed to have a constitutional antipathy to those bungalows.

No, the bungalows might be safer and dryer and warmer at night; they might be cleaner and healthier and more comfortable all the time; but he wanted a tent and he meant to put it where he wanted it. So, at great expense of time and labour on the part of natives, but very little expenditure of money on his part, he succeeded in hoisting a tent from Bombay to the top of the Western Ghat mountains, of a size and of an age and of a strength which suggested a military mess-camp.

The tent was set up in the Jungle at the edge of Khandalla. The servants would find quarters in Khandalla village; a cook, a cook's servant-boy and a butler for the entire household; a boy for the small son, an ayah for the wee girl and a very expensive ayah for the lady herself.

If an ayah is expensive enough, she is usually a very intelligent person, thoroughly informed on most general subjects pertaining to her own country and entirely competent to impart that information. It is understood she will always interpret the native standpoint relative to any matter under discussion. Her value as a servant may be great, but her value as an instructor will be greater. It was necessary that each of the ayahs should be wife to one of the men servants, but it is always possible to make a temporary arrangement of that sort to accommodate the customs of a high official.

So the present Mrs. Hichens was to be established in the tent, very comfortably matted as to the floor and furnished with all necessary appointments of a satisfying quality and wealthy appearance. Men of high rank must do all things with a certain pomp and circumstance, otherwise the ignorant might sometimes forget their rank. And rank must never be allowed to be forgotten.

Police Commissioner Hichens would spend all week-ends with her; that is to say, he would leave Bombay by the first train going up after Court closed on Saturday and would be obliged to take the Sunday evening train down. The two children so recently come into the care of a second mother, would be occupied and entertained by their servants; and the little girl, not quite three years old, would be under the additional guardianship of a Great Dane dog who had once belonged to her own mother.

It will be observed that the Great Dane dog is spoken of as a personality. He was so. He seemed to have quite fixed conclusions about the family. He ignored the servants (excepting Bhanah the cook, who was a servant as far out of the ordinary as the lady's own ayah). He tolerated the small boy. He approved of the new lady. He never ceased to mourn for his dead mistress; especially in the presence of the man.

He would extend his great length on the floor in a low couchant position, not too close to where the man sat—and search the strong human face with eyes more strong. Without the twitch of a muscle anywhere in his whole body, he would endure the man's gaze as long as the man chose, with a level look of cold, untiring rebuke. There was no anger in it, no flash of light, no flame of passion—but it had a way of eating in.

The servants bear common witness that it is the only thing they have ever known to drive the Sahib away from the delightful relaxations of his own home, which he claimed as sanctuary from the stress and grind of his official days. But the Great Dane Nels had done it more than once. Afterward the Sahib would sometimes take Nels on a hunting-furlough.

It was the first Mrs. Hichens who took the puppy with her, when she went to India with Police Commissioner Hichens; and before she died he was made to promise her on his honour, that he would care for and protect Nels as if Nels were is own son, so long as Nels should live. There was no help for it.

Especially as it was quite well known among the servants, that on the very day of her death she had made the Sahib with his own hands lay the sleeping child over on the bed underneath Nels' out-stretched paws; because this was done in the presence of Baby's ayah and of her own ayah also, and therefore two witnesses had heard her say:

"Nels, I am giving my baby to you. The Sahib her father is not able to be with her, much. But you are to care for my baby for me. Do you understand, my dear?" She often called Nels "my dear" with a peculiar inflection on the *dear* and an upward lilt of tone.

And Nels had agreed, because he pressed the little body hard and lifted up his big grey head and cried a long, low cry. And the lady had laughed a little and wiped glistening tears from her death-misted face, for her baby would be—not *quite* alone.

So all the servants knew that Nels had owned the child from that day. Now it is not a wise thing to antagonise a body of East Indian servants in matters which they consider sacred; and Police Commissioner Hichens was a lawyer and a judge and a wise man. He might fear Nels as he feared death itself, the two being equivalent in his mind, but he might not destroy Nels with his own hand, nor let it be known that he had caused the great dog's death. Still, if he took Nels with him on hunting-furloughs, as often as possible setting him to charge most deadly game, there was always the possibility of an accident.

To many it seemed strange that the present Mrs. Hichens, a regal young English thing, was made to live in a lonely tent, well back among dense jungle growths, quite out of sight or call away from any human habitation, with her husband's little son and littler daughter and the Great Dane dog. Certainly the servants were about during the daytime; as much out of sight as possible, according to their good teaching. But at night there were no servants about; they were all far away at the other end of the village, because the natives who lived at this side were low caste.

And it was at night the thing developed. A slow-driving inquisition, night after night. It drove her through and beyond the deadly fever lassitude. She was not building up out of it;

she was beaten down below it. She was beaten through all the successive stages of breaking nerves. She used all the known arguments, all the intellectual methods to sustain pure courage, to hold herself immune. She used them all up.

At first, when her husband came up for his weekends, he was quite evidently pleased with his arrangement. And it would take a self-confidence which had long since gone a-glimmering out of her, to break in on his enthusiasm with any criticism of his provisions for her comfort; certainly no criticism on any basis of noise. It has been said that Police Commissioner Hichens was an unapproachable man; and some things are impossible. One can die, you know, any death. But some things are entirely impossible.

The day came when she dragged her weary weight up from the couch and drove her unsteady frame along the new pathway through jungle thickets toward the village. The idea had been gnawing in her consciousness for days; to find the nearest house or hut or any kind of place where human beings lived, so as to have it in her mind where to run when the time came. It had come to that. It went in circles through her brain; when the time came to run, she positively must know where to run.

Her progress was slow and painful. When her limbs shook so she could not stand alone, she leaned against a tree. She must not lie down on the ground on account of the centipedes and scorpions.

"Hello—"

Startled a little, she turned toward the voice. A man's voice, very low. It came from somewhere behind her. She broke away from her support and the fever-surge caught her and whipped her from head to foot. Her balance was going—

"I'm sorry. I didn't mean to frighten you."

She was kept from falling by the arm of the stranger.

"No. It's the fever. I assure you it's the fever."

Now he just steadied her with one hand. The fever was filling her brain with a dull haze. . . . He was slender and not tall. He was much bronzed. She could see only his eyes and his mouth. He spoke again:

"Why are you alone in this jungle—with such a fever?"

The words dropped into her consciousness; even, smooth, like pebbles gently released into water.

Then the blackness of outer darkness came up between.

. . . That was how the present Mrs. Hichens began to know Skag.

He carried her back along the path, fresh-marked by her own footsteps, to the tent.

Next afternoon he called to learn how she was. He had a sheaf of wild mountain lilac-blooms in his hand.

"Oh, lovely! I haven't seen lilacs since England."

"They make me think of my mother," he said, giving the flowers into her hands.

"I would so much like to hear about your mother."

Skag had not the habit of much speaking, but he found it easy to tell this English girl about the mother who had died when he was a child. She leaned against banked pillows and watched the changes flow across his face. They were almost startling and yet so clean, so wholesome, that she felt inwardly refreshed, as by a breath from mountain heights.

Naturally he went on to tell her about Carlin; but when at last he spoke her name, the English girl interrupted him:

"Is it possible you are meaning Doctor Carlin Deal?"

"Yes; do you know her?" Skag asked.

"I have met her several times—quite frightened at first, because I had heard about her—you know she is very learned, even for one much older."

"I know she is a physician."

"Yes; London Medical. But it's not just her profession; it's herself. She's really wonderful; her sweetness is so strong and—all her strengths are so lovely."

"She is wonderful to me," Skag said.

"I'm congratulating you, you understand?" The present Mrs. Hichens smiled as she added: "I've heard that she has a fine discernment of men."

He went before sunset. After he had gone she asked her ayah to find out about who he was and whatever concerning him.

When Police Commissioner Hichens came up that week-end, he was so seriously dissatisfied with the tediousness of her recovery, that she had no inclination to tell him about having gone out from the tent on her own unsteady feet, at all. Certainly it would be calamitous for him to hear of her having been carried in by a perfect stranger. For which reason she called her ayah, while the Sahib was in his bath before dinner and said to her hurriedly:

"Ayah, will you do a thing for my sake?"

"To the shedding of my blood, Thou Shining."

"Then guard from the master that he shall not learn of my going out, or of the stranger who appeared."

"He shall never learn. Never while he lives shall he learn, unless from your own lips."

"Will all the other servants help you, Ayah dear?"

"It is already considered and determined among us. He shall never learn from us."

"Why are you all good to me?"

"Because by the hand of our master, who is our father and our mother, our bodies live; but by the grace of thy soul our hearts are glad. *It is better to have joy in the heart one day than to endure upon the fatness which grows out of a full stomach for ten years.*"

"Oh, Ayah, don't tell me things like that, because they are never to be forgotten."

"That is a great saying, oh Flower-of-Life. A saying come down from many generations. My people have found in it much food. The most poor among us go empty many days by the strength in it. And it is known that holy men have lived long years of holy life, without any satisfaction to the body at all, dwelling in that courage by which the unutterable of suffering may be endured, entirely by the *memory of one day*."

The ayah's voice finished in the tones of ceremony; and she moved smoothly from the room, unconscious that she had not been dismissed.

The following evening, after the police commissioner had gone down, the ayah brought report concerning the stranger. His name was Sanford Hantee Sahib. He was an American Sahib. He did not consort with any of his own people, nor with Europeans. Of all human beings he had only one friend and associate, Cadman Sahib, who was a great man among men—as was well known by even the ignorant. Cadman Sahib had been heard to call him "Skag," but Cadman Sahib would permit no one to call him by that title excepting himself; therefore it was a sealed title, to pronounce which few are worthy. Five days ago Sanford Hantee Sahib had come by train from far in the interior, beyond the Grass Jungle country, to meet an Indian Sahib of high rank in the railway service, at Poona. It was an appointment personal to himself; no one knew the purpose. Also, why Cadman Sahib had not come together with him was not known, unless—

"Oh, Ayah! I don't care a bit about Cadman Sahib—*will* you be good enough. What about the man? Now go on."

"Most illustrious lady, the thing is an exaltation. I am poor and ignorant. My head is at your feet. One like I am should not approach power like his save turning fresh from a bath."

"Ayah dear! I am prepared."

"He has the power to control all wild animals. So great is his power that not long ago, when he and his so-fortunate friend Cadman Sahib had both fallen into a tiger pit-trap and a mighty young tiger in his full strength had come after them, falling bodily down upon them and being full of fright and fury, had turned upon them to destroy them, beholding his master's face, the beast had become subject to him in the instant and had sat quietly before him the whole night, without moving to hurt them. What man will require more than this?"

"For Heaven's sake! What a tale. But Ayah, what sort of man is he?"

"Who will be able to know what sort of man? Is it not enough?"

"We require much more than that."

"Lady, I—who am not as you are—I have not bathed since dawn. Surely calamity will fall on me, if I set my tongue to the nature of such an one."

"If he is holy, then he will be willing to help."

"The knowledge of him among men is that he *is that*."

"Then, Ayah, I will take the danger of calamity away from you, for I have need. Speak."

"It is known that he resembles the most high masters themselves, in that he is *always kind*. And yet there was a strange saying, that he permitted his friend Cadman Sahib to destroy the head of a mighty serpent who had feasted upon the creatures and children of a Grass Jungle village. Now these things could not both be true at the same time, unless he had taken a vow to protect the children of men. In that case his presence in the land was a benediction beyond the benediction of twenty years of full rains. He might even be one of the high gods, incarnated to serve Vishnu the Great Preserver, if what they said was true, that he had been recognised by Neela Deo, the Blue god—king of all the elephants—in *his own place*."

"Then, Ayah, fasten it all into one word."

"That he is a very great mystic. Not one of the yogis who are unclean and scrap-fed, but a true mystic; a master and an adept in one of the greatest of all powers."

"*Have no fear*. I alone shall carry the burden of speaking."

Since there are few more potent benedictions than "Have no fear," the ayah withdrew in deep content.

While Skag sat in the tent next day, the police commissioner's wife said to him:

"I have learned that you are a wonder man."

"That is a mistake."

"Is it true that you and a friend spent the night in a pit-trap with a living, unchained tiger and that he did not hurt you?"

"A part of the night, yes."

"Will you explain it on any ordinary grounds?"

"Maybe not quite ordinary. I travelled several years with a circus in America; and I learned to handle animals, especially big cats of different sorts."

"How do you do it?"

"A man does it by first mastering the wild animals in himself. Then he must have learned never to be afraid."

"Is that all?"

"He must always be fair to them. I mean he must never take advantage of them; never do anything to them that would make him fight back, if he were in their place."

"I am thinking what a difference there is between your standpoint and that of the hunters of wild animals I know. But tell me—have you ever been afraid?"

"Yes, once."

"Really afraid?"

"Yes."

"I want to hear about it some day, if you will be so good; but first I want to tell you a story of fear; two kinds of fear. There has been no one I could speak to—and I am in need of help."

"I would like to help you. Tell on."

"Do you know much about hyenas?"

"I know they are the most unclean of all beasts. I have never heard that they are dangerous to men."

"Sometimes they are. Only a little way from where we sit in this jungle, a woman was killed and eaten last year, by a hyena. But I am not afraid for myself. I have said my fear is of two kinds. First, I am seriously concerned for the children; especially the baby. She is frail at her best and if it were not for her long afternoon naps, I am unwilling to think what would come to her just from the sort of thing which has been happening. She is highly organised; and one has heard that any kind of nerve-shock is most dangerous to such children. Then, there is a different kind of fear, *quite* different; it is for her Great Dane dog."

"Won't he charge them?"

"That is the most awful part of it. Of all creatures I have ever known, I may as well say of all people I have ever known, he has the most splendid courage. One night in every week he is taken to Bhanah's own quarters, so that his master shall not be disturbed. The change seemed to relieve him, at first. But—one who had not seen could never conceive how gradually, through the long, long nights—I have watched his almost super-human courage—breaking."

Skag opened his lips to speak, but she put up her hand.

"This is hard to tell because I have never known that I could be afraid. I have always supposed that I had perfect courage. But while Nels' courage has been in the wrecking, my own has been wrecked—quite!"

Her voice was very low and very bitter.

"I don't believe it's as bad as that."

She glanced up and smiled the slow smile of extreme age upon extreme youth.

"My husband, the police commissioner, has hunted in India more than twenty years; some of his friends longer than that. I suppose they are as familiar with the natures and doings of most animals in this country as foreign hunters can become. But of course the natives know jungle creatures even better. We have two servants, born in these hills, my ayah and Bhanah the old cook; I have much from both of them. But my experience here in this tent, has—as the natives would say—established it all in me. You will have heard that hyenas are almost always the scouts for tigers."

"Yes, Mr. Cadman told me that."

"Jackals run with them. The hunters say that between the hyena, whose stench is beyond description awful, and the jackal, whose stench is strong dog, they obliterate the tiger smell and so prevent the desperate panic coming in time to the hunted creatures, who fear the tiger more than anything."

"Hyenas in captivity do not smell so exceptionally bad."

"One has heard that all flesh-eating animals in captivity are fed clean meat, reasonably fresh—"

"They are; and for the moment I forgot their reputation—that would make a difference."

"It is claimed here, that they eat only two kinds of flesh, at once—human and dog. They say that the hyena entices and betrays to the killing, the tiger kills and eats his fill, then the jackals come in and leave only bones and tendon-stuff for the hyena. This is what he devours as soon as it is old enough to suit his taste."

"Are all these animals here in this jungle?"

"Plenty of jackals; but the tigers have been killed out of all this part of these Ghats by the European sportsmen of Bombay and Poona. The hunters disregard hyenas; so there are many left, with no killer to kill for them."

"That might make them dangerous."

"And they will tell you that when a hyena is forced to kill for himself, he invariably hunts for a dog. It has become very important to me that dog flesh is their first choice. And dogs never fight hyenas; never even to defend their own lives. They may bark or howl while the hyena is some distance away, but as soon as it comes near they are silent; and when it approaches them, they simply cower and submit. Not only that, but it is beyond question that hyenas have the power to call dogs to them. . . . For five weeks I have been alone in this tent six nights in every week all night, with two children and the spartan soul of Nels the Great Dane dog; and I have seen and I have heard the *process* of the hyena's lure."

"That is what I want to hear about."

"You shall hear; but will you be good enough to remember, please, Nels is no average dog. There is nothing better in lineage than his. Also, he is a thoroughly trained hunting dog. My husband, the police commissioner, has used him in hunting tigers and cheetahs, black panthers and leopards of the long sort, the big black bears of Himalaya and jungle pigs, which we call wild boars at Home. To different famous hunting districts of the country he has taken Nels, on many hunting-furloughs; and Nels' courage stands to him and to his friends, the very last word in courage. I have often heard him say he does not know a man with courage to equal that which has never once failed in Nels."

"I should like to know that dog."

"You shall certainly meet him; and it may be you are the one to know him. I am confident no one does, now."

"About the hyenas?"

"The hyena has three kinds of call. The most common is the bark of a puppy. (If you ever hear it you will not wonder why mother dogs go out to it, to their death.) Presently the bark breaks into a puppy's cry. It whimpers, then it climbs up into heart-breaking desolation; the wailing cry of a lost puppy. It snaps out in distraction futile little yappings; then it whimpers again, like sobbing. So on for hours.

"The next most common is a laugh; a harsh, senseless laugh. The effect is to terrorise, to paralyse its prey. It is wicked. It climbs up into piercing, high, falsetto tones; all maniacal. . . . So insane that though one knows perfectly well what it is, it chills one's blood. This keeps on a long time, with variations. Every change seems worse than the last. But sooner or later it brings one up standing with a laugh impossible to describe, unless it is devilish—so clear, so keen, so intelligent, so beyond expression malicious. Toward morning this sometimes brings sweat. Oh, maybe not if one were alone; but with Nels, watching Nels—indeed yes!

"The last and least often heard—I mean they do not do it every night, sometimes not for several nights, sometimes they do all three in one night—is the cry of a little native baby; the cry of a lost baby; the cry of a deserted baby; the cry of a baby alone out in the jungle shadows and frightened to death."

She stopped and lay quite still; seeming to forget he was there.

"And what then?"

"Nothing, only it keeps on sometimes the rest of that night. They never mix the three kinds together. Even when they do them all in one night, they are usually in this order as I am telling you. Sometimes the baby is still for a few minutes; then it begins again and goes on."

Again she stopped a long time. Suddenly she flung up her hand and spoke faster:

"No, there's nothing more about that little deserted native baby's cry, excepting that I've started up in broad daylight afterward, with a cold panic in my heart that it had really been a baby, a true baby and I had failed to go and save it. And—the nights, the long nights I have fastened my weight on Nels' neck to keep him inside of this door!"

She pointed to the opening by her couch.

"Why don't you chain him?"

"He goes on a leash perfectly, but he has never been taught to be chained up. My husband has never permitted the servants to do it. I tried it here myself, but he suffers and cries; and that keeps both the children awake. It would jeopardise Baby's life to force him. On account of the ceremony which occurred a few hours before her mother died, the servants believe she belongs to Nels. They claim that he acknowledges the ownership. I will admit that he behaves like it. She has often kept him back. He goes from this tent door to her cot yonder, to look at her. But always he comes back to the door. Some night my weight will not be sufficient. That is my fear."

"The situation is clear and I think I can manage it, if you will leave it to me for a night or two. These beasts must be kin to a big snake I met in the Grass Jungle country. My friend Mr. Cadman shot him. That was when I found fear—"

At that moment Skag heard the clear, treble tones of a child's voice:

"Nels-s, Nels-s, Nels-s!"

And the veriest fairy thing his eyes had ever looked upon came flying in the tent door before him. Her head was a halo of gold made of the finest kind of baby curls. She was unbelievable. She was like a flame, beside the couch.

"This is Betty, our baby."

The child lifted intensely blue eyes and while Skag smiled into them, he was without words before the vivid whiteness of her face. She was sent with her ayah to the back of the tent for her nap. Then Nels came in.

Skag had never seen such a dog. For size, for proportions, for power, for dignity, he was quite beyond comparison.

"This is Nels, one of the four greatest hunters in India."

Nels came to him at once. With a searching regard he looked into Skag's face one long moment, then a glow came up in his eyes and he swung about and stretched himself alongside Skag's chair, reached his arms out before him and laid his chin on them, almost touching the man's foot. Skag leaned over and stroked the big head. It felt like sealskin, but it was soft clean grey colour.

"Nels has adopted you, Wonder Man!"

The lady on the couch spoke like a small child, marvelling.

"I am glad to have his friendship. But I wish, if you will excuse me, I wish that you wouldn't call me by that name. Skag is not my real name, but the few friends I have call me Skag. I'd be pleased if you would call me that."

"That's very nice of you, but do you much mind? I like Wonder Man better."

"I don't believe I quite understand why."

"Partly from things I've heard about you. But rather more on account of what I've seen just now. I fancy the natives are not far wrong and you are a wonder man to them. . . . If you do this sort of thing, delivering people who are in danger of their lives, and getting the devotion of creatures as hard to win as Nels, I can see that you are going to have a great reputation in this India. And you are not to be in the least disturbed if I call you Wonder Man; I am believing the title is prophetic at least."

"What I'm doing for you is only what any man would do. If you hear me outside to-night, don't be startled. I'll get the beast as soon as I can. If there's more than one, I'll stay around till they're cleaned out."

Soon after dusk Skag circled out into the jungle. He carried one of the best hunting-pieces made and plenty of ammunition. Taking a position in sight of the tent on the jungle side, he waited. Within half an hour a little puppy began to bark. No man alive could ever know it was anything but a puppy. It yapped and whimpered a while and then it began to get frightened. He moved toward it, but it stopped. For several minutes there was silence. Then another one began back of him. He slipped through the shadows with the utmost caution, but before he got near it, it also stopped. This occurred several times. At last, away in another direction, a wild, grating laugh broke out. He turned at once and moved carefully but swiftly to come in range between it and the tent.

This laugh-thing was torture. It couldn't stop. It was insane. He thought it would never be done. In a few minutes it was important to have it done. She had said it was to paralyse its prey. It was enough to paralyse anything. Then he jumped. Now *that* was devilish! But he was coming closer to the sound and getting interested, when it stopped. So he followed it from place to place. Always, when he got near possible range, it stopped. Always it began in a few minutes in some other spot. There might be a dozen. . . .

And a woman, alone with two children and a dog, had endured this six nights out of seven, night after night all night, for five weeks. . . .

Near morning, toward the front, a sick baby began to cry. While he made his way around, his steps quickened to the very urge of its need. He was quite near the tent when—a clear, high, agonised shriek. It was the girl! And he ran.

There was an instant when he did not realise anything. He just saw. Fifty feet from the tent, the Great Dane dog, his head low, almost touching the ground, moving slowly, step by step—with a long, slender, white figure dragged bodily on his neck. Then he heard:

"Rodger! Keep back! Take care of Baby. Nels, *Nels*! Nels, you must *listen* to me. . . . *Nels*!"

He caught hold of her and the dog at the same moment.

"Don't let him go. *Don't let go of Nels*!"

"All right, I won't. Now will you go back to the tent, please? I've got Nels. I'm going with him."

"No, *the thing has happened*! I tell you, he doesn't even know me! Why do you want him to go at all?"

"Because they keep out of my range, alone. He'll lead me to this one. I'll take care of him. Now go; will you please go back?"

"I don't—"

A frantic scream from a boy's throat and in the same instant the lifting cry of a younger child. Clear in the door-space of the tent, behind them, two little figures clung together in the opening—and just at one side, close to the children, a dark, ungainly shape! Skag sprang three jumps toward the opposite side, dropped on one knee and fired. The shape bounced up, crumpled over and lay still.

They both ran to the children. Skag had just made sure the beast was dead, when he heard:

"Nels, Nels!—He is gone!"

"If you'll shut the door safely, I'll take care of Nels."

"It won't fasten, but I'll stay."

The Great Dane was not in sight but Skag knew the direction. He ran almost upon them. Nels stood, but crouched toward the ground. A shape rose against him—above his shoulders on the other side. Skag slipped around to reach it without hitting the dog. In the same instant Nels took a blow from the jungle beast's head. The two swerved over toward one side. Skag set his gun-muzzle against the hyena's neck—he could see that much—and blew it away from him. (There wouldn't be much danger but it was dead.) Then he knelt, his hand instantly wet at Nels' throat. But the blood was not gushing, it was streaming. He put his arms underneath to lift him, but couldn't do it alone. There was nothing to do but go for the girl.

"I'm sorry. I need your help. Dare we leave the children a minute?"

"Yes, Baby is falling asleep; and Rodger is brave, he will watch her. . . . Tell me, is Nels killed?"

"No, I think we can save him. But we must be quick."

She was by his side running, as he added:

"I know how to do it, when we get him to the light."

They worked together and it was all they could do, but they got Nels into the tent. She brought the materials he asked for, and while he stopped the flow of blood and dressed the wound, she went to the baby. When he rose she was leaning over the child.

"I'm afraid something has happened to her! Her face is strange Her breath is not right. I wish Ayah would come; I don't know a thing about babies!"

"Is there a doctor near?"

"Not this side Poona."

"I can go after him."

"You're awfully good, but there will be no train before the one my husband comes up on. It's a holiday. He would have been up last evening, only he had important business. I am not at liberty to determine about a physician, because he will be here so soon."

"Shall I go after the ayah?"

"That might help—thank you so much!"

Skag learned in the next two hours that there is nothing in life more difficult for a man to find, than servants' quarters in a native village. By full daylight he gave up and tramped back a considerable distance. As he approached the tent, an Englishman came out walking rapidly toward him. Police Commissioner Hichens had a very red face. He spoke before Skag could see his eyes:

"Sir, I take pleasure in ordering you to leave my premises. You will be good enough not to be seen again in this vicinity."

"Yes? You—are—finding—fault—with—me?"

"What occurs to mine does not in the least concern you! You are occupying yourself with my affairs. I will not permit it. Am I explicit enough?"

"You are explicit enough."

Skag wheeled on the path and walked away from the police commissioner under a sharp revelation that if he didn't get away at once, he would do a thing he had never been inclined to do before. He was amazed by his own fury. Unconsciously he spoke aloud:

"I never wanted to—"

"*Remember, it is not necessary to touch the unclean.*"

Low tones of strange vibration. Skag looked up. A brown-robed man stood before him. (The long straight lines of the garment were made of a material hand-woven of camel's hair, known in the High Himalayas as *puttoo*.) The quiet face was in chiselled lines. The level dark eyes were looking deep into the place where Skag's soul lived. Skag was intensely conscious that he stood in a Presence. He endured the eyes. They made him feel better. The robed man spoke again:

"I speak to give you assurance that those you have served will be cared for. Also, a responsibility may fall upon you. If you accept, a great good will come to you in this life."

"I will do what I can."

"*Peace be with thee.*"

"Shall I see you again?"

"Never."

Skag stood aside and the robed man walked toward the tent.

Skag went back to Poona. Carlin's eldest brother Roderick Deal had not come yet. Still waiting, a week later, he walked one morning on the stone causeway, which is a most attractive unit in the architecture of Poona's great waterworks, and filled his eyes with the Ghat vistas toward the north and west. Joyous dog tones made him glance back. It was Nels, straining forward on a heavy chain-leash in the old cook's hand.

"Let him go."

Now Skag noticed that the dog moved with some effort, possibly with some pain; but when he arrived, Nels reared his mighty body and set his paws on Skag's two shoulders. Skag hugged him and eased him down. The old cook handed Skag a note. It read:

To the Wonder Man, by the hand of Bhanah the cook, who is a gift to the Man from the gods. Together with Nels the beautiful, a gift to the Man from Eleanor Beatrice (Hichens)—who is free!

Bhanah the cook will tell his master the rest. Save this, that Eleanor Beatrice is grateful with her full heart to the Man.

He is to remember that he has been adopted by Nels. He is to walk softly because he is on the way to be adopted—of course it is past belief, but also it is past question—by the mightiest of all mystic orders, whose messengers have accomplished this thing.

N.B. The Sahib is to enquire of his servant Bhanah what is the native meaning of "walk softly." He will find Bhanah entirely trustworthy in all matters of information.

Skag looked up and the old cook spoke:

"I, who am speaking to Sanford Hantee Sahib, am Bhanah—entered into covenant before the gods that I am his servant to serve him with my strength, so long as I endure to live.

"I bring from the shining lady who was my mistress, whom may the gods protect! certain messages for him alone.

"The child is dead. Her body lies deep in a metal case beside her mother's, near one of the old bungalows."

"I am sorry to hear that."

"Death does not snare the soul. If she were still here, Nels would not be free to come to my master. And my master has become his heart's desire."

"I am glad to have him and you."

The old cook laid his hand on his forehead and bent low before Skag.

"The lady-beautiful will sail from Bombay in a few days, returning to her own mother's house. She is forever free from Police Commissioner Hichens Sahib, who was my master only for her sake and for the sake of Nels. The lady's own ayah will go with her to her own country, to serve her as I serve thee.

"These things are accomplished by a Power which works through those who are seldom seen and never known of men.

"I have spoken and it is finished. Have I permission to take Nels to my quarters where he can rest? He is well; but not yet fully strong. If my master will tell us his place, we will come to him in the morning."

Skag told them. The recognition of Nels as a personality amused him; but he did not quarrel with it.

CHAPTER VII

THE HUNTING CHEETAH

Since Bhanah and Nels had come to him, Skag had fallen into the way of taking Nels out quite early for a full day's tramp through the broken shelving Ghats. (This helped to bear the weight of the days till Carlin's eldest brother should reach Poona.) The contours were different from anything he had seen along the top or toward the sea; as if in the beginning the whole range had been dropped on the planet and its own weight had shattered the eastern side, to settle from the cracks or roll over upon the plains. Nels would travel close beside him for hours; but if he ever did break away, Skag had only to call quietly, "Nels, steady!" and Nels would return joyfully. He never sulked.

Every morning now, Bhanah carefully stowed in Skag's coat, neat packets of good and sufficient food for himself and the dog at noontime. Skag had never been cared for in his life; he had neither training nor inclination to direct a servant. But there was no need. Bhanah knew perfectly well what was right to be done; and he was committed with his whole heart to do it.

The order of Skag's life was being softly changed; but he only knew his servant did many kind things for him which were very comfortable. He was a little bothered when Bhanah called him "My Master"—having not yet learned that servants in India never use that title, excepting in affection which has nothing to do with servitude.

The morning came, when Roderick Deal arrived. Carlin had said that all arrangements must be made with her eldest brother; and some tone within her tone had impressed Skag with concern which amounted to apprehension. But when he walked into Roderick Deal's office and met the hand of Carlin's eldest brother—there was a light in his eye which that Indian Sahib found good to see.

Roderick Deal overtopped the American by two inches. He was slender and lithe. His countenance was extraordinary to Skag's eye for its peculiar pallor; as if the dense black hair cast a shadow on intensely white flesh—especially below the temples and across the forehead. There was attraction; there was power. Skag saw this much while he found the eyes; then he saw little else. He decided that Sanford Hantee had never seen really black eyes before; the size startled him, but the blackness shocked. (It was in the fortune of his life that he should never solve the mystery of those eyes.) Skag felt the impact of dynamic force, before he spoke:

"You will not expect enthusiasm from me, my son, when as the head of one of the proudest families in all India, I render official consent, upon conditions, to your marriage with my sister Carlin. . . . You are too different from other men."

Skag had something to say, but he found no words.

"You are to be informed that the only sister of seven brothers is a most important person. She is called the Seal of Fortune in India; which is to say that good fortune for all her brothers is vested in her. If calamity befalls her, there is no possible escape for them. This is the established tradition of our Indian ancestors.

"We smile among ourselves at this tradition, as much as you do; but there are reasons why we choose to preserve it, among many things from those same Indian ancestors. We have no cause to hate them. Hate is not in our family as in others of our class; but we never forget that it is *our class*."

The brooding pain in the man was a revelation. Carlin had said, ". . . there are things you must understand."

"You are already aware that we are English and Indian. But you do not conceive what that means. It is my duty to speak. All life appears to me first from the English standpoint; but you see the *shadow of India under my skin*. All life appears to my sister first in the Indian concept; but you will not easily find the shadow of India under her skin. We have one brother—darker than the average native. . . . Are you prepared to find such colour in one of your own?"

The question was gently spoken, but the eyes were like destiny.

"Any child of hers will be good to me," Skag answered softly.

A glow loomed in the blacknesses and Roderick Deal flashed Skag a smile which reminded him, at last, of Carlin.

"European men, in the early days, were responsible for the branding, now carried by thousands in India—carried with shame and the bitterest sort of curses. But our line is unique in this regard. We are conditioned by a pride, as great as the shame I have spoken of. On account of it, no one of us may enter marriage without public ceremony of as much circumstance as is expedient."

The storm-lights had gone down and a half-deprecatory, half-embarrassed expression, made the face look so quite like any other man's, that Skag smiled.

". . . Because we are descended from two extraordinary romances, both of which were celebrated by the marriage of an imperial Indian woman—one Brahmin, one Rajput—with a British man of noble family—one Scotch, one Irish. Carlin will tell you the stories; she loves them."

Again the smile like Carlin's.

"So she must come down to Poona, where she was born; and the ceremony must be performed in the cathedral here, by the Bishop himself—who is a real man by the way, as well as distinguished."

. . . That was all right.

"You are to be published at the time of your marriage, in all the English and vernacular printed sheets throughout India, specifically as a scientist whose research will take you much into jungle life."

Roderick Deal paused for reply. Skag considered a moment and said tentatively:

"If my work will come under that head?"

"Oh, quite! there is no question. And now I am come to the explanation of my delay. There have been preparations to make; dealings with Indian government. As you will understand, Government would be entirely unapproachable by any man himself desiring such an appointment. But influence is able to set in operation the examination of his records; and if they are good enough, the rest can be accomplished.

"Carlin convinced me that you would make no serious protest; and I am assuring you that these conditions are really good fortune to you. But they are imperative; it must be this way or not at all."

Skag was given opportunity to speak, but he had nothing to say, yet.

"You must enter the service of Indian government in the department of Natural Research. The appointment will give you distinction not to be scorned and a salary better than my own—which is very good."

After a moment's thought, Skag said:

"Will it tie me up?"

"Not in the least. On the contrary, it will make you free."

"What about my obligations?"

"Your obligations will be entirely vested in reports, which you will turn in at your discretion. I understand that you already have materials which would be considered highly valuable. Also, I hear that you have fallen heir to Nels, the great hunting dog. Of the four that are well known, he is easily the best. And he is young; he will bring you experiences out of the jungle such as no man could find alone. What the Indian Research department wants, is *knowledge of animals.*"

"That's exactly what I want."

"Your Department will facilitate you, immensely. I speak positively, because the initial work is finished; there remains nothing, but that you shall come with me to the department offices and become enrolled. However, not before you are properly outfitted. My tailoring-house will take care of you."

"A uniform?"

"Not a uniform exactly, but strictly correct; rather military, but more hunting; perfectly suitable and very comfortable. You'll be quite at home in it. It's the sort for you."

The eyes measured Skag's outlines appraisingly, but betrayed nothing.

"We have not finished. The matter of clothing is adjacent to another not less important. A foreigner in this country is nothing better than a wild man, without a servant."

"I have one—" Skag spoke with inward satisfaction: "—Bhanah the old cook, who did serve Police—"

"Not Police Commissioner Hichens' *Bhanah*?"

"Yes."

"How?"

"He came to me."

"Did you negotiate with him?"

"No."

"Then will you kindly tell me, why?"

"I do not know."

There was a marked pause. The eyes had become wide.

"Well—really . . . *Are* you the sort-of-thing I've been hearing about?"

Roderick Deal's expression was kindly-quaint; and Skag answered the look rather than the words:

"How should I know what that is?"

"You *have* astonished me. And I am pleased. From Bombay to Calcutta and from Himalaya to Madras—you will find no more valuable man, than that same Bhanah. He is called old, but he is not old. If you have noticed, the term is always spoken as if it were one with his name—because of his learning. He is the man of men for you. *How* did he come to you?"

"He brought Nels with the note, that the dog was a gift. When he spoke, he said he was committed before the gods to serve me as long as he lived."

"How did his voice sound?"

"A queer, level tone."

"There is no doubt. *It is enough for one day.*"

The words were spoken with almost affectionate inflections. Skag was puzzled. Roderick Deal stepped to the door and spoke to a servant; returning to his seat, he smiled openly into Skag's eyes before speaking:

"Now you will come with me. We must lose no time."

"Yes, I want to get back to Hurda as soon as I can."

"Not before the monsoon breaks. It is due any day now, any hour. Till ten days after it has broken, no sane man will take train."

"I want to get back. I think I will risk it."

"You will pardon me, you are not allowed."

The tone was perfect authority. The eyes smouldered, but the lips smiled.

"You are not used to be in any way conditioned, I understand that; but I am not willing to be responsible to my only sister for the smashed body of her one man. Oh, I assure you *not*! And you may one day grant that the guardianship of an elder brother is not a bad thing to have. Why—I beg your pardon, but of course you are not here long enough to know the situation."

He stopped abruptly and looked away, considering.

"I will put it in one word and tell you that *one* moment *any* train, on *any* track, may be perfectly safe; and the next moment, it may be going down the khud with half a mountain. Again, we exercise the utmost care in all bridge-building—with no reservation of resources; but almost every year a bridge or more goes with the crash."

"The crash?"

"The reason why we say the great monsoon 'breaks' is not because itself breaks, but because—whatever happens to be underneath, you understand."

The floor of protest had dropped away. Skag's face said as much.

"The tailors will need till the rails are safe to get you fitted; and before the monsoon comes, I suggest that you take your hunter up into the cheetah hills. Cheetahs are not supposed, by those at Home, to attack men. Many of them will not; but they are unreliable. The forfeits they have taken from unbelief have made them a bad reputation, among the English."

"The cheetahs I have seen in cages have been mild, compared with tigers."

"Cheetah kittens are snared and broken at once by hard handling; meaning that it is not the cheetah himself, but what is left of him, one sees either in the kennels of the princes or in the foreign cages. You will remember my warning about his character?"

"Thank you, yes."

"Good. I have known men to prefer not . . . Then you will carry yourself alert in any kind of jungle. If you sight a cheetah, be prepared; he may *not* attack. He may. Few men have eyes good enough to follow him after his first spring. One should be a perfect shot; are you that?"

"I am a good shot, but I don't like to kill animals."

"Then I am the last man to commend you to the cheetah hills . . . if it were not for Nels. He is entirely competent to take care of you, unless in one possible emergency. They sometimes, but rarely, work in pairs. If ever the dog should be occupied with one and another should be in *sight*—be sure your unwillingness to kill does not delay you to the instant of charge."

"You imply that it is necessary to carry a gun in any kind of jungle—always?"

"Always wise, of *course*; but I consider it less imperative just now, because the animals are not what we call fighting. They are waiting for the great monsoon. So—you might take your dog up into the cheetah hills—"

"I don't see how a dog—"

"He'll break the cheetah's back and cut his throat, before the real start is made at you. But Bhanah will tell you whatever; and he is entirely reliable. You may depend upon him, without reservation."

"That's a big thing to know."

"India has many good servants, but Bhanah is a rare man."

The unquenchable fires in Roderick Deal's eyes began to feed upon some enigma in Skag's own; he endured it a moment and then interruption became expedient:

"Does the monsoon come on schedule?"

"It does."

"What is it like?"

"It is as much an experience as a spectacle. I'm not attempting to describe the thing itself; it should be seen. But across the southwestern part of India, it includes the procession of the animals. All animals from all covers, running together."

"There is something like that in the far north of America," Skag said. "It is called the passage of the Barren Ground Caribou. They move south before the first winter storms in thousands. I've heard that sometimes their lines extend out of sight. They have no food, but they do not stop to forage. Our northern hunters say that nothing will stop them."

"That's interesting; immensely. I've not heard of it."

"But I didn't mean to interrupt you."

"Our creatures move in a trance of panic, straight away from the coming rains. I say a trance, because they appear to be oblivious of each other; hunter and hunted go side by side, without noticing."

The drive of Skag's life-quest was working in him, as if nothing had ever given it pause.

"Do they go fast?"

"The timid and lumbering come out first, hurrying; they increase in numbers, all sorts, and run faster till those near the end go at top speed—it's a thing to see. Bhanah will tell you when and where to watch it; but be careful and get under good roofing in time. And then, after the tracks are set right, if you must reach Hurda in order to come back with Carlin . . . Man, God help you if you do not give my sister the best of your gifts!"

"Why, I belong to her—"

Their hands met; and Skag's soul rose up without words, to answer a white flame in the inscrutable eyes.

Early the following morning, Sanford Hantee Sahib said to his servant:

"Bhanah, what do you know about cheetahs?"

"Such little things as a man may know, Sahib."

"Are you willing to give some of it to me?"

"All that I am and all that I can, belongs to my master."

"Is that—the regular—"

"Nay, *nay*! It is right for my master to consider, that I serve him not for a price. This is true service—as men in my land bring to things holy. Those who serve for the weight of silver, render the weight of their hands."

"I don't want you to begin thinking that I'm holy though—you understand that."

"There are meanings which will appear to the Sahib in time; it is not suitable that they come from me. But this much may be spoken: if my master serves in a great service—then I, who am a poor man and ignorant, may give something if I serve him."

"If that's what you mean, it's all right. Then we won't go out this morning, Nels and I. It'll be the time to get some of that little knowledge of yours about cheetahs."

It seemed to Skag that the uncertainty about just why Bhanah had come to him, was cleared away; and there was a dignity about the man which he liked. It was all right.

"Sanford Hantee Sahib should not go to find cheetahs before he knows his dog," Bhanah began.

"Just what are you getting at?"

"My master is a preserver of life and Nels is a great hunter."

"I've thought of that. Is there any danger that he will kill when I don't want him to?"

"Sahib, I, Bhanah, have known Nels since he was a puppy, I have seen him take his training to kill; therefore I believe he will quickly be taught to work together with my master, who is his heart's desire. This is the chief thing, that my master is his heart's desire. But also I know—he will kill when there is need for him to kill."

"Does he ever fail?"

"If he had ever failed, he would not be here. The Police Commissioner Hichens Sahib—to whom may the gods render his due!—has many times set him in the teeth of death; when occasion could be prepared, always."

"He did not fight the hyena."

"Now the Sahib speaks of an evil thing. For *that* reason he was made to live in a tent in the Jungle."

"But what—"

"The hyena is *evil-itself*; and a dog has no hope in him to fight with it. We may not 'speak *a name* in the same breath of common-judgment'; but I say that the living fear in a man's body made secret covenant with the knowledge of this fact—because the man had long desired that Nels should die. The lady-beautiful and his small children—all together—I say they were made to live in danger—that some hyena might destroy Nels!"

Only Bhanah's voice showed feeling as he finished.

"So that's what I interfered with; and that's why he let the dog be given to me."

"It is straightly spoken. But the Sahib will not hold Nels less, for courage or for power? There is not one to equal him."

"Bhanah, we'll put that hope into Nels, against when he hears a hyena."

"That will be with the good hunting-piece in my master's hands, at first—to teach him confidence. Then he will fear—*not anything on earth.* Then it will be *all* like the cheetah hills to him. Sahib, it is more satisfying than food."

"Where are the cheetah hills from here?"

"South and West; not the way the Sahib has gone before."

"You haven't told me about them before."

"Because Nels was not come to full strength, since his hurt."

"I'd hate to have him meet an accident."

"To-morrow he will go safe. He rose up last night and listened to a hunting cheetah's cry."

"Are they close as that?"

"Not to a European Sahib's ear; but to Nels, yes."

"Deal Sahib said you would tell me about the cheetahs."

"What I have of value is by the common wayside; but *fortune causes wealth to flow down mountain streams for those who climb.* There are several things to consider, Sahib."

Skag was amused; he had not yet heard that only the ignorant teach without apology. As seriously as possible, he said:

"I am listening."

Bhanah spoke gravely; his words falling like weights:

"That he is—seldom seen—till it is too late—to prepare. He is treacherous."

"Where does he hide?"

"In the large-leaved trees which stretch their branches like that." And Bhanah held his arms out horizontally, one above the other, parallel.

"All right."

"That he is quicker than a man's eye."

Skag waited.

"And that he is more deadly than the tiger."

"How is that?"

"Because he is more quick. Because he is equal in power, even when he is not equal in weight. Because he fights not only for food, not only for life, but for the love of killing. Of all living things, he is the creature of blood-lust. He is the name-of-fear, incarnate. It would not be a good thing for my master to hear, nor for his servant to tell—the cheetah's ways with a body from which life is gone out."

"You've made a strong argument for the cheetah as a fighter, Bhanah, but you don't seem to stand much for his character."

"Who faces the hunting cheetah, Sahib, faces death. If the cheetah falls upon him from above, or comes upon him from behind, he will know death; but he will never know the cheetah. A hunter's first shot must do its work; he will not often have time to fire again."

"I've got that. But I don't quite see what chance a dog has

with him."

"Only four dogs in this my land, have any chance with him, Sahib."

"And the others?"

"They live because they have not met a cheetah."

"How does Nels do it?"

"My master must look upon that, to understand. I have seen, but I cannot show it. It—" and a rare smile lighted the dark shadows of Bhanah's face, "is *soon.*"

"I've heard the Indian princes use them for hunting."

"Yes, Sahib, many Indian princes keep hunting cheetahs as English Sahibs keep hunting horses. They go out after small things; and innocent—mostly deer, of all kinds; even the *neel gai,* the great blue cow."

"Will Nels attack such things?"

"Nels will not attack the defenseless; he has not been used for it. His ways are established in that; there is no fear. If he should be ranging at any time, he will return at the first call; but if he does not, my Master, let him go. Be certain, *Nels knows.*"

"That's good. I'm in this country to get acquainted with animals—"

"But to the preserving of men?"

"When I find it's necessary, I've no objection then—"

Bhanah stooped quickly and touched Skag's feet.

"Vishnu, the Great Preserver, has sent another Hand to this my India."

Skag looked into the man's face and found high light in it.

Next dawn was hot, but there was a stimulation in it; not like the mountains, not like the sea. The air was full of a mellow enticement, like strange incense; or romance. Skag enquired of his servant if the day would be right for the cheetah hills.

Bhanah turned to the southeast and scanned the horizon line. Then he held up his hand, palm toward the same direction, for a minute. At last he walked to a shrub and looked at its leaves, closely.

"It may be that one day is left for my master to go into the cheetah hills; but the earth makes ready for the breaking of the great monsoon."

Skag was getting interested in the Indian standpoint; he was finding something in it. Quite innocently, he used the subtlest method known to learn.

"What is the great monsoon?"

"Beneficence."

"What is the earth doing?"

"Now, she is holding very still. When it breaks, she will shake. Having endured three days, she will rise up and cast off her old garments, putting on new covering—entirely clean."

"Will I be able to see that?"

"Nay, Sahib! The wall of the waters will be between your eye and every leaf."

. . . The wall of the waters; like the tones of a bell far off, the words sank into some deep place in Skag. This day they would recur to him; and in the years to come, they would recur again and yet again.

Swinging along out of Poona toward the cheetah hills, Skag was buoyant with healthy energy. His heart was like the heart of a boy. Consistent with his old philosophical dogma, this present was certainly the best he had ever known. Carlin was in it, as surely as if she were present. Roderick Deal had proved to be a man to respect; and to love, secretly . . . "the guardianship of an elder brother."

Looking back, he saw that Poona City was beautiful, lying close against the eastern side of the Ghats, just as they begin to fold away toward the plains. No breath of plague or pestilence from Bombay could reach across the ramparts of that mountain range.

The air was getting hotter every minute; but it was good. The vistas stretched far—all satisfying. Bhanah said the monsoon was close. "Beneficence"; the Indian idea of a deluge. He liked it all.

They came up into the hills through some stretches of stiff climbing; and on the margin of a broad shelf Skag stopped for breath. The panorama behind had widened and extended immensely. The face of a planet seemed to reach from his feet across to the eastern horizon, descending. He sat down on a flat rock and Nels comfortably extended himself near by.

It was all good. The great golden jewel back in his heart, full of afterglows—Carlin. The finding of a real man. The ways, the reservations, the revelations, of Bhanah. The beauty and character of the dog at his foot . . .

Nels had lifted his head. His eyes were fixed intently on the empty white distances of the sky. His pointed ears were set at a queer angle. There was nothing unusual to be seen, nothing Skag himself could hear. He paid closer attention; and presently, began to get a perfume. It was the great, good earth-smell; richer and fuller every minute.

Then Nels stood up and faced the southeast. Skag looked where the dog seemed to be looking. Along the horizon line he saw an edge of dark grey. No, the horizon line was cut; this thing lay against the earth as straight as the blade of a knife.

Now Skag began to feel something in the air. He couldn't recognise it, nor define it, but it was imperative—some kind of urge. There was the sense of emergency, perfectly clear; so much that he turned and looked about, listening for a call. He thought of Carlin; could she be in any need? He was glad she wasn't here; this was a good place to get away from . . . Ah, that was it! *The urge to run.*

"How is it, Nels, old man, does the great monsoon make us feel like moving?"

Nels stood like a thing carved out of solid pewter. He did not hear. He faced the southeast. But Skag understood why the animals were due to make a procession; the chief thing was to get away. Then Skag settled into a perfect calm.

Four spotted deer came trotting up the shoulder of a near incline, almost directly toward them. The dog watched them with a casual eye. They went by, sixty feet away. Nels was looking further on to where a big brown bear ambled along, making good time for one of her build—behind her, a yearling. Still Nels showed no inclination to leave his place.

As if it were a vision of the night, the whole landscape before Skag became dotted with specks; all moving. All moving in the same direction, almost toward him. As the numbers increased, he saw that they ran straight; there was no swerving. In spite of what Roderick Deal had told him, his mind demanded the reassurance of his own voice.

"Nels, is it real? Are we asleep?"

The dog was a stoic; he moved one ear, but he did not lift an eye.

Skag noticed that the hush in the air seemed to have laid a bond of silence on all these creatures. He had heard no calls, no cries. And these were the calling, crying animals of the world.

Here and there at some distance, he saw the ungainly, shambling gait of hyenas, in twos and fours and threes together, or alone. Once when four passed quite near, he felt Nels' shoulder against his thigh.

"Nels, old man, buck up. I tell you, get a grip. They may be the devil, but he isn't hard to kill. I'll show you. Do you get me, son?"

Nels looked up into the man's face, a long look. Then he pressed his head close, under Skag's hand.

Spotted deer ran in small groups; they came into sight and passed out quickly. More swift and more beautiful, were slender deer with single horns, twisted spirally; sometimes very long. Skag thrilled to their pride of action; but Nels seemed in no wise interested.

There was another kind of deer seen at some distance; the bucks were full-antlered and from where Skag stood, they looked light grey colour. Rabbits scuttled in and out of sight constantly, all over the landscape.

Between the parallel lines of seven spotted deer on one side and a small herd of grey deer on the other, he saw a great, low-leaping beast; plainly yellow with black stripes—one tiger the sportsmen had not bagged.

Evidently some mighty thing had transcended enmity and annihilated fear—*for one day.*

Little things held his eye one while. Creatures like monster rats—they were really mongooses—racing for their lives. Lizards from two to eighteen inches long; and he saw one with rainbow colours in his skin, mostly red. He learned afterward it was a great-chameleon; and angry. He saw one small scaled thing, rather like a crocodile in shape, but with a sharp-pointed nose; it waddled by, near enough to show two little black beads in its face.

When Skag lifted his eyes the earth seemed to have given up a score of packs of jackals. Their action was not like the wolf nor like the dog; it was a short, high leap—giving to a running pack the effect of *bobbing*. They were more perfect wolves than the American coyote, but smaller; and they looked to have much fuller coats. Searching the location of these groups of bobbing runners, his eye lifted toward the southeast.

. . . The grey knife-blade had cut away half the world. It lay straight across the earth, midway between his feet and where the horizon line should curve. Without any look of motion, without any shine or sheen, smooth as a wall of dull-polished granite, it rose to beyond sight in the sky—the utterly true line of its base upon the ground.

. . . So this was *the wall of the waters.*

No man dare interpret it to any other man; but Skag found perfect awe. Then he grew very quiet—his faculties alert as never before.

When he noticed the landscape again, the bobbing packs were gone. Slender spotted things in pairs and alone, were leopards—leaping long and low. A great dark creature, going like the wind, was a black panther.

Then he saw, right before him, the unthinkable. Majesty in miniature. A perfect East Indian musk buck—the most beautiful of living things. The wee fellow came on, leaping to the utmost of his strength; his nostrils wide, his lips apart, his eyes immense. He swayed a little, wavered and fell.

Skag ran and leaned over him—the little heart was driving out the little life. It seemed a pity out of all proportion. . . . He held the tiny breathless thing tenderly, as if it were a dead child. . . . So he laid it down reluctantly, at last; and straight-tened—to see a hunting cheetah coming toward him, not far away.

He glanced down, Nels was not there. He looked all about, Nels was not in sight. Then the reserves in Skag's nature came up. All histraining flashed across his brain. Every nerve, every muscle in his body, was instantly adjusted to emergency. There was no failure in co-ordination.

He stood quietly watching the cheetah. It appeared not to have seen him. If it kept on, it would pass about seventy feet away. But Skag knew it would not keep on. With his mind he might think it would, but something in him knew it would not.

He remembered Carlin; no, he must not think of her now. He remembered that Nels was gone; no, he must not think of that either. All the weapons he had were in his heart, in his head. He set himself in order, ready. Recalling, while he waited, with what joy he had been ready to face the tiger that coughed near the monkey glen, to stand between Carlin and it—he was aware that now he faced a hunting cheetah *as much for her.*

The cheetah stopped, and turning toward him direct, laid itself along the ground so tight he could see only a line of colour among the grasses. There it seemed to stay.

When a man deals with a cat, to allay fear or to establish any common ground of sympathy, he ought to see its eyes. While realising this fact, Skag heard a piercing cat-scream, some distance back of him. He had not heard sounds from any of the animals before. . . . He found himself calculating whether the monsoon or night or the cheetah, would reach him first.

Changing sun-rays had laid a sheen resembling silver upon the wall; not dazzling, but softly bright. After a while the cheetah showed, nearer than when it settled into the grass. The wall was moving forward surely—as surely as time—but the cheetah would reach him first.

At last he saw two yellow discs. Then he worked with his power—his supreme confidence. He had never been more quiet, never more fearless in his life.

The hunting cheetah moved toward him without pause, till he could see the whole body along the ground; the broad, short head; the wide, sun-lit eyes. And while he sent his steady force of human-kindly thought into those eyes, they *narrowed into slits*. In that instant Skag knew that the beast had no fear to allay; no quality of nature he could touch. It was a murderer, pure and simple.

Then he thought of Carlin. . . . Of her brother. . . . Of Nels. He opened his lips to speak, but the name did not pass his throat.

Carlin, Carlin! It was only a question of time; and Skag folded his arms.

And high against the wall of the waters rolled the clarion challenge-call of Nels, the Great Dane dog. The cheetah leaped and settled back. Skag turned to look the way it faced. A grey line flashed along the ground. Skag did not know it, but he was racing toward their meeting.

The cheetah lifted and met Nels, body against body, in mid-air—Skag heard the impact. Nels had risen full stretch, his head low between his shoulders; the cheetah's wide-spread arms went round him, but his entire length closed upon the cheetah's entire length—like a jack-knife—folding it backward. Skag heard a dull sound, the same instant with a keen cat-scream—cut short as the two bodies struck the earth. When he reached them, Nels was still doubled tight over the cheetah's backward-bent body; his grey iron-jaws locked deep in the tawny throat.

"Sahib! Sanford *Han*—tee Sahib!"

"Hi, Bhanah; this way!"

Bhanah came with a rain-coat in his hand. Stooping to examine Nels a moment and rising to glance at the wall, he spoke rapidly:

"The Sahib has seen his Great Dane Nels kill a second cheetah in one day. There are two cuts on each leg. Also because Nels must not lose his strength on a fast journey to his master's place—I, Bhanah, will uncover mine honour in the presence of a man."

And quickly casting his turban from his head, he proceeded to tear it down the middle. While he worked, he talked—as if to himself—in half chanting tones:

"Men in my country do *not*—this thing; but I do it. Of a certainty Nels has accomplished that I could not, though I would. This night two cheetahs remain not—the gods witness—to destroy little tender children of men. And when the so-insignificant cuts of Nels shall be presently wrapped with the covering of mine own honour, I shall be exalted not less! *The gods witness.* Then we return swiftly into a safe place."

This was no ordinary exultation. Skag's ears were wide open; and he heard grief—and hate.

"How did you know where I was?" he asked quietly.

"I heard the first cheetah's death cry; and I knew he was not far from you, Sahib."

"I thought he was pretty far, one little while."

Skag had spoken, thinking of Nels. Bhanah searched his face while the look of a frightened child grew in his own. Again he stooped quickly and touched the man's feet. He had done it once before—to Skag's acute discomfort.

"What's the meaning of that?"

"That a man's life is in thy breath, my Master."

"Bhanah, I'll find out—how to answer you."

Then Bhanah laughed a low exultant chuckle, while he finished binding Nels' legs with a part of his own turban.

"It is well, Sahib; the *fortune which never fails* is thine. And now, if we are wise, we will run."

Nels led, all the way; and they were barely under cover, when the earth indeed shook. The stone walls of the building rocked; the dull thunder of a solid, continuous impact of dense water upon its roof, filled their ears. The light of the sun was cut off.

"Bhanah, you and Nels will camp with me to-night. This has been the hunting cheetah-day of my life; and—Nels is responsible that he didn't get me."

"My master is the heart of kindness."

While Bhanah was busy, later, Skag laughed:

"I'm remembering that you said Nels did it *soon*. How did he do it?"

"By the drive of his weight against the cheetah's body; and the strength of his limbs, in the action my master saw."

They had eaten and Nels was properly cared for, when Bhanah spoke softly:

"Shall we have tales, Sahib?"

Skag roused from a moment's abstraction to answer:

"Bhanah, I don't remember anything I could talk about to-night, but the hunting cheetah—Nels got."

"The hunting cheetah is one, Sahib; *there are many.* Telling is in knowledge and in speech; finding is in the man. I will tell, if the Sahib pleases; but he shall find."

So they had tales that night.

CHAPTER VIII

THE MONSTER KABULI

Skag had learned, in finding Carlin, that it wasn't like a man in America finding the one particular and inimitable girl, not even if she were the *laurus nobilis* and he the eagle of the same coin. In India, where people have pride of race, and time to keep it shining, there are formalities. . . . The two had arranged to meet in the jungle—not deep in the glen where the tiger had coughed, but at the edge toward Hurda, when Skag returned from Poona. He was to go straight into the jungle from the railway station. Carlin would be watching and follow there. . . .

Sanford Hantee of the Natural Research Department, after much opportunity to wrestle with the subtle and gritty and hard-testing demon of delay, came at last to Hurda again, and stepped out of the coach with a throb in his chest and a knot in his throat which only the best and bravest soldiers have brought in from the field. As the moments of waiting at the edge of the jungle passed, it dawned upon him that something had happened, or Carlin already would be with him, at least crossing the big sun-shot area from the walled city. . . . What had happened is this story of the monster Kabuli, which is an animal story even without the entrance of the racing elephant, Gunpat Rao.

Many months before, five merchants came in from far Kabul and sat down in the market-place at Hurda, day by day unfolding more of their packs. They brought nuts from High Himalaya, foot-hill raisins and the long white Kabuli grapes themselves, packed in cotton, a dozen to fifteen in the box. Then there were dried figs and dates, pomegranates picked up far this side of the Hills, Kabuli weaves of cloth, and silks inwoven with gold thread. They were small packs, but worth a great price; which is important to relate in any company.

Now these five Kabulies were usually together (not too far from the kadamba tree where Ratna Ram sat); and their turbans were of different colours, but their hearts were mainly of one kind of hell. Sometimes they stood and sometimes they moved one by one among the bazaars; but Hurda thought of them as one alien presence, and signified that the hugest of them, the monster himself, was also the most hateful and dangerous, which he was.

If I should tell how tall he was exactly, and this in the midst of Sikhs and other of the tallest people of the world, you would think it one of the high lights of a writer-man, and if I should tell you of the face of this monster; the soft folds of fury resting there in the main; the bulk of loose greyish lids over the whites of eyes flecked with brown pigments; of the sunken upper lip and the nose drooping against it, you would say long before I had finished, "Let up on the poor beast—"

And this was a rich man, this Kabuli; richer than any of these brothers, and deeper-minded; so that he could think with keener power to make his thought come true. Also, life was more full to him than to the others, so that he could look over the world of his packs; and when he slept in the midst of his packs, all his treasure was not there. You really should have seen him smile as the head-missionary, Mr. Maurice, approached, and you should have seen the smile change to a sneer, without a flick of difference in the expression of the eyes. And perhaps it is just as well that you missed the look that came into the eyes of the monster Kabuli when the beautiful English missionary, Margaret Annesley, passed.

Miss Annesley was Carlin's closest friend in Hurda. They worked together among the women and children, among the sick and hungry, and found much to do, without entering the deeper concerns of soul-wellbeing which Mr. Maurice attended. These last were rather reticent concerns of Carlin, especially. Mr. Maurice protested against their moving through certain parts of the city, against entering Mohammedan households, or the quarters of the bazaar women—all of which talk was well-listened to. Miss Annesley had no fear, because she was essentially clean. She was effective and tireless, a thrilling sort of saint; but she could see no evil, not even in the monster Kabuli. Carlin had no fear because she was Carlin; but she had a clear eye for jungle shadows—for beasts, saints, and men. As for the Kabuli, she quietly remarked:

"Why, Margaret, can't you see he's a mad dog?"

In other words, Carlin used the optic nerve as well as the vision said to be of the soul.

"But, my dear, he seemed really stirred," Miss Annesley protested.

"I do not doubt he was stirred," Carlin replied. Her mind was the mind of India, with Western contrasts; also it was familiar from both angles with the various attractive attributes of her friend. . . . But Margaret Annesley continued to greet the monster Kabuli from time to time. Having great means and worldly goods and riotous health, he had nothing to discuss but his soul—which few beside Margaret would have found ostensible.

"I tell you he has *rabies*," Carlin once repeated.

This did no good; so she went to Deenah who was Miss Annesley's servant, a Hindu of the Hindus and priceless. Deenah declared that he was already aware of the danger; that he missed nothing; also that he was watchful as one who feared the worst.

Deenah was a small man, swift and noiseless. He had an invincible equilibrium and authority in his own world, which was a considerable establishment back of the dining-room, including a most delectable little creature even smaller than Deenah, but quite as important, and sharing all light and shadow by his side. Deenah had a look of forked lightning and a mellow voice. The more angry he became, the more caressing his tones.

One day while he was down in the bazaars buying provisions, the monster Kabuli beckoned Deenah to come closer. They stood together—terrier and blood-hound—and Deenah listened while the form and colour of better conditions was outlined for his sake. . . . The Kabuli had heard that Deenah was a great servant; he had heard it from many sources, even that Deenah was favourably compared with the chief commissioner's favourite servant—who was a picked man of ten thousand.

Deenah inclined his head, hearkening for the tone within the tone, but gravely acknowledged that he had heard much in this life harder to listen to.

The Kabuli continued that Deenah was no doubt appreciated on a small scale in the house of Annesley Sahiba; but the establishment itself, as well as the people, was inadequate to offer scope for the talents of such a man as Deenah; also that Deenah was remiss in making no better provision for the future of his own household; also, the gifts should be considered—and now the Kabuli was opening his packs.

Deenah granted that life was not all sumptuous as he might wish, but he had been given to understand no man's life was so in this world; he would be glad now, to hear the plan by which all that he lacked could appear and all that he hoped for, come to pass.

The Kabuli opened wider his treasures. Deenah's narrow-lidded eyes feasted upon the wealths and crafts of many men. . . . And the plan had to do, not with this night nor with the next, but with the night after these two nights were passed, and Deenah's Sahiba and the Hakima (literally, the physician, which meant Carlin) were to be brought for the evening to the house of the Kabuli's friend, one Mirza Khan, a Mohammedan, whose soul also was in great need.

Deenah's voice was gentle as he enquired how he was to be used—why riches accrued to him, since it was the life of the life of his mistress to serve those ill or in need, body or soul. The Kabuli replied that he was not sure that the Sahiba would go to a Mohammedan house, even with her friend the Hakima, unless Deenah could assure his mistress that the Mohammedan was well known to him and honourable, his house an abode of fellowship and peace.

Deenah considered well, in soft tones saying presently that he could not accomplish this thing alone, but must advise with his fellow-servants who were trustworthy. In fact, if the Kabuli could come this afternoon—when the Sahiba and the Hakima would be away—and tell his story once more, in the presence of the utterly reliable among the servants—all might be brought to pass.

The Kabuli did not care for the plan, but Deenah repeated that he could not do this thing alone; his voice admirably gentle, as he reiterated his own helplessness. . . . Still he granted with hesitation that the Sahiba deigned to trust him to a degree. . . . At this moment the Kabuli saw Deenah's eyes forking at the treasure-pack. There was longing in them that was pain. The face of Deenah was the face of one struck and crippled with his own needs, which point helped the Kabuli to decision.

The terms of the agreement were made straight and fixed. Deenah went back to his house where he made the monster's plan known to the servants. In the afternoon, when the house was empty, the monster Kabuli called and opened a small pack in the quiet shade of the compound, before the eyes of six men and one woman, as much Deenah as himself. . . . When the time in the story came that Deenah was to use his influence upon the mind of his mistress, there seemed a slowness of understanding among the other servants; so that the Kabuli had to speak again and very clearly.

Just now the head of Deenah bent low over the open pack, the movement of his hand instantly drawing and filling the eye of the trader from Kabul; and then it was that the Sahiba's *syce*, who was a huge man, materialised a *lakri* from under his long cotton tunic—the *lakri* being a stick of olive-wood from High Himalaya and very hard. This he brought down with great force upon the hugest and ugliest head in all Central Provinces at that time.

Merely a beginning. Six other *lakris* were drawn from five other tunics—the extra one for Deenah.

The great body was dragged farther back toward the servants' quarters. Here Deenah officiated. With each blow he enunciated in caressing tones, some term of the agreement . . . until he heard the protest of the mother of his little son:

"Shall you, Deenah, who are only her man-servant, have all the privilege of defending the Sahiba—to whom I, Shanti, am as her own child?"

And Deenah, not missing a count, cried:

"Come and defend!"

So Deenah's wife and the other women came, bringing the smooth hand stones with which they ground the spices into curry powder. . . . And when the beating was over, they carefully tied up the pack of the Kabuli and sealed it without a single article missing. Then they carried the body out of the compound, across the main highway, beyond the parallel bridle-road, and let it slide softly down into the little *khud* beyond, deeper and deeper each year from erosion.

A little afterward, that same afternoon, Margaret Annesley and Carlin Deal were walking along the bridle-path. Hearing a moan they looked over into the khud, where the monster Kabuli was coming to. He managed to raise one hand, but the movement of the fingers somehow struck the pity from Carlin's heart. It was not a clean gesture of a chastened man. Even though his body was terribly bruised and broken, the face was that of Ravage in person. Carlin pulled her companion on. They hastened to the bungalow where the tied pack was in evidence and strange sounds reached them from the servants' compound.

It was the picture of a tranced group that they saw—Deenah sitting upon the ground, uttering frightful low curses securely coupled together—in the language of all languages for this ancient art. The others were around him, even two or three of the women.

"Deenah!" Miss Annesley called.

The concentration was not to be broken.

"Deenah—is a madness come to this place?"

The head of her priceless servant was bowing close to the ground, but his mind was still away; and in high concord to his tones, were the tones of the small delectable one, whose eyes, dark and vivid, were the eyes of Jael singing her song after slaying Sisera. Margaret turned to her *syce.* There were tears and sweat in his eyes, but no answering human gleam.

"Carlin—" she said. "Help me carry the *daik-ji*—"

It was a huge vessel containing several gallons of cool water; and this was lifted by four hands and poured upon Deenah, whose eyes met them at once with the light of reason.

"Bear witness, I am cursing softly," he said.

"Are you my head servant?"

"I am thy servant."

"And you permit this bazaar-tamasha in your compound?"

Deenah observed that this was not an affair upon which he could speak to the Sahiba, his mistress. Meanwhile Carlin watched Deenah's eyes fill with the keen reds of bloody memory.

"Go away, Margaret," Carlin said. "He will talk to me. Please go now. In six breaths he will be back in his trance again—"

So it happened. Deenah watched his mistress depart, then he raised his eyes to Carlin, saying:

"The Hakima will understand. These things are not for the Sahiba—"

"Speak—"

Deenah arose, saying: "It is not good for you to set foot in my house, but come to the threshold; then neither my voice nor the voices of these shall enter her understanding—"

Deenah pointed to the rest of the servants who gathered around.

The tale of the monster Kabuli was unfolded to Carlin without a single interruption for several moments; in fact, until Margaret Annesley came running forth, crying:

"Are you never going to cease talk and carry help to the Kabuli—who is hurt?"

Carlin beckoned her back. "Not hurt, dear. He is ill. He has hydrophobia."

"Our protection depends upon you," Deenah concluded, to Carlin. "We commit ourselves to you; we render our lives and honour into your care. You alone, Hakima-ji, can present the story of these doings to the chief commissioner, whose name we hold in honour above other men. Will you see that it be known—not one thread has been taken or changed from the pack of the Kabuli; also, the chief commissioner—out of his equity which has never failed—shall judge us, *knowing* that we did the beating for the Sahiba's sake."

The chief commissioner at Hurda was a good and a just man. He listened seriously and spoke to Carlin of the value of good Indian servants in the houses of the English; of the dangers of the tiger in the grass and the serpent upon the rock and the Kabuli in the khud—to whom he would attend at once.

It was many weeks after that when the case was called, and Deenah's eyes grew red-rimmed like a pit-terrier's as he told the story again, but his voice fondled the ears of those present in the court-room. . . . One by one, the other four Kabulies left the market-place in Hurda; and when the monster himself had been made to pay and his healing had been uninterrupted for many weeks, there came, a day when the unwalled city of Hurda knew him no more.

He was not forgotten, even though months sped by; for in Miss Annesley's heart was a pang over the big man who had been horribly hurt. . . . Meanwhile for Carlin all life was changed—as the magic of swift afterglow changes every twig and leaf and stem. Then came her hard days, watching for Skag's return—the weeks passing while he waited in Poona.Every morning from a distance, she observed the train come in from the South. When Skag did not appear, sometimes she would go alone for a while to the edge of the jungle, but never deep, because he had asked her not to. Sometimes it was an hour or two before she was ready to look out at the world or the light again. . . .

One early morning as she crossed the market-place, Carlin saw a strange elephant there with his mahout; and a messenger approached deferentially, asking if she were the Hakima, and if she could lead the way to Annesley Sahiba. . . . Four hours' journey away—this was the messenger's story—a native prince whose dignity included the keeping of one elephant, an honourable dispensation from Indian Government, had called in great need for the ministration of the Hakima, and that of her friend, Annesley Sahiba—for lo, unto him a child was to be born.

Carlin asked if she were needed at once—thinking of the many days and the train at noontime. The messenger said that within four hours he was told to deliver the Hakima and Annesley Sahiba at the palace door. He followed along, and the elephant came behind him, as she walked toward Margaret's bungalow. . . . If Skag were to come this day, she thought! . . . Deenah was away, but Carlin left word with his wife that she would be back that night, or early the next day. Margaret was ready. Carlin was in the howdah beside her, before there was really a chance to think.

CHAPTER IX

THE MONSTER KABULI (CONTINUED)

Skag did arrive from Poona that day. When Carlin did not come to the jungle-edge, and the vivid open area between him and the city showed no movement, he did not linger many minutes. Power had come to him from the waiting days, and this hour was the acid test. All his life he had refused to look back or look ahead, making the *Now*—the present moving point, his world—wasting no energy otherwise.

In the long waiting days, he had learned what many a man afield had been forced to learn in loneliness, that when he was very still, and feeling *high*, not too tired—in fact, when he could forget himself—something of Carlin came to him, over the miles.

But in spite of all he knew, much force of his life had strained forward to this moment of meeting. The shock of disappointment dazed him. His first thought was that there was some good reason; but after that, the misery of faint-heartedness stole in, and he wondered the old sad wonder—if love had changed.

Skag hurried back to the station where he had left the Great Dane, Nels, with Bhanah, who would have to find quarters for himself. Nels stood between the two, waiting for his orders; and wheeled with a dip of the head almost puppy-like when the man decided. So Skag walked on toward the road where

Carlin lived; and at his heels, with dignity, strode one of the four great hunting dogs in India. Presently he saw Miss Annesley's head-servant, Deenah, running toward him—face grey with calamity.

And now Skag heard of the coming of the messenger with the strange elephant; and the black edging began to run about Deenah's tale, as he revealed the ugly possibilities in his own mind that the Monster Kabuli had his part in this sending:

". . . Now Hantee Sahib must learn," Deenah finished, "that not within four hours' journey from Hurda; nay, not within six hours' journey from Hurda, is there any native prince with the dignity of one elephant."

. . . They were walking rapidly toward the house of the chief commissioner whom Deenah said was away in the villages. Their hope of life and death fell upon the Deputy Commissioner-Sahib. Always as he spoke, Deenah's face steadily grew more grey, the rims of his eyes more red. His memories of the monster were flooding in like the rains over old river-beds, and there was no mercy for Skag in anything he said.

The Deputy Commissioner, a perfectly groomed man, leisurely appeared. He did not wear spectacle or glass; still there was a glisten about his eyes, as if one were there. He came out into the verandah opening a heavy cigarette-case of soft Indian gold. His head tilted back as if sipping from a cup, as he lit and inbreathed the cigarette. To Skag he seemed so utterly aloof, so irreparably out of touch with a man's needs at a moment like this, that he could not have asked a favour or adequately stated his case. Deenah took this part, however. If there were drama or any interest in the tale, there was no sign from the Deputy, whose eyes now cooled upon Nels, and widened. Presently he interrupted Deenah to inquire who owned this dog.

The servant signified the American, and Skag took the straight glisten of the Englishman's glance for the first time.

"May I inquire? From whom?"

Skag coldly told him that the dog had been owned by Police Commissioner Hichens of Bombay. . . . The deputy regretfully ordered Deenah to continue his narrative, and in the silence afterward, presently spoke the name:

"Neela Deo, of course—"

This meant the Blue God, the leader of the caravan; and signified the lordliest elephant in all India. . . . The Deputy, after a slight pause, answered himself:

"But Neela Deo is away with the chief commissioner. . . . itha Baba—"

There was another lilting pause. This referred to a female elephant, the meaning of whose name was "Sweet Baby." The Deputy capitulated:

"Mitha Baba, yes; especially since she knows the Hakima—and oh, I say, that's a strange tale, you know—"

He glanced from Deenah to Nels, to Skag; but received no encouragement to narrate same. Not in the least unbalanced, he tipped back his head and took another drink from between his smoky fingers; then his glassless eye glittered out through the white burning of the noon, as he added:

"But Mitha Baba would not chase a strange elephant, unless she positively knew the creature was running off with her own Gul Moti. . . . She's discriminating, is Mitha Baba. But I say, Gunpat Rao came from the Vindhas, you know."

It dawned upon Skag that this wasn't monologue, but conversation; also that it had some vague bearing upon his own affairs. The pause was very slight, when the Deputy resumed:

"Yes, Gunpat Rao is from the Vindha Hills, within the

life-time of one man. . . . Mitha Baba is as fast, but she won't do it; so there's an end. Gunpat Rao. . . . Gunpat Rao. The mahouts say young male elephants will follow a strange male for the chance of a fight. It's consistent enough. Yes, we'll call in Chakkra. . . . Are you ready to travel, sir?"

This was to Skag.

No array of terms could express how ready to travel was Sanford Hantee. The Bengali mahout, Chakkra, appeared; a sturdy little man with blue turban, red kummerband, and a scarf and tunic of white.

The Deputy flicked away his cigarette and now spoke fast—talk having to do with Nels, with the Hakima, with Gunpat Rao, who was his particular mahout's master, and of the strange elephant who had carried the two Sahibas away.

Chakkra reported at this point that he had seen this elephant in the market place, an old male—with a woman's howdah, covering too few of his wrinkles—and a mahout who would ruin the disposition of anything but a man-killer. Chakkra appeared to have an actual hatred toward this man, for he enquired of the Deputy:

"Have I your permission to deal with the mahout of this thief elephant?"

"Out of your own blood-lust—no. Out of necessity—yes."

A queer moment. It was as if one supposed only to crawl, had suddenly revealed wings. Not until this instant did Skag realise that a Chief Commissioner had the flower of England to pick his deputies from, and had made no mistake in this man. . . . A moment later, Nels had been given preliminary instruction, and Skag was lifted, with a playful flourish of the trunk, by Gunpat Rao himself, into the light hunting howdah. Chakkra was also in place, when the Deputy waved his hand with the remark:

"Oh, I say, I'd be glad of the chase, myself, but an official, you know, . . . and Lord, what a dog!"

The last was as Nels swung around in front of Gunpat Rao's trunk as if formally to remark: "You see we are to travel together to-day."

The Deputy detained them a second or two longer, while he brought his gun-case and a pair of pistols, to save the time of Skag procuring his own at the station. They heard him call, after the start:

"It might be a running fight, you know. . . ."

A little out, Nels was given the scent of the strange elephant and Deenah left them, with nothing to mitigate the evil discovery that Carlin and her friend had been carried straight through the open jungle country, toward the Vindhas; not at all in the direction the messenger had stated within hearing of the other servants.

A steady beat through Skag's tortured mind—was Deenah's story of the monster Kabuli; no softness nor mercy in those details. He had watched, in the Deputy, a man unfold, after the mysterious manner of the English. He had entered suddenly, abruptly into one of the most enthralling centres of fascination in Indian life—the elephant service. He had seen the exalted and complicated mechanism of a Chief Commissioner's Headquarters get down to individual business with remarkable speed and not the loss of an ounce of dignity. But under every feeling and thought—was the slow bass beat of Deenah's story about the monster Kabuli.

Nels had been called to the trail in the very hour of his arrival. Skag would have supposed their movement leisurely, except that he saw Nels steadily at work. Gunpat Rao, the most magnificent elephant in the Chief Commissioner's stockades—excepting Neela Deo and Mitha Baba—was making speed under him, at this moment. (Gunpat Rao had approved of him instantly, swinging him up into the howdah with a glad grace and a touch that would not unfreshen evening wear.)

Chakkra, the mahout, was singing the praises of Gunpat Rao, his master, as they rolled forward; flapping an ear to keep time and waving his ankas—the steel hook of which was never used.

"Kin to Neela Deo, is Gunpat Rao; liege-son to Neela Deo, the King!" he repeated.

It appeared that he was reminding Gunpat Rao, rather than informing the American, of this honour.

"Did I not hear the Deputy Commissioner Sahib say that he came from the Vindhas, and that Neela Deo is from High Himalaya?" Skag asked.

The mahout's face turned back; his trailing lids did not widen in the fierce sunlight. It was the face of a man still singing.

"The kinship is of honour, not of blood, Sahib," he answered.

Then Chakkra informed Skag that Kudrat Sharif, Neela Deo's mahout, was the third of his line to serve the Blue God, who was not yet nearly in the ictus of his power and beauty; while he, Chakkra, was the only mahout Gunpat Rao had known—since he came down from the Vindhian trap-stockades, where he was snared. He was about thirty years younger than Neela Deo, the King. Would the Sahib bear in mind that an elephant continues to increase in strength and wisdom for an hundred years? And now would he consider Gunpat Rao's size—the perfection of his shape? Might not such a Prince claim relationship to such a King?

. . . Chakkra then pointed out that when the grandson of his own little son should sit just here, behind the incomparable ears of his beloved—the ears with linings like flower-petals—so, looking out upon the world from a greater height than this—then doubtless people would have learned that another mighty elephant had come into the world.

Skag missed nothing of the talk. Another time it would have filled him with deep delight. It belonged to his own craft. A man might use all the words, of all the languages in all their flexibilities and never tell the whole truth of his own craft. In fact, a man can only drop a point here and there about his life work. One never comes to the end.

Also before his eyes was the joy of Nels in action—the big fellow leaping to his task, steadily drawing them on, it appeared; and always a breath of ease would blow across Skag's being as he noted the quickening; but when that was merely sustained for a while, the hope of it wore away, and he wanted more and more speed—past any giving of man or beast. . . . The old drum of the Kabuli tale constantly recurred, as if a trap door to the deeps were often lifted. Skag would brush his hand across his brow, shading his head with his helmet lifted apart for a moment, to let the sunless air circulate.

They passed through the open jungle merging into a country of low hills and frequent villages. The rains that had broken in Poona had not yet reached this country. . . . The sun went down and the afterglow changed the world. Carlin's afterglow, it was to Skag, from their moment at the edge of the jungle—on the evening of the troth; there was pain about it now. India had a different look to him—alien, sinister, of a depth of suffering undreamed of, because of the beating bass of the Kabuli tale, intensified by the sense that falling night would slacken the chase. . . .

Skag had lost the magic of externals, the drift of his great interest. All his lights were around Carlin, and powers of hatred, altogether foreign to his faculties, pressed upon him in the threat of the hour. . . . Yes, Chakkra remembered the five Kabuli men who had sat in the market-place. Yes, he remembered the story of the beating of the monster, the long slow healing after that; and his last look, as he left Hurda for the last time. . . .

It was well, Chakkra said, that they had open country for the chase. It was well that the Kabuli did not call to the Sahibas, and hide them in one of the great Mohammedan households of Hurda—where even Indian Government might not search. It was well that the Kabuli did not dare to come closer to Hurda than this, so that they had a chance to overtake his elephant afield, before the walls of the *purdah* closed. . . .

Such was the burden of Chakkra's ramble, and there was no balm in it for Skag. The weight settled heavier and heavier upon him with the ending of the day. Nels was a phantom of grey before them in the shadows, leisurely showing his powers. At times, while he ranged far ahead, they would not hear him for several minutes; then possibly a half-humorous sniff in the immediate dark, and they knew the big fellow waited for Gunpat Rao to catch up. Once he was lost ahead so long that Skag spoke:

"Nels—"

The answer was a bound of feet and a whine below that pulled the man's hand over the rim of the howdah, as if to reach and touch his good friend.

"Take it, Nels—good work, old man," Skag said.

They passed through zones of coolness as the trail sank into hollows between the hills, and Gunpat Rao rolled forward. Pitch and roll, pitch and roll—as many movements as a solar system and the painful illusion of slowness over all. Often in Skag's nostrils one of the subtlest of all scents made itself known, but most elusively—a suggestion of shocking power—like an instant's glimpse into another dimension. If you answer at all to an expression which at best only intimates—*the smell of living dust*—you will have something of the thing that Skag sensed in the emanation of Gunpat Rao, warming to action.

Occasionally as they crossed the streams there was delay in finding the trail on the other side. Once in the dark after a ford, when Nels had rushed along the left bank to find the scent, Gunpat Rao plunged straight on to the right without waiting; and the mahout sang his praises with low but fiery intensity:

"He is coming. He is coming into his own!"

"What do you mean, Chakkra? Make it clear to me who have not many words of Hindi—"

"The meaning of our journey appears to him, Sahib; from our minds, from the thief ahead and from the great dog,—the thing that we do is appearing to him. He knows the way—see—"

Nels had come in from the lateral and found that Gunpat Rao was right. An amazing point to Skag, this. The great head before him, with Chakkra's legs dangling behind the ears, had grasped something of the urge of their chase. A vast and mysterious mechanism was locked in the great grey skull. Actually Gunpat Rao seemed to laugh that he had shown the way to Nels.

"You don't mean, Chakkra, that he goes into the silence like a holy man?"

"It is like."

Skag had seen something of this in his India—the yogi men shutting their eyes and bowing their heads and seeming to sink their consciousness into themselves, in order to ascertain some fact *without* and afar off.

"Our lord gives his mind to the matter and the truth unfolds—" Chakkra added.

"Will the other elephant travel through the night so steadily?"

(The sense of his own powerlessness was in him like a spear.)

"Not like this, Sahib," said Chakkra.

The hint, however, was that the thief elephant would make all speed; that the lead of the four hours would be conserved as carefully as possible by the other mahout.

"But he has a woman's howdah," Chakkra invariably added. "Two Sahibas, as well as the mahout himself. . . . To-morrow will tell—hai, to-morrow will tell, if they go that far!"

That was always the point of the blackest fear—that the elephant ahead should come to some Mohammedan household, and leave Carlin where no one could pass the veil.

"But what of the messenger who brought word to the Sahibas?" Skag asked.

"He would slip away. Some hiding place for him—possibly back at Hurda."

Chakkra seemed sure of this.

That was Skag's long night. He tried to think of the Kabuli as if he were an animal. A man might have a destroying enmity against a cobra or a tiger or a python; but it was not black and self-defiling like this thing which crept over him, out of the miasma of Deenah's tale.

In the dawn they reached a small river. Skag saw Nels lose his tread in the deepening centre, swing down with the current an instant and then strike his balance, swimming. Here was coolness and silence. To-night he would know. To-night, if he did not have Carlin—

. . . Gunpat Rao stood shoulder-deep in the stream. Skag fancied a gleam of deep massive humour under the tilt of the great ear below him, as the elephant, none too delicately, set his foot forward into the deeper part of the stream. His trunk and Chakkra's voice were raised together—for Chakkra was slipping:

"Hai, my Prince, would you go without me? Would you leave the Sahib alone in his proving-time? Would you leave my children fatherless? . . . There is none other—"

They stood in the lifting day overlooking a broad sloping country—the Vindha peaks faintly outlined in the far distance.

"It is the broad valley of Nerbudda," Chakkra said, "full of milk and wine against the seasons. One good day of travel ahead to the bank of Holy Nerbudda, Sahib, before the fall of night—if the chase holds so long."

Skag did not eat this day. It was not until high noon that they halted by a spring of sweet water, and the American thought of his thirst. Nels was leaner. He plunged to the water; then back to the scent again with a far challenge call. (It was like the echo of his challenge to the cheetah as the wall of the waters loomed across the hills, above Poona.) On he went, seriously; his mouth open in the great heat, his tongue rocking on its centre like nothing else.

Gunpat Rao seemed gradually overcoming obstructions; as if his great idea mounted and cleared, his body requiring time to strike its rhythm. Chakkra sang to him. The sun became hotter and higher—until it hung at the very top of the universe and forgot nothing. There was a stillness in the hills that would frighten anything but a fever bird to silence. To Skag it was a weight against speech and he sat rigidly for many moments at a time—all his life of forest and city, of man and creature, passing before his tortured eyes. . . . And the words Carlin had spoken; all the mysteries of his nights near Poona when she had seemed to draw near as he fell asleep—seemed to be there as he came forth from a dream. Always he had thought he could never forget the dreams—only to find them gone utterly, before he stood upon his feet. Past all, was the marvel of the hunting cheetah day, when he looked at the beast that gave no answer to his force; only murder in its savage heart—and Carlin's name was his very breath in that peril, something of her spirit like a whisper from within his own heart.

All that afternoon Skag's eyes strained ahead, and his respect grew for the thief elephant with his greater burden, and his wonder increased for Nels and Gunpat Rao. One dim far peak held his eyes from time to time; but Skag lived in the low beat of India's misery—the fever and famine; the world of veils and the miseries beyond knowledge of the world. He sank and sank until he was chilled, even though the sweat of the day's fierce burning was upon him. He understood hate and death, the thirst to kill; the slow ruin that comes at first to the human mind, suddenly cut off from the one held more dear than life. It seemed all boyish dazzle that he had ever found loveliness in this place. That boyishness had passed. In this hour he saw only hatred ahead and mockery, if Carlin—. . . but the far dim peak of misty light held his aching eyes.

"Go on, Nels—on, old man," he would call.

And Chakkra would turn with protest that could not find words—his tongue silenced by the lean terrible face in the howdah behind him. Presently Chakkra would fall to talking to his master, muttering in a kind of thrall at the thing he saw in the countenance of the American who had touched bottom.

Sanford Hantee was facing the worst of the past and an impossible future, having neither hate nor pity, now. Yet from time to time with a glance at the gun-case at his feet, he spoke with cold clearness:

"We must overtake them before night."

Chakkra, who had ceased singing, would bow, saying:

"The trail is hot, Sahib. They are not far."

Steadily beneath them, Gunpat Rao straightened out,

lengthening his roll, softening his pitch. Nels was not trotting now, but in a long low run. Skag was aghast at himself, that his heart did not go out to these magnificent servants. There was not *feeling* within him to answer these verities of courage and endurance; yet he could remember the human that had been in his heart.

The low hills had broken away behind them; the first veil of twilight in the air. A shelving dip opened, showing the bottom of the valley. Skag could see nothing ahead—but Nels lying closer to the trail. Chakkra's shoulder was suddenly within reach of Skag's hand, for the head of his master was lifted.

As the great curve of Gunpat Rao's trumpet arched before his face—two things happened to Skag. A full blast of hot breath drove through him; and a keen high vibrant tone pierced every nerve. Then Chakkra shouted:

"Gunpat Rao, prince of Vindha—declares the chase is on! Hold fast, Sahib,—we go!"

The earth rose up and the heavens tipped. There was no foundation; the bulwarks of earth's crust had given away. The landscape was racing past—but backward—and Nels, yet ahead, was a still, whirring streak. The thing hardly believed and never seen in America—that the elephant is speed-king of the world—was revelation now! No pitch or roll; a long curving sweep this—seeming scarcely to touch the ground. This was the going Skag had called for—a night and a day. And Nels was labouring beside them now, but seeming to miss his tread—seeming to run on ice.

"Hai!" yelled Chakkra. "Who says there is none other than Neela Deo?"

A thread of silver stretched before them, crossing the line of their course. It broadened in a man's breath. They turned the curve of the last slope, and heard the shout of the mahout far ahead. The thief elephant was running along Nerbudda's margin to a ford.

A roar was about Skag's head and shoulders like a storm—Gunpat Rao trumpeting again! The landscape blurred. The forward beast was growing large . . . two standing figures above him—the fling of a white arm!

The huge red howdah rocked as the thief elephant entered the river; a moment more, only the howdah showing. Distantly like the hum of furious insects, Skag heard Chakkra's chant:

"The thief is snared! Holy Nerbudda herself weaved the snare. . . .The hand of destiny is ours, Sahib. Nay, mine, not thine! Did not the Deputy Commissioner Sahib say *by necessity*? . . . Plunge in! . . . Hai, but softly. Prince of thy kind, take the water softly, I say—"

And Gunpat Rao entered the river at a swimming stroke. Skag's eyes had hardly turned from the great red howdah. There was a keen squeal from ahead, answered by a fiery hissing intake of Chakkra's breath:

"That, Sahib, is the murderous mahout using his steel hook. . . . Yes, it was *by necessity*, the Deputy Sahib said. Certainly it was *by necessity*!"

The fling of a white arm again. Sanford Hantee was standing.

"Carlin!" he called.

The answer came back to him in some mystery of imperishable vibration.

"I am here."

The two great beasts were moiled together against the stream. . . . The man and woman, whose eyes still held, might have missed the flash of steel that Chakkra parried with his ankas. In fact, it was the sound of a quick gasp of Margaret

Annesley that made them turn, just as Chakkra shouted:

"*By necessity*, Sahib! . . . It is accomplished!"

The other's blade had whirled into the water. They had heard the welt as Chakkra's ankas came down. The strange mahout looked drunken and spineless for a second; then there was a red gush under his white cloth as he pitched into the stream.

The Great Dane had just caught up. He was in the river below them—not doubting his part had come.

"Nels, steady! Let him go!" Skag called. "Don't touch, old man!"

And then, after the thief elephant, having no fight in him, was made fast, they heard Chakkra singing his song, but paid no attention. . . .

It was a longer journey back to Hurda, for they came slowly, but there was no haste; and two, at least, in the hunting howdah could transcend passing time, each by the grace of the other. Gunpat Rao was returned to the Deputy Sahib with an amulet to add to his trophy-winnings; and a sentence or two that might have been taken from the record of Neela Deo himself. The thief elephant was found to be a runaway that had fallen into native hands. And Nels was restored to Bhanah by the way of the heart of Carlin Deal. . . .

They never found out how far the two women would have been taken beyond the Nerbudda. After they had first mounted into the red howdah at Hurda, the messenger of the Kabuli had disappeared into the crowd and was not seen again. . . . As for the monster himself, he had suffered enough to plan craftily. (The Nerbudda took his mahout and covered him quite as deeply as the crowd had covered his messenger at Hurda.)

Much in his silence afterward, and in the great still joy that had come to him, Sanford Hantee chose to reflect upon the mystery of pain he had known on the lonely out-journey—the spiritless incapacity to cope with life—the loss even of his mastercraft with animals. He would look toward Carlin in such moments and then look away, or possibly look within. By her, the meanings of all life were sharpened—jungle and jungle-beast, monster, saint and man—the breath of all life more keen.

CHAPTER X

HAND-OF-A-GOD

Skag and Carlin had come back from Poona where five of Carlin's seven brothers had been present at her marriage. There were weeks in Hurda now, while Skag's equipment for jungle work arrived bit by bit. They lived some distance from the city and back from the great Highway-of-all-India, in Malcolm M'Cord's bungalow, a house to remember for several reasons.

The Indian jungles were showing Skag deep secrets about wild animals—knowledge beyond his hopes. Some things that he thought he knew in the old days as a circus-trainer were beginning to look curious and obsolete, but much still held good, even became more and more significant. The things he had known intuitively did not diminish. These had to do with mysterious talents of his own, and dated back to the moment he stood for the first time before one of the "big cat" cages at the Lincoln Park Zoo in Chicago. That was his initiation-day in a craft in which he had since gone very far as white men go—even into the endless fascination of the cobra-craft.

Skag was meeting now from time to time in his jungle work some of the big hunters of India, men whose lives were a-seethe with tales of adventure. When they talked, however, Skag slowly but surely grasped the fact that what they had was "outside stuff." They knew trails, defensive and fighting habits, species and calls; they knew a great collection of detached facts about animals but it was all like what one would see in a strange city—watching from outside its wall. There was a certain boundary of observation which they never passed. All that Skag cared to know was across, on the inner side of the wall.

As for the many little hunters, they were tame; only their bags were "wild." They never even approached the boundary. Skag reflected much on these affairs. It dawned on him at last, that when you go out with the idea of killing a creature, you may get its attitude toward death, but you won't learn about how it regards life.

The more you give, the more you get from any relation. This is not only common knowledge among school-teachers, but among stock-raisers and rose-growers. Almost every man has had experience with a real teacher, at least once in his life—possibly only a few weeks or even days, but a bit of real teaching—when something within opened and answered as never before. It was like an extension of consciousness. If you look back you'll find that you loved that teacher—at least, liked that one differently, very deep.

Skag wanted a great deal. He wanted more from the jungle doubtless than was ever formulated in a white man's mind before. He wanted to know what certain holy men know; men who dare to walk to and fro in the jungles without arms, apparently without fear. He wanted to know what the priests of Hanuman know about monkeys; and what *mahouts* of famous elephants like Neela Deo and Mithi Baba and Gunpat Rao of the Chief Commissioner's stockades, know about elephants.

At this point one reflection was irresistible. The priests of Hanuman gave all they had—care, patience, tenderness, even their lives, to the monkey people. There were no two ways about the *mahouts*; they loved the elephants reverently; even regarding them as beings more exalted than men. As for the holy men—the sign manual of their order was love for all creatures. No, there was no getting away from the fact that you must give yourself to a thing if you want to know it. . . . Skag would come up breathless out of this contemplation—only to find it was the easiest thing he did—to love wild animals. . . .

Skag had reason to hold high his trust in animals. He had entered the big cat cages countless times and always had himself and the animals in hand. He had made good in the tiger pit-trap and certainly the loose tiger near the monkey glen didn't charge. All this might have established the idea that all animals were bound to answer his love for them.

But India was teaching him otherwise.

In the hills back of Poona he had met a murderer. That cat-scream at the last chilled him to the very centre of things. Cheetahs were malignant; no two ways about that. Skag hadn't failed. He never was better. There was no fear nor any lack of concentration in his work upon the cheetah beast. Any tiger he knew would have answered to his cool force, but the cheetah didn't.

It was the same with the big snake in the grass jungle. Skag had met fear there—something of monstrous proportion, more powerful than will, harder to deal with by a wide margin than any plain adjustment to death. It stayed with him. It was more formidable than pain. He had talked with Cadman about a peculiar inadequacy he felt in dealing with the snake—as if his force did not penetrate. Cadman knew too much to hoot at Skag's dilemma. The more a man knows, the more he can believe.

"It would be easier with a cobra than a constrictor," Cadman had said. "You'd have to strike just the right key, son. This is what I mean: The wireless instruments of the Swastika Line answer to one pitch; the ships of the Blue Toll to another. . . . But I've seen things done—yes, I've seen things done in this man's India. . . . I saw a man from one of the little brotherhoods of the Vindhas breathe a nest of cobras into repose; also I have seen other brothers pass through places where the deadly little karait is supposed to watch and wait and turn red-eyed."

The more Skag listened and learned and watched in India, the more he realised that if he knew all there was to know about the different orders of holy men, all the rest of knowledge would be included, even the lore of the jungle animals. He had come into his own considerable awe through what he had seen in the forest with the priests of Hanuman, but things-to-learn stretched away and away before him like range upon range of High Himalaya.

Malcolm M'Cord was the best rifle-shot in India. The natives called him Hand-of-a-God. As usual they meant a lot more than a mere decoration. M'Cord was one of the big master mechanics—especially serving Indian Government in engine building—a Scot nearing fifty now. For many years he had answered the cries of the natives for help against the destroyers of human life. Sometimes it was a mugger, sometimes a cobra, a cheetah, often a man-eating tiger that terrorized the countryside. There are many sizeable Indian villages where there is not a single rifle or short piece in the place; repeated instances where one pampered beast has taken his tolls of cattle and children of men, for several years.

The natives are slow to take life of any creature. They are suspicious toward anyone who does it thoughtlessly, or for pastime; but the Hindu also believes that one is within the equity of preservation in doing away with those ravagers that learn to hunt men.

In the early days M'Cord began to take the famous shoot trophies. Time came when this sort of thing was no longer a gamesome event, but a foregone conclusion. His rifle work was a revelation of genius—like the work of a prodigious young pianist or billiardist in the midst of mere natural excellence.

He had wearied of the game-bag end of shooting, even before

his prowess in the tournaments became a bore. . . . So there was only the big philanthropy left. The silent steady Scot gave himself more and more to this work for the hunted villagers as the years went on. It sufficed. Many a man has stopped riding or walking for mere exercise, but joyously, and with much profit, taken it up again as a means to get somewhere.

It was Carlin who helped Skag to a deep understanding of her old friend, the Scot, and the famous bungalow in which he lived.

"It is 'papered' and carpeted and curtained with the skins of animals, but you would have to know what the taking of those skins has meant to the natives and how different it is from the usual hunter-man's house. The M'Cord bungalow is a book of man-eater tales—with leather leaves."

Carlin, who had been one of M'Cord's favourites since she was a child, saw the man with the magic of the native standpoint upon him. . . . With all its richness there was nothing of the effect of the taxidermist's shop about the place. Altogether the finest private set of gun-racks Skag had looked upon was in the dim front hall. Bhanah and Nels had a comfortable lodge to themselves, and there was a tiny summerhouse at the far end of the lawn that had been an ideal of Carlin's when she was small. The playhouse had but one door, which was turned modestly away from the great Highway. It was vined and partly sequestered in garden growths, its threshold to the west. The Scottish bachelor had turned this little house over to the child Carlin years ago, as eagerly as his entire establishment now. Yet the woman was no less partial to the playhouse than the child had been.

. . . They hardly saw the Scot. In fact it was only a moment in the station oval. Skag looked into a grey eye that seemed so steady as to have a life all its own and apart, in the midst of a weathered countenance both kindly and grim. . . . There was a tiny locked room on the south side of the bungalow, vividly sunlit—a room which in itself formed a cabinet for mounted cobras—eight or ten specimens with marvellous bodies and patchy-looking heads. . . . The place was heavily glazed, but not with windows that opened. Skag caught the hint before Carlin spoke—that the display might have a queer attraction for cobras that had not suffered the art of the taxidermist.

Skag turned to the girl as they stood together at the low heavy door, leading into the library. Something in her face held him utterly—something of wisdom, something of dread—if one could, imagine a fear founded on knowledge. . . . A brilliant mid-afternoon. Bhanah and Nels had gone to the stockades. Since the chase and rescue of Carlin, Nels and the young elephant Gunpat Rao were becoming friends—peculiar dignities and untellable reservations between them—but undoubtedly friends.

There was a kind of stillness in the place and hour, as they stood together, that made it seem they had never been alone before. Deep awe had come to Skag. As he looked now upon her beauty and health and courage, with eyes that saw another loveliness weaving all wonders together—he knew a kind of bewildered revolt that life was actually bounded by a mere few years; that it could be subject to change and chance. Thus he learned what has come to many a man in the first hours after bringing his great comrade home—that there must be some inner fold of romance to make straight the insistent torture at the thought of illness and accident and death itself—something somehow to enable a man to transcend all three-score and ten affairs and know that birth and death are mere hurdles for the runners of real romance.

. . . The sunlight brought out faint but marvellous gleamings from the serpents. It was as if every scale had been a jewel. . . . Skag looked closer. It wasn't bad mounting. It was really marvelous mounting. His eye ran from one to another. Every cobra's head had been shattered by a bullet. The broken tissues had been gathered together, pieced and sewn—the art of the workman not covering the dramatic effect entirely, yet smoothing the excess of the horror away.

". . . I've heard of cobras always, yet I never tire and never seem any nearer them," Carlin was saying. "I remember the word *cobra* when I heard it the first time—almost the first memory. It never becomes familiar. They are mysterious. One can never tell the why or when about *them*. One never gets beyond the fascination. The more you know the more you prepare for them in India. It's like this—any other room would have windows that open. . . . Cobras have much fidelity. We think of them as reptiles; and yet they are life-and-death-mates, like the best of tiger pairs. One who kills a cobra must kill two or look out—"

Carlin had strange lore about mated pairs; about moths and birds and other creatures (as well as men-things) finding each other and living and working together; about a tiger that had mourned for many seasons alone, after some sportsman had killed his female; about another rollicking young tiger pair that leaped an eight foot wall into a native yard in early evening, made their kill together of a plump young cow, and passed it up and over the wall between them.

"The cubs were hungry," Carlin had said.

Still they did not leave the door-way of the cobra room. Skag saw that something more was coming. Once more he was drawn to the mystery of the holy men by her tale:

". . . I was a little girl. It was here in Hurda. . . . I had strayed away into the open jungle, not toward our monkey glen, but farther south where the trees were scarce. . . . Of course I shouldn't have been alone—"

Skag was staring straight at one of the cobras. Carlin turned and placed her hand upon his sleeve. She knew that he was fighting that old dread that had come upon him on the day of the elephant pursuit—a dread well enough founded, grounded upon many tragedies—of the pitfalls and menaces and miasmas of old Mother India; the infinite variety, craft, swiftness and violence of her deaths. (White hands were certainly clinging to Skag.) One's vast careless attitudes to life are fearfully complicated when life means two and not the self alone.

"This isn't a horrible story—" she said.

He cleared his throat; then laughed.

"I'll get past all this," he muttered. "Go on, Carlin—"

"I heard a step behind," she said. "It was my uncle—the most wonderful of many uncles. I have not seen him since that day. He is a little older than my eldest brother—possibly thirty at that time—tall, dark, silent; a frowning man, but not to me. Even then he belonged to one of the little brotherhoods of the Vindhas—lesser, you know, in relation to the great brotherhoods of the Himalayas. In fact it is from the Vindha Hills that they move on when they are called—up the great way and beyond—"

Another of Carlin's themes—always the dream in her mind of climbing to the heights.

"We walked on together through one of the paths—some time I will show you. It was not like anyone else coming to find a child, or coming to take it back. A most memorable thing to a little one, this elaborate consideration from a great man. He did not suggest that I turn. He made himself over to my adventure."

She waited for Skag to see more of the picture from her mind than her words suggested:

"Ahead on the path—leisurely, like nothing else, a cobra reared, a king cobra, as great as any of these. He barred our way. There comes a penetrating cold from the first glance. It's like an icy lance to the centre of consciousness. Then I felt the man's presence beside me. My confidence was that which only a child can give. What the mind knows and fears has too much dominion afterward. . . . The appalling power and beauty of the cobra fascinated me. I have never quite forgotten. There was a lolling trailing grace about the lifted length, the head slightly inclined to us, the hood but partly spread—something winged in the undulation, a suggestion of that which we could not see, faintly like the whir of a humming bird's wings. That is it—an intimation of forces we had not senses to register—also colours and sounds! . . . My hand was lost in the great hand. My uncle did not turn back. He was speaking. There was that about his tones which you had to listen for—a low softness that you had to listen to get. Yes, it was to the cobra that he spoke.

". . . There was never a poem to me like those words, but they did not leave themselves in continuity. I could not say the sentences again. I seem to remember the vibration—some sense of the mysterious, kindred with all creatures—and a vast flung scroll of wisdom and poetry, as if the serpents had been a great and glorious people of blinding, incredible knowledges—never like us—but all the more marvellous for their difference! . . . And the cobra hung there, his eyes darkening under the gentleness of the voice—then reddening again like fanned embers. . . .

"Then I heard my uncle ask to be permitted to pass, saying that he brought no harm to the mother, undoubtedly near, nor to the baby cobras—only good-will; but that it was not well for a man and a little girl to be prevented from passing along a man-path. . . . It was only a moment more that the way was held from us. There was no rising at all, to fighting anger. A cobra doesn't, you know, until actual attack. In leisurely undulations, he turned and entered the deeper growths. A moment later my uncle pointed to the lifted head in the shadows. One had need to be magic-eyed to see. We went on a little way and walked back. It was not that we had to pass—but that we must not be obstructed." . . .

This was the India that astonished Skag more than all hunter tales, more than any hunter prowess; but there were always two sides. . . . The weeks were unlike any others he had ever known. The mystery deepened between him and Carlin. Almost the first he had heard of her was that she was "unattainable"—yet *they* had known each other at once. . . . Still Carlin *was* unattainable; forever above and beyond. Such a woman is no sooner comprehended on one problem than she unfolds another; much of man's growth is from one to another of her mysteries. And always when he has passed one, he thinks all is known; and always as another looms, he realises how little he knows after all. . . .

A thousand times Skag recalled the words of the learned man who had spoken to Cadman and himself on their way to the grass jungle. "You will acknowledge love, but you will not know love until it is revealed by supreme danger. The way of your feet is in the ascending path. Hold fast to the purposes of your own heart and you will come into the heights."

Could Carlin be more to him than now? . . . Yes, she was more to-day than yesterday. It would always be so. Love is always love, but it is always different. . . . Sometimes he would stay away from the bungalow for several hours. He was of a nature that could not be pleased with himself when he gave way tumultuously to the thing he wanted—which was continually to be in Carlin's presence. His every step in the market-place, or in the bazaar, had its own twitch back toward Malcolm M'Cord's bungalow; his every thought encountering a pressure of weight to hurry home.

Carlin was full of deep joys of understanding. One did not have to finish sentences for her. She meant India—its hidden wisdom. She had the thing called education in great tiers and folds. Skag's education was of the kind that accumulates when a man does not know he is being educated. . . . Certainly Carlin was unattainable—this was an often recurring thought as he learned Hindi from her and something of Urdu; the usages of her world, its castes and cults.

Down in the unwalled city one mid-afternoon, he finished

certain errands and started for the bungalow. Had he let himself go, his feet would have stormed along. He laughed at the joy of the thing; and he had only been away since tiffin. Yet there was tension too—the old mystery. A man cannot feel all still and calm and powerful, when there has suddenly descended upon him realisation of all that can possibly happen to take away one so much more important than one's own life as to make contrast absurd. Skag was looking ahead into stark days, when he would be called upon to take big journeys alone into the jungle for the service. It was very clear there might be many weeks of separation . . . and now it was only a matter of hours. He was nearing the little gate. . . .

These are affairs men seldom speak about—seldom write; yet his experience was one that a multitude of men have felt vaguely at least. There was a laugh about it, a sense of self-deprecation; but above all, Skag knew for the sake of the future that he must get himself better in hand against this incredible pull to the place where she was. It seemed quite enough to reach the compound or the grass plot and hear her step.

She was not at the gate. He halted. Malcolm M'Cord was expected home this day. He might have come. Surely he might give two such rare good friends a chance to have a chat together . . . in Malcolm's own house, too. Besides there was no better chance than now for a bit of moral calisthenics. Skag turned back. No one was very near to note that he was a bit pale. Still he was laughing. Even Nels, his Great Dane, would have thought him weird, he reflected. Had Bhanah been along, there could have been no possible explanation. . . . He was walking toward the city, but his eyes were called back again. Carlin had come to the gate. She held up her right arm full and straight—her signal always, such an impulse of joy in it.

He waved and made a broken sort of gesture toward Hurda, as if he had forgotten something. Minute by minute he fought them out after that—sixty of them, ninety of them, good measure, sixty seconds each, before he started at last to the bungalow again. The sun was low. The bazaars were but a little distance back, when he met Bhanah and Nels out for their evening exercise. . . . No, M'Cord-Sahib had not yet come. . . . Yes, all was quite well with the Hakima, Hantee-Sahiba, who was reading in the playhouse. . . .

Quite alone. Skag quickened, but repressed himself again. It was business for contemplation—the way Bhanah had spoken of Carlin as Hantee Sahiba, after her usual title. . . . He heard the birds. The great Highway was deserted; the noise of the city all behind. . . . If he had merely "acknowledged love" so far, as the learned man had said—what must be the nature of the emotion that would reveal the full secret to him? Always when his thoughts fled away like this, his steps seized the advantage and he would find himself in full stride like a man doing road-work for the ring.

She wasn't at the gate this time. Just now Skag felt the first coolness of evening, the shadow of the great trees. . . . She did not come to the gate. His hand touched its latch and still he had not heard her voice. On the lawn path—in that strange lovely wash of light—he stood, as the sun sank and the afterglow mounted. This was always Carlin's hour to him—the magic moment of the afterglow. In such an hour in the outer paths of the tree jungle, they had spoken life to life.

"Malcolm M'Cord—is that you, Malcolm?"

Her voice was from the playhouse. It was steady but startling. Something cold in it—very weary. Still he did not see her. The door was on the western side.

Skag answered.

"Oh—" came from Carlin.

There was an instant intense silence; then he heard:

"Go into the house. I thought it was Malcolm. . . . I'll join you. Don't come here—"

He turned obediently. He had the male's absurd sense of not belonging. . . . He might at least be silent and do as she said. A keener gust of reality then shot through him. His steps would not go on. She must have heard his change from the gravel to the grass, for she called:

"It's all right, go right in—"

"But, Carlin—"

"Don't come here, dear! It's—not for you to see now!"

He halted, an indescribable chill upon him. The low threshold was in sight, yet Carlin did not appear in the doorway. It was not more than sixty feet away, across the lawn. It may have been something that she had on. . . . A gold something. This came because of a fallen bit of gold-brown tapestry on the threshold. It had folds. Out of the cone of it, was a rising sheen like thin gold smoke. A fallen garment was the first thing that came to Skag's mind, keyed to the suggestion of some fabric which Carlin was to put on. The thing actually before his eyes had not dislodged for an instant, the thought-picture in his mind.

Right then Skag made a mistake. He had not taken ten running steps before he knew it, and halted. That which had been like rising gold smoke was a hooded head—lifting just now, dilating. Already he knew, almost fully, what the running had done. The thought of Carlin in the playhouse had overbalanced his own genius. He walked forward now, for the time not hearing Carlin's words from within. . . . The door was open; the windows were screened. The girl was held within by the coiled one on the stone. . . . She was imploring Skag to go back:

". . . to the house!" he heard at last. "Wait there—don't come! It is death to come to me!"

He could not see her.

"Where are you standing, Carlin?"

"Far back—by the sewing machine! . . . Will you not—will you not, for me?"

He spoke very coldly:

"While he watches me from the stone—you come forward slowly and shut the door!"

"That would anger him into flying at you—"

Quite as slowly, his next words:

"I do not think he is angry with me—"

Yet Skag was not in utter truth right there, even in his own knowledge. His voice did not carry conviction of truth. . . . The thing unsteadied his concentration. The fact that he had started to run and thus ruffled the cobra, was still upon him like shame. It reacted to divide his forces now, at least to make tardier his self-command. Back of everything—Carlin's danger. There was a quick turn of his eye for a weapon, even as he heard a deep tone from Carlin—something immortal in the resonance:

". . . You might save me . . . but, don't you see—I want you more!"

A *lakri* of Bhanah's leaned against the playhouse at the side towards the road.

The cobra had lifted himself erect upon his tail almost to the level of Skag's eyes, hood spread. Carlin talked to him—low tones—no words which she or Skag should know again. . . .

The *lakri* was of iron-wood from the North, thick as the man's wrist at the top. It pulled Skag's eye a second time. It meant the surrender of his faith in his own free-handed powers to reach for the *lakri*; it meant the fight to death. It meant he must disappear from the cobra's eye an instant behind the playhouse. . . . Carlin's tones were in the air. He could not live or breathe until the threshold was clear—no concentration but that. . . . Like the last outburst before a breaking heart, he heard:

"If you would only go—go, my dear!"

He had chosen—or the weakness for him. There was an instant—as his hand closed upon the *lakri*, the corner of the playhouse wall shutting him off from the cobra—an instant that was doom-long, age-long, long enough for him to picture *in his own thoughts* the king turning upon the threshold—entering, rising before Carlin! . . . The threshold was empty as he stepped back, but the cobra had not entered. Perturbed that the man had vanished, he had slid down into the path to look. Skag breathed. "And now if you will shut the door, Carlin—"

A great cry from Carlin answered.

Thick and viperine, the thing looked, as it hurled forward. It was like the fling of a lash. Four feet away, Skag looked into the hooded head poised to strike, the eyes flaming into an altogether different dimension for battle.

The head played before him. The breadth of the hood alone held it at all in the range of the human eye—so swift was the lateral vibration, a sparring movement. The whole head seemed delicately veiled in a grey magnetic haze. Its background was Carlin—standing on the threshold.

"I won't fail—if you stay there!" he called.

It was like a wraith that answered—again the old mystery, as if the words came up from his own heart:

"I—shall—not—come—to—you—until—the—end!"

Skag was back in the indefinite past—all the dear hushed moments he had ever known massed in her voice.

"Stay there—not nearer—and I can't fail!"

He was saying it like a song—his eyes not leaving the narrow veiled head before him. It was like a brown sealed lily-bud of hardened enamel, brown yet iridescent—set off by two jewels of flaming rose. There was no haste. The king's mouth was not tight with strain. It was the look of one certain of victory, certain from a life that knew no failures—the look of one that had learned the hunt so well as to make it play. . . .

The brown bud vanished. Skag struck at the same time. His *lakri* touched the hood. With all his strength, though with a loose whipping wrist, he had struck. The *lakri* had touched the hood, but there was no violence to the impact. . . . Carlin's love tones were in his heart. Skag laughed.

The head went out of sight. Skag struck again. It was as if his *lakri* were caught in a swift hand and held for just the fraction of a second. No force to the man's blow. The cobra was no nearer; no show of haste. Skag's stick was a barrier of fury, yet twice the king struck between . . . twice and again. Skag felt a laming blow upon a muscle of his arm as from sharp knuckles.

And now they were fast at it. The man heard Carlin's cry but not the words:

"Stay there!" he sang in answer. "Not nearer—just there and I can't lose! . . . It isn't in the cards to lose, Carlin—"

Yet his mind knew he could not win. The cobra's head and hood recoiled with each blow. It took Skag's highest speed—as an outfielder takes a drive bare-handed, his hands giving with the ball. The head moved past all swiftness, even the speed greatest swordsmen know. It was like something that laughed. Before the whirring *lakri*, the cobra head played like a flung veil between and through and around.

. . . So, for many seconds. The grey magnetic haze was a dirty brown now. The man was seeing through blood. He could not make a blow tell. He could not see Carlin. . . . She was not talking to him. . . . She was calling upon some strange name. . . . His arm was numbed again—like a blow from a leaden sling. There was a suffocating knot in his throat and the smell of blood in his head . . . that old smell of blood he had known when his father whipped him long ago. . . .

He tried to chop straight down to break in upon the king's rhythm. It answered quicker than his thought. . . . Yes, it was Malcolm M'Cord, she was calling. . . . He saw her like a ghost now. She was utterly tall—her arms raised! . . . Then he heard a rifle crack—then a breath of moisture upon his face—the sealed bud smashed before him—the rest whipping the ground.

Skag went to Carlin who had fallen, but he was pulled off abruptly.

"I say, Lad, let me have a look at you. . . . The child's right enough. Let her rest—"

The grim face was before him, two steady hands at work on him, pulling back his collar, taking one of Skag's hands after another—looking even between the fingers, feeling his thighs.

"I can't find that he cut you, Lad," he said gently.

Skag pushed him away. Carlin was moaning.

"I'm thinking your lad's sound, deerie," M'Cord called to her. "A minute more, to be sure." . . .

He kept a trailing hold of Skag's wrist, staring a last minute in his eyes.

No break anywhere in the younger man's flesh.

The afterglow was thickening. A servant came down the path to call them to dinner. The servant had never seen such a spectacle—the Hakima sitting with Hand-of-a-God and Son-of-Power, together—on the lawn already wet with dew—their knees almost touching. . . .

"The like's not been known before, Lad—even of a man with a sword," Malcolm M'Cord was saying. "You must have stood up to him two minutes. No swordsman has done as much. . . . And it was only a *lakri* you had—and a swordsman's blade goes soft and flat against a cobra's scales! . . . You see, they take wings when the fighting rage flows into them. It's like wings, sir. . . . Yes, you'll have a lame arm where the hood grazed. It couldn't have been the drive of the head or he would have bitten through—"

Even Skag, as he glanced into Carlin's face from time to time, forgot that Hand-of-a-God had done it again—one more king cobra with a patched |head and a life and death story to be added to the sunny cabinet in the bungalow. . . . Carlin rose to lead them to dinner at last, but Malcolm shook his head.

"On you go, you two. I'll sit out a bit in the lamplight, just here by the playhouse door. . . . She'll be looking for him soon. . . . She won't be far. She won't be long coming—to look for him. . . . She'd find him and then set out to look for you, Lad."

The lights of the bungalow windows were like vague cloths upon the lawn. . . . Carlin and Skag hadn't thought of dinner. They were in the shadow of the deep verandah. Once Carlin whispered:

"I loved the way he said 'Lad' to you."

It was hours afterwards that the shot was heard. . . . Carlin was closer. He felt her shivering. He could not be sure of the words, yet the spirit of them never left his heart:

"If I were she—and I had found you so—upon the lawn—I should want Hand-of-a-God to wait for me—like that!"

CHAPTER XI

ELEPHANT CONCERNS

"Only the altogether ignorant do not know that the women of my line have been chaste."

It was the youngest mahout of the Chief Commissioner's elephant stockades of Hurda, who spoke.

They sat in comfort under the feathery branches of tall tamarisk trees, smoking their water-pipes, after the sunset meal. It was the time for talk.

"A good beginning," said a very old man near by, "it being wise, in case of doubt, to stop the mouth of—who might speak afterward."

"And the men of my line," proceeded the youngest mahout, without embarrassment, "have been illustrious—save those who are forgotten. They all have been of High Himalaya; yet I am the least among you. I render homage of Hill blood, hot and full, to every one of you—my elders—because you are all mahouts of High Himalaya, even as my fathers were."

The men of the stockades bowed their heads in grave acknowledgment.

"Then by what curse of what gods falls this calamity," the boy went on, "that we of the Chief Commissioner's stockades are forced to receive a mahout from the Vindha Hills; and an unreputed elephant—from the hills without repute?"

"Softly, young one, softly!" a mahout in his full prime made swift answer. "Truly it is well the young are not permitted to use that untamed strength in speech, which is best governed by the waste of sinew!"

The youngest mahout bent his head in humility and said with soft reverence:

"Will he who is most wise among us, enlighten the darkness of him who is most foolish?"

"It is that elephants of great repute have come from the Vindha Hills; and mahouts of great learning. Also, there is a luminous tradition that the most exalted creatures of their kind—those who travelled far from the high lands of Persia long ago—chose place for their future generations in the Vindha Hills; and not in High Himalaya."

This man who had first rebuked sternly and afterward explained with extreme gentleness, was Kudrat Sharif, the mahout of Neela Deo—mighty leader of their caravan. He was malik—which is to say, governing mahout—over them all; and best qualified among them. Therefore a clamour rose for more. The youngest mahout went from his place and sat near, as Kudrat Sharif continued:

"The black elephants are all but gone. Not more than one in a generation of men is seen any more. They are seldom toiled into the trap-stockades, in which the less wary are taken. The natures of those who have been snared are strange to us of the High Hills. They sometimes destroy men in their anger; they sometimes destroy themselves in their grief."

"What is the heart of this knowledge?" asked a man who had not spoken before.

"That these stockades are distinguished by Government," Kudrat Sharif replied. "The elephant who is to reach us this evening, is a black elephant—descended from the lines of ancient Persia."

A chorus of exclamations swept the circle, before the gurgle of hookahs took the moment, as the mahouts gave themselves to meditation and water-winnowed smoke.

Then the trumpet tones of an elephant were heard from far out in the gathering gloom.

"May Vishnu, the great Preserver, save us from a killer!"

The man who said these words was not less than magical in his power to control the unruly; but he never took credit to himself. "That is the voice of a fighter—smooth as curds of cream—and it reaches from far out; very far out."

The challenge-call sounded again; and the big males of the stockade answered without hesitation.

These mahouts had trained ears; and they listened—computing the stranger's rate of speed. The fullness of tone increased; and presently one said:

"He comes fast."

But they were not prepared to see the elephant that rolled into the glare of their torches out of the night.

He came to pause in the centre of the exercise arena—a vast sanded disk just front of the stockade buildings—and stood rocking his huge body, tamping the ground with his feet as if still travelling. The mahout on his neck spoke to him patiently:

"Now will my master use his intelligence to understand that we have arrived?"

Then turning to the men on the ground, the strange mahout said wistfully:

"Look on me with compassion, oh men of honour and of fame! I have heard of you, but you have not heard of me."

"We have heard of you, that you are the making of a master-mahout, in due time," answered Kudrat Sharif.

"Then the gods who preserved my fathers to old age, have not forgotten that I learned patience in my extreme youth," sighed the man.

Seeing that the elephant was not quieting, Kudrat Sharif spoke now in pacifying tones—to the mahout:

"Come down among us who are your brothers; we have prepared all things for your refreshment."

"I will come down with a full heart and an empty stomach, most beneficent, when this Majesty will permit," the strange mahout assented wearily.

"Is he rough, son—to sit?" asked the very old man, coming closer.

The elephant shied a step and his mahout cuddled one ear with his fingers, as he replied:

"He is the smoothest thing that ever moved upon the surface of the earth—like a wind driven by fiends. But he never stops."

The elephant was rolling more widely if anything, than at first; so the mahouts stood back a little and considered him.

His blackness was like very old bronze, with certain metallic gleams in it—like time-veiled copper and brass. His flawless frame was covered with tight-banded muscle. There was no appearance of fat. His skin was smooth—without wrinkles. He was young; about forty years, or less. But there was the nick of a tusk-stroke in one ear; and a small red devil in his eye.

Without warning, he flicked his mahout off his neck and set him precisely on the ground—the movement so quick no eye could follow his trunk as it did it.

The youngest mahout brought a sheaf of tender branches—such as are most desirable—and laid them near, but not too near; and when the elephant began to eat, they removed the burden of his mahout's possessions from his back.

Then the man received their ministrations—keeping an eye on the elephant. When he was ready to smoke, he began slowly:

"Ram Yaksahn is my name; and my ancestors—from the first far breath of tradition—have been servants of the elephant people. We were of High Himalaya till the man who was the man before my father. Since then we serve in the Vindha Hills. My twin brother was called with his master, to the teak jungles of the South; but I have been with the trap-stockades till now, when they send me down to these plains with the catch of all seasons."

"It is a good hearing," said the very old man, as they all bent their heads; and the youngest mahout carefully arranged some specially good tobacco in Ram Yaksahn's hookah.

"Now what is his record?" one asked.

"First, there is a record," Ram Yaksahn replied, "which may be his or another's. It is your right to know.

"Four monsoons before this elephant was trapped, the body of a forest reserve officer was found on a mountain slope. The head was broken; and the ribs. Rains had washed away all earth-marks, but small trees had been uprooted near that place; therefore the thing had been done by an elephant. Close by, a dead dog lay; entirely battered—and a split stick. Burial was given to that man with few words. He was not mourned. May the gods render to him his due!"

The mahouts assented, as Ram Yaksahn smoked a moment.

"Be patient with me, most honourable," he went on, in strained tones. "I come to you serving a strange master. The record I tell now, is truly your right to know."

"Have no fear; we serve with you!" Kudrat Sharif reassured him.

"Some months after this elephant was trapped," he continued, "they had him picketed in the working grounds—to learn the voices of men. It was there, in the midst of us all, that he killed his first mahout. No man could prevent.

"That mahout was a violent man. He had just struck his own child an unlawful blow. She lay on the ground as the dead lie. Then it was that this elephant moved before any man could move. We heard his picket stakes come up, but we did not see them come up. No man could prevent.

"He gathered the child's dead body in his trunk and swung it back and forth—back and forth. It hung like a cloth. Slowly he came nearer to his mahout, while he swung the body of the child. When he was close, he laid the body between his own front feet. The violent man stood watching like one in a dream.

"Then this elephant who is now my master, caught the man who stood watching—as you saw him take me down, swiftly—and swung him, but in a circle. The man struck the ground on his head and it was broken; also his ribs."

Low murmurs of appreciation swelled among the listening mahouts. Ram Yaksahn bent his head.

"It was determined," he said with satisfaction, "by wise men of authority who rule such matters at the trap-stockades, that this elephant had done just judgment; because the man had done murder.

"But we could not come close to this elephant—to link with his leg-chains—for his threatening eye. That night and the next day, he kept the body between his feet—the body of the little child he kept—save when he swung it. No man could prevent.

"Then he left it" (Ram Yaksahn's voice suddenly went husky), "and came to me—and put me on his neck. For this reason I am his to him; and he is mine to me!"

"Well done, well done!" the mellow voice of Kudrat Sharif spoke softly; and the mahouts of the Chief Commissioner's stockades assented.

"There is yet one thing," Ram Yaksahn resumed, "and I should cover my face to tell it. But if you learn that I am a fool of fools, consider my foolishness. His blackness is strange; his strength is mighty—it took four to handle him, not two, in the beginning—and his quickness is more quick than a man can think. Also, he has a red devil in his eye.

"When my name was spoken after his name and my duty rendered me to serve him, I found he was indeed my master. We consider the creatures of his kind are exalted above men; but I thought him a son of darkness, come up out of the pit. In my fool heart I did; and I do not know yet.

"At the time when he was trapped, I was in High Himalaya finding a fair woman of lineage as good as my own—as my fathers have done. So when this last thing happened, not many weeks ago, a son of mine lay on his mother's breast. She came out with the child and sat near me. She was teaching me that my son laughed. I saw only her; and knew only that her babe was strong.

"I forgot that this elephant browsed close by, having long picket chains to reach the tender branches. He came toward where we sat and stood looking at us; and I called on her to behold the red devil in his eye. But I looked—not into his eye; and I did not see him upon us—till he lifted my son from her breast. I saw the little body swing up, far above my head—the so very little body—and I heard her cry in the same breath."

Ram Yaksahn laid his forehead against his fists and softly beat his head. Looking up with drawn features, he went on:

"My face was in the grasses when I heard her laugh. Then I saw the babe—not longer than a man's arm—slowly swinging in my master's trunk, back and forth—back and forth. The little one was making noises of content—such as babes use—when my master laid him very gently between his own front feet. The child spread his hands, reaching up for the curling tip above his face.

"Now it has been said that I am not lacking in courage; but in that hour I was without sense to know courage or fear. The fingers of cold death felt along my veins and searched out the marrow of my bones; for when I leaped to take the babe—I met the red threat in my master's eye. But the mother of my son went like a blown leaf and stooped between this elephant's feet, to lift up her first man-child.

"She came away with him safe; and this elephant swayed before us, at the end of his picket chains, stretching his quivering trumpet-tip toward the babe—with flaming fires in his eyes.

"The daughter of High Himalayan mahouts called this black majesty 'Nut Kut'; and they have added that name on the Government books. But they will not take his first name away. I have finished."

And Ram Yaksahn gave himself to his hookah—still keeping his eye on Nut Kut.

"His first name has not been told," mildly reminded the very old man.

"His first name is Nut Kut!" said Ram Yaksahn with decision. "But his last name is Pyar-awaz."

All the mahouts laughed; translating the double name in their own minds—-Mischief, the Voice-of-Love.

"We have no violent men in these stockades," said Kudrat Sharif, speaking to them all. "And we do not find that Ram Yaksahn was lacking in courage. We will prove the nature of Nut Kut with kindness."

His decision was conclusive; and they proceeded to encourage the mighty black into his own enclosure.

This was the coming of Nut Kut to the Chief Commissioner's elephant stockades at Hurda. As time went by, the attraction of his mysterious nature inflamed the mahouts with interest; and also with concern—for he was a fearsome fighter.

Carlin had gone to a sick sister-in-law for a few days; and as soon as he heard of it, Dickson Sahib had driven to the M'Cord bungalow—realising that without her it would be desolate to his young American friend. Protesting that he needed someone to come and break his own loneliness, he carried Skag home.

So just now Skag was smoking his after-tiffin cigarette in the verandah of Dickson Sahib's big bungalow. The great Highway-of-all-India, with its triple avenue, its monarch trees, swept past the front of the grounds. Several times from here, he had seen a big elephant go joyously rolling by. He could tell it was joyous; and the man on its neck was usually singing.

The very smell of elephants had always stirred Skag—like all clean good earth-smells in one. When he was animal trainer in the circus, the elephants had not been his special charge; but he had seen a good deal of them. They looked to him like convicts; or manikins—moving to the pull of the hour-string. They were incessantly being loaded, unloaded, made to march; cooped in small, stuffy places—chained.

He wanted to see elephants—herds of them! He wanted to see them in multitudes, working for men in their own way; using their own intelligence. He wanted to see them in their own jungles—living their own lives.

Sooner or later he meant to see them, all ways. He had come to India, the land of elephants, partly for that reason; but in the Mahadeo mountains he had found none—nor in the great Grass Jungle. Yet he had learned that when he wanted anything—way back in the inside of himself—he was due to get it. To-day this thing was gnawing more than ever before; he wanted elephants—hard.

Dickson Sahib came out on his way back to the offices and stopped to finish their tiffin conversation:

"I'm glad you're interested in young Horace; you're going to be no end good for him, I can see that. You'll find him far too mature for his years. His brain's too active; but he's not abnormal. His tutors call him insatiable; but from his babyhood the breath of his life has been elephants. He's taken a lot from the learned natives; they talk with him as if he were quite grown—half of it I couldn't follow myself."

"That is extraordinary to me," said Skag.

"Of course it is. But there's been nothing else for it. My own days are quite tied up, and his mother—the climate, you know. So you see what I mean, he's really needing—just you."

Dickson's eyes turned on a little fellow who stood alone, further down the verandah. Then his face shadowed, as he spoke in a lower tone:

"I said he's not abnormal—that should be qualified. Several years ago he was carried home from the Chief Commissioner's elephant stockades by their governing mahout, Kudrat Sharif. The servants said he was crying and fighting to go back; but otherwise seemed quite himself. When I came from the offices in the evening, however, he was in a fever; raving about Nut Kut—raving about Nut Kut for days—always wanting to go back to Nut Kut.

"I went after the governing mahout and he said the child had played too hard; and that was why they brought him home. Kudrat Sharif is a graceful man, with much dignity; but I always felt he held something in reservation."

"What about Nut Kut?" Skag asked.

"Nut Kut is a great black elephant, trapped in the Vindha Hills only a few years ago. He's young and I've heard he's a dangerous fighter. My son likes him; but I can't get over believing he's responsible for the high nerve tension the boy always carries. But don't let Horace annoy you." Dickson Sahib finished hurriedly. "You're his first love, you know!"

Any man knows the kind of thrill when he's told that a boy has fallen in love with him; but the lad's interest in elephants—reminding Skag of his own—made him specially worth considering. The little figure suggested dynamic power rather than physical strength. The hair was dull brown, with an overcast of pale flame on it; the skin too white. But the eyes held Skag. They were pure grey, full of smouldering shadows and high lights—forever contending with each other. At this moment the boy was leaning his head toward the road, listening.

"She's petulant to-day, the lady!" he chuckled. "Wait till you see Mitha Baba, Skag Sahib."

Down through the great trees a handsome female elephant approached, careering at a curious choppy gait. With her trunk well up, she was trumpeting every third step.

"What's the matter with her?" Skag asked.

"She's abused, Skag Sahib." The boy became a bit embarrassed; hesitating, before he went on: "The Hakima used to speak to her whenever she passed Miss Annesley's bungalow; and now—she's not there to do it."

Horace waved his hand to Mitha Baba's mahout; and the mahout shouted something in a dialect Skag did not know.

"He's awfully proud of Mitha Baba; and it's true, Skag Sahib, there isn't anything in grey beyond her; but—" Horace stopped, suddenly gone wistful.

"What's the trouble?" Skag asked, startled.

"They won't let me near him—they won't let me! I want him more than anything I know—"

"Then you'll get him!" interrupted Skag.

It must have been the sureness in Skag's voice, that made some choking tightness way back in the boy's soul let go; whole vistas of possibilities opened up.

"We're going to get on, you know—I'm sure of it!" he said breathlessly. "If only I were old enough to be your friend!"

Skag remembered the father's words.

"I've never had a friend younger than myself," he answered, "and there are only a few years difference—why not?"

Their hands met as men. And it was still early in the afternoon.

Horace went into the house and spoke with a servant. Coming out, he took a long minute to get some excitement well in hand before speaking:

"I've arranged for one thing to show you, already! My boy will be back from the bazaar soon, to let me know whether the time will be to-day or to-morrow. It's a surprise—if you don't mind, Skag Sahib."

"All right, then what is the most interesting thing you know about?" Skag asked.

"Elephants. No question."

"Have you many here in Hurda?"

"Not any belonging to Hurda; but our Chief Commissioner has forty Government elephants in his stockades—the finest ever. Neela Deo, the Blue God—who is the leader of the caravan—the mahouts say there isn't an elephant in the world to touch him; and Mitha Baba and Gunpat Rao—they're famous in all India. And Nut Kut; indeed, Skag Sahib, you should see Nut Kut. They don't allow strangers about where he is; he's the one—the mahouts won't let me go near him."

"What's wrong with him?" Skag asked.

"I don't know; I'm always wondering. In the beginning—when I was little—but I don't believe it was—wrong."

The boy spoke haltingly, frowning; but went on:

"That's between Nut Kut and—Horace Dickson! I like him better than anything I know. The mahouts have tried every way to discourage me—yes, they have!"

"What does he do?" Skag questioned.

"You know Government does *not* permit elephant fighting," the boy began solemnly, "but—Nut Kut doesn't know it! His pet scheme is to break away out of his own stockades, if there are any elephants across the river—that's where the regiments camp—and get in among the military elephants. He's a frightful fighter."

"How do they handle him?" Skag asked.

"It takes more than two of their best males to do it—big trained fellows, you understand. Even then, usually, one of the great females comes with her chain—the kind they call 'mother-things'—she handles it with her trunk. Just one little flick across his ears and any fighter will be willing to stop—even Nut Kut. But it's to see, Skag Sahib; never twice the same—it can't be told."

A servant came in from the highway, salaaming before Horace and reporting that the *tamasha* would occur at the usual time this afternoon—afternoon; not evening.

"Then we'll have tea, at once!" Horace interrupted him. "Quick! Tell the butler."

After tea they walked along the great Highway-of-all-India, by the edge of the native town and over the low stone bridge. Beyond the river, they passed acres of tenting. A glamour of dust lay in the slanting sun-rays. An intense earth-smell penetrated Skag's senses. A feel of excitement was in the air.

"Where are the elephants?" Skag asked.

"How do you know it's elephants?" the boy countered.

"Several ways; but last of all, I smell 'em."

"It is elephants—much elephants. You are to see them in one of their big works in the Indian elephant-military department."

This announcement of the programme instantly made Skag forget that he had come out with a lad in need of healthy comradeship.

"What work?" he asked.

"This is elephant concerns, Skag Sahib," the boy replied; "they work with men and they work for men, but no one knows what they think about the man-end of it; because they are always and always doing things men never expect. They do funny things and strange things and wonderful things. It's the inside working of an elephant regiment, that makes it so different from anything else.

"It's all tied up with men on the outside; but you mustn't notice the outside. Inside is what I mean—the elephant concerns. No one knows what it will be to-day."

"Have you forgotten Nut Kut?" smiled Skag.

"Not ever!" the boy answered quickly, "but even if he doesn't come—they almost always do something interesting. That's why we never call them animals or beasts, but sometimes creatures—because they have a kind of intelligence we have not. And that's why we *always* speak of them as persons."

"I like that," Skag put in.

"From end to end of India," the boy went on, "down Bombay side and up Calcutta side, regiments of elephants go with regiments of men—in the never-ending fatigue marching that keeps them all fit.

"The tenting and commissariat-stuff is carried by the elephants, straight from camp to camp, safe and sure and in proper time—always. That's the point, you understand, Skag Sahib—they never run away with it, or lose it, or go aside into the jungle to eat. You're going to see one regiment start out to-day.

"The man-regiment will go another road—a little longer, but not so rough. The elephant regiment will go by themselves, just one mahout on each neck—like you would carry a mouse. Really, they go on their own honour; because men have no power to control them—only with their voices. You know

Government doesn't permit elephants to be shot, for anything—only in case one is court-martialled and sentenced to die."

"Don't the mahouts ever punish them?" Skag asked.

"They're not allowed to torture them—never mind what! And men can't punish elephants any other way—they're not big enough."

Then a voice rolled out of the dust-glamour before them. In quality and reach and power, it reminded Skag of a marvel voice that used to call newspapers in the big railway station in Chicago.

"Whose voice?" he asked Horace.

"That's the master-mahout. He calls the elephants; you'll see. He's the only kind of mahout who ever gets pay for himself."

"How's that?"

"It's what makes the elephant-military a proper department. Only elephant names on the books; the pay goes to them. The mahout is always an elephant's servant; he eats from his master, of course. From the outside it saves a lot of trouble, to be sure."

Skag laughed. From the elephant standpoint, a small Englishman was conceding a certain amount of convenience to men.

"You see," the boy went on, "an elephant lives anyway more than a hundred years; and his name stays just like that and draws pay without changing. Always a mahout's son takes his place, when he gets too old or dies. I can recall when Mitha Baba's mahout was one of the most wonderful of them all. Now he has gone old, as they say; and his son is on her neck."

There was a moment when Skag would have given his soul—almost—if he might have grown up in India, as this child was growing up; in the heart of her ancient knowledges—in the breath of her mystic power. Then a great plain opened before them. It appeared at first glance, completely full of elephants.

. . . The glamour of sun-drenched dust hung over all.

Looking more closely, Skag saw nothing but elephant ranks toward the right, and nothing but elephant ranks toward the left; but in the centre, a large area was covered with separate piles of dunnage, evenly distributed.

From where he stood toward where the sun would set—a broad division stretched; and in the middle of this division, a single line of loaded elephants filed away and away to the horizon.

. . . Skag became oblivious. He was so thralled with the sight that he did not notice what was nearer. The whole panorama held his breath till right before him a great creature rose from sitting—without a sound. There was a dignity about its movement not less than majestic. It was a mighty load; but the huge shape slid away as smooth as flowing water—as easy as a drifting cloud.

A deep voice said quietly:

"Peace, master; go thy way. Peace, son."

"Did he speak to both of them?" Skag asked of Horace.

"Yes; the first part was to the elephant and the last part was to the mahout. This mahout must be one of the great ones, else the master-mahout would not have spoken to him. But he will always speak to the elephants—something."

A strange name filled the air, rolling up and away. It was followed by a courteous request, in softer tones; and Skag watched another big elephant approach from the unpicketed lines. It came to where the master-mahout stood, close to a pile of tenting, wheeled to face the way it should go presently, and sank down to be loaded.

Men did the lifting into place and the lashing on. There was detail in the process, to which the elephant adjusted his body as intelligently as they adjusted theirs. When they required to reach under with the broad canvas bands, he rose a little without being told. Indeed they seldom spoke even to each other; and then in undertones. The elephant's mahout sat in his place on the neck, as if he were a part of the neck itself.

The smoothness, the ease of it all, amazed Skag. That every good night, spoken to every separate elephant, was different—peculiar to itself—was no less astounding. It was never as if addressed to an animal, or even to a child; but always as if to a mature and understanding intelligence. As when the master-mahout said to one female:

"Fortune to thee, great Lady. May the gods guard that foot. And have a care in going down the khuds—it is that mercy should be shown us, thy friends."

And again to a young male, whose movements were very self-conscious:

"Remember there is to be no tamasha to-night, thou son of destiny. It is not yet in thy head—to determine when shall be tamasha. Fifty years hence, and when wisdom shall be come to thee, thou heir of ancient learning, then we shall have tamasha at thy bidding."

. . . A monster female came at the call of her name, with a long heavy chain—one end securely attached to her. The other end she handled with her trunk. Advancing to within a few feet of the master-mahout, she stood facing him, teetering her whole body from side to side, swinging her chain as she rolled.

Horace flashed away and ran in among the massed elephants and mahouts. Coming back to Skag, he said breathlessly:

"A mahout says the other one went before we came! That means, if Nut Kut comes—there'll be no one to manage him. You remember, Skag Sahib, I told you about the 'mother-thing'—if anyone starts a fight, she breaks it up with her chain; better than any two or three fighting males. Two tuskers just wake Nut Kut up!"

Then he stood staring at the female with her chain—getting red in the face as he spoke:

"Oh, I say! She doesn't want to be loaded; and she knows! Why, they know she knows! . . . Master-mahout!" he called in brave tones that trembled, "I am Dickson Sahib's son—of the grain-foods department—"

"We know you, Sahib, salaam!" interrupted the master-mahout, with a smile.

"Is it not the unwritten-law that the great 'mother-thing' shall be obeyed?" the boy quavered.

"It is the unwritten-law, Sahib; and we will not impose our will on her. It is this, there is no sign of what she means; the masters are all quiet to-day—there is no warning of *tamasha*."

The master-mahout spoke with grave consideration; but just as he finished, the "mother-thing" wheeled into place and went down to take her load.

"Cheer up, son, I guess it's all right," comforted Skag.

"It's all right—if Nut Kut doesn't come," said the boy, whimsically.

"So 'tamasha' sometimes means trouble?" queried Skag, remembering the tamer definition he had learned.

"It means anything anybody considers entertaining!" answered Horace. "By preference—an elephant fight! Remember, Government doesn't allow 'em; but sometimes they just happen anyway."

Then an elephant failed to answer. Several mahouts left their places and went to one spot; and Skag saw the one who had been called. He was sitting low against the ground, slowly rocking his head from side to side. A mahout was examining his ears—folding them back and feeling of them—laying his cheek against the inside surface.

"Is he sick?" Skag asked.

But the boy's eyes were wide upon the broad avenue before them, where the loaded elephants went marching away. Then he burst out, in choking excitement:

"Look, Skag Sahib! See that loaded elephant coming back from the line? I think you are going to see one of the most wonderful things that ever happened. They say it has been done; but I've never seen it—I've never seen it myself."

Skag saw a powerful elephant coming back alongside the loaded line. He did not move with the same smooth flowing motion as the others. He walked as if he were coming on important business. With a load on his back, he returned and sank down beside the pile of tenting intended for another elephant.

"What's the meaning of it?" Skag asked.

Little Horace Dickson answered in a hushed way—as one in the presence of a miracle:

"It is one of the regulars, come back to take a part of what belongs to the sick elephant."

Skag looked at the boy's face, in incredulous amazement. It

was lit—awe and exaltation were both there. Then he noticed the look of the master-mahout—that was a revelation.

. . . They were putting half as much again on top of the already loaded elephant.

. . . Certain phrases went through Skag's brain, as he watched the thing done—over and over. *No one had called this elephant back. He came before they knew themselves that an elephant was sick. When the mahouts first went to examine the sick one—this one was already on the way. How did he know?*

The extra loaded elephant rose and started again. Then a great shout went up. Tones of many voices filled the slanting sunrays in all the glamour of dust. The wonderful voice of the master-mahout loomed above all:

"Wisdom and excellence are thy parts, oh Thou! Justice and kindness—we who are poor in them—will learn of thee! Thou son of strength, thou child of ancient knowledges and worth!"

And the mahouts shouted again!

At that moment Skag knew as well as he knew anything in life, that he stood somewhere in the outer courts of a great animal-cult; and he was convinced that it was of a mystic nature—however that could be. He swore in his heart that he would never give up, till he got further in.

The master-mahout's voice ascended now on a strange call. It was a lift-lift-lifting tone.

"What does that mean?" Skag asked.

"All the elephants know that—it's the lifting call," Horace explained. "When an elephant is sick—unless they have an extra number in the regiment—they always call for two to volunteer; and they divide the load of the sick elephant between them. They use these tones instead of a name—just for that. There comes a male now, to take the rest of this load."

Skag watched the added load going into place on the volunteer. It was almost finished, when a trumpet blast sounded directly behind him—toward Hurda. Several elephants answered from the regiment; and many mahouts called to each other.

"Is that the bad fighter coming?" Skag asked.

"Yes, Skag Sahib, that's Nut Kut. But I don't know just what you're going to see—the ones who ought to handle him are all gone."

The master-mahout's voice was rising up into the vault of heaven and falling over upon the horizon. It seemed to Skag the like was never heard before.

"He's calling the two big tuskers back," Horace chuckled, "but there'll be doings on before they get here! Will you listen to Nut Kut's challenge?"

Skag turned to face the looming trumpet tones. There were no tones behind him like them. Smooth and mellow, they were yet so full of power as to make all the others sound insignificant. They were like love-tones translated into thunder.

But when Nut Kut came in sight, Skag caught his breath. The shape was made of gleaming bronze. No detail showed; it was a thing that took the eye and the breath and the blood. There was no look of effort in its inscrutable motion.

They stood in the open, between this thing and the regiment behind. There was no obstruction. And Skag moved to be between it and Horace—when it should pass them on its way. The regiment of thoroughly trained elephants were standing firmly in their places; but they were making the welkin ring with a thousand trumpets in the air.

Certainly Skag knew that this incredible thing before him—bigger every second—was Nut Kut. He looked to see why the great challenge-tones had stopped, and revelation went through him—like an explosion. Nut Kut had seen Horace and was coming straight for him.

Skag leaped to meet Nut Kut first, but he couldn't catch the elephant's eye. The huge shape was upon him and he was flung aside. Recovering himself almost instantly, he got around in time to see—but not in time to prevent.

Horace lifted both arms and leaned forward—his grey eyes gone black—as Nut Kut's trunk caught him. A little broken cry came from him and his death-white face hung down an instant—from high up.

Then, backing away, swaying from side to side, Nut Kut set his eyes on the man who followed—his red eyes, blazing with red warning. The American animal trainer did not fail to understand; he paused.

Slowly the great bronze trunk curled and cuddled about Horace Dickson's body and began to swing him. Skag knew that elephants swing men when they intend to kill them; and he heard a low moaning—like wind—rise up from the multitude of mahouts behind.

. . . Further and further the boy swung in the elephant's trunk, back and forth—back and forth. Unnatural tones startled Skag—sounding like delirium. Nut Kut put little Horace Dickson down, close under his own throat, his long trunk curling outside—always curling about—feeling up and down the boy's limbs, his frame, his face. The small mouth was open; the little red tongue—flickering.

Horace seemed oblivious; but when he laughed aloud. Nut Kut caught him up again—lightning quick. This time he swung the boy higher, till he rounded a perfect circle in the air; backing still further away and lifting his head. Nut Kut flung him round and round and yet around—faster and yet faster.

The moaning—like wind—still came from behind.

After endless time—like perdition—Skag heard Horace gasping, choking. He thought there were words; but couldn't be sure. And while this was going on. Nut Kut brought the boy down—flat on the ground. The impact must have broken a man. But Horace got to his feet—staggering in the circle of the trunk—looking dazed.

Now Skag moved forward, holding his hands out—as he came nearer to the big black head.

"I know you now, Nut Kut," he said quietly, "you're white inside all right. You're not meaning to hurt him. You like him—so do I."

But Nut Kut backed away, gathering the boy with him, looking down into the American's eyes—the red danger signals flaring up in his own again.

"Nut Kut, old man," Skag reasoned in perfectly natural tones, "you can't bluff me. I tell you, I know you. I know you as well as if we came out of the same egg!"

Nut Kut was still backing away and Skag was following up.

"You may take me, if you want—I can't let you wear him out, you know."

And then, while Nut Kut wrapped about and drew Horace in closer, Skag laid his fingers on the great bronze trunk, gently but firmly stroking—the red eyes focused in his own. For seconds the man and the elephant looked into each other. Suddenly Nut Kut loosed Horace and laid hold on Skag.

The moaning ascended and broke—like wind going up a mountain khud. There was nothing certain to the mahouts, but that this man of courage would be dashed to death before their eyes.

Skag squirmed in the grip about his body as Nut Kut held him high. It looked as if he were being crushed. But when he got his hands on the trunk again, he laughed. Now Nut Kut lowered him quickly—holding him before his own red eyes. The touch of the elephant was the touch of a master. But the eyes of the man were mastership itself.

. . . They were just so, when Ram Yaksahn—with a ghastly haggard face—lurched from behind Nut Kut, fairly sobbing. Nut Kut jerked Skag tight (it was like a hug), released him deliberately and turning, put his own sick mahout up on his own neck, with a movement that looked like a flick of his trunk.

"Now easy, Majesty, go easy with me—indeed I am very ill!" Ram Yaksahn protested in plaintive tones, as Nut Kut wheeled away with him.

Seeing Horace in the hands of a strange native—and certainly recovering—Skag looked away toward Hurda and wonder aloud if Nut Kut would be punished. It was the master-mahout who answered him:

"Nay, Sahib. He has done no harm."

"I'd like to have a chance with him," said Skag.

The master-mahout smiled—a mystic-musical smile, like his voice.

"I have come from my place for a moment," he said, looking intently into Skag's eyes, "for a purpose. We have heard of you, Son-of-Power. The wisdom of the ages is to know the instant when to act; not too late, not too soon. We have seen you work this day; and the fame of it will go before and after you, the length and breadth of India—among the mahouts."

He turned, pointing toward the elephant regiment. Many mahouts were shouting something together; their right hands flung high.

"It is right for you to know," the master-mahout went on, "that mahouts are a kind of men by themselves apart. Their knowledges are of elephants—sealed—not open to those from without. Yet I speak as one of my kind, being qualified, if in the future you have need of anything from us—it is yours."

And without giving Skag a chance to answer him, but with a stately gesture of salaam, the master-mahout had returned to his place and was calling another elephant.

Skag turned toward Horace, who was drawing a fine looking native forward by the hand. The boy spoke with repressed excitement—otherwise showing no sign of Nut Kut's strenuous handling:

"Skag Sahib, I want you to know Kudrat Sharif, the malik of the Chief Commissioner's elephant stockades. It is not known, you understand—meaning my father—but the malik has always been very wonderful to me."

Kudrat Sharif smiled with frank affection on the boy, as he drew his right hand away, to touch his forehead in the Indian salaam. The gesture showed both grace and dignity—as Dickson Sahib had said.

"I am exalted to carry back to my stockades the story of the manner of your work, Son-of-Power," he began.

"My name is Sanford Hantee," Skag deprecated gently.

"But you will always be known to Indians of India as Son-of-Power!" Kudrat Sharif protested. "It is a lofty title, yet you have established it before many."

Just then a great elephant came near, playfully reaching for

Kudrat Sharif with his trunk.

"And this is Neela Deo, the leader of the caravan!" laughed Horace.

"It is my shame that there is no howdah on him to carry you; we came like flight, when Nut Kut's escape was known," Kudrat Sharif apologised. "But after some days, when Nut Kut's excitement sleeps, we shall be distinguished if Son-of-Power chooses to come to the stockades and consider him.

"I heard your judgment of his nature, Sahib; and I say with humilitythat I shall remember it, in what I have to do with the most strange elephant I have ever met. Truly we are not sure of Nut Kut, whether he is a mighty being of extreme exaltation, above others of his kind in the world, or—a prince from the pit!"

Kudrat Sharif salaamed again; and Neela Deo lifted him to his great neck and carried him away.

Walking home, Horace expressed himself to his friend—as the heart of a boy may be expressed; and Skag dropped his arm about the slender shoulders, speaking softly:

"Remember, son, a little more—would have been too much."

"All right, Skag Sahib, because now you understand; but—isn't he interesting?"

Knowing well what the boy meant about the great strange creature—more than his fighting propensities, deeper than his physical might—Skag assented thoughtfully:

"Yes; I would like to know him better."

CHAPTER XII

BLUE BEAST

Across the river at the military camp, the cavalry outfits were preparing for a jungle outing. It isn't easy to name the thing they contemplated. Pig-sticking couldn't be called a quest, yet there are "cracks" at the game, quite the same as at polo or billiards.

Horse and man carry their lives on the outside, so to speak. The trick of it all is that a man never knows what the tusker will do. You can't even count on him doing the opposite. And he does it quick. Often he sniffs first, but you don't hear that until after it is done. Men have heard that sniff as they lay under a horse that was kicking its life out; yet the sniff really sounded while they were still in the saddle—the horse still whole.

All the words that have to do with this sport are ugly. It's more like a snort than a sniff. . . . You really must see it. A trampled place in the jungle—tusker at bay—-a mounted sticker on each side waiting for the move. The tusker stands still. He looks nowhere, out of eyes like burning cellars. That is as near as you can come with words—trapdoors opening into cellars, smoke and flame below.

At this moment you are like a negative, being exposed. There is filmed among your enduring pictures thereafter, the raking curving snout, yellow tusks, blue bristling hollows from which the eyes burn. The lances glint green from the creepers. . . .

Then the flick of the head that goes with the snort. The boar isn't there—lanced doubtless. . . . Yes, the cavalry "cracks" get him for the most part and then you hear men's laughter and bits of comment and the strike of a match or two, for very much relished cigarettes. But now and then, the scene shifts too quickly and the *other* rider may see his friend's mount stand up incredibly gashed—a white horse possibly—and this *other* must charge and lance true right now, for the boar is waiting for the man in the saddle to come down.

Nobody ever thinks of the boar's part. Queer about that. It's the bad revolting curve that goes with a tusker's snout, in the sag of which the eye is set, that puts him out of reach of decent regard. Only two other curves touch it for malignity—the curve of a hyena's shoulder and the curve of a shark's jaw. Three scavengers that haven't had a real chance. They weren't bred right.

Among the visitors that came in for the jungle play was Ian Deal, one of the younger of Carlin's seven brothers; one of the two who hadn't appeared for her marriage. The other missing brother was in Australia, but Ian Deal had been in India at the time of the ceremony and not the full-length of India away. Skag had thought about this; Carlin had doubtless done more than that. Once she had flushed, when someone had marked Ian's absence to the point of speaking of it. Before that, Skag had only heard that Ian was one of the best-loved of all. . . .

He watched the meeting of the brother and sister. It was at the railway station in Hurda, and Skag couldn't very well get away. There was something almost like anguish in the face of the young man as he hastened forward—anguish of devotion that never hoped to express itself; anguish by no means sure of itself, because it burned with the thought of Carlin being nearer to any man. Ian didn't speak, as he stopped with a rush before his sister. He merely touched her cheek, but his eyes were the eyes of a man whose heart was starving. The English observe that this jealous affection occasionally exists between twins; the Hindus suggest certain mysterious spiritual relations as accounting for it. . . . Finally Skag realised that Carlin's eyes were turned to him, something of pity in them and something of appeal.

It was all very quick then. Skag's hand was out to her brother. Ian didn't see it. Only his right elbow raised the slightest bit; his dark face flushed and paled that second. The stare was refined; it wasn't hate so much as astonishment that any man could ever bring the thing about to touch Carlin's heart. Back of it all was the matter that Ian Deal would have died before confessing—the pain and powerlessness of a brother who loves jealously.

Few beings of his years would have seen so deep and kept his nerve that instant, but Skag had been different since his battle with the cobra. He had decided never to lose his nerve again. This was the first test since that day. . . . His throat tightened a second, so that he had to clear it. All he knew then was that her brother was striding away, having muttered something about the need to see after unshipping Kala Khan, his Arab mount, which was aboard the train. There was a sort of shimmer between Skag's eyes and Ian Deal's vanishing legs that made them seem lifted out of all proportion. Then Carlin caught his arm, carried him forward and to her at the same time, as she whispered:

"You were perfect, Skag-ji. I never loved you so much as that moment, when poor Ian refused to take your hand—"

Skag cleared his throat a second time. . . . Carlin had used that name only once or twice before; and only in moments of her greater joy in him. He had been told by Horace Dickson that "ji" used intimately was "nicer" than any English word.

Something in this experience threw Skag back to the point of the cobra and the last experience with crippling nerves. Of course, it was the thought of Carlin imprisoned in the playhouse that broke him. Starting to run when he first saw the cobra on the threshold, he counted Failure. That burst of speed for ten steps had put the king into fighting mood. Skag had beaten thin in his own mind the possibility of ever committing Failure again. A man must not lose his nerve in the stress of a loved one's peril. One doesn't act so well to bring the event to a winning. In fact, there is no excuse and no advantage and no decency in losing one's nerve, any time, any place. . . .

Skag had *known* things in certain seconds of his duel with the cobra. (Mostly, a man only thinks he knows.) Carlin had stood on the threshold, not more than fifteen feet away, while he was engaged. No one had told him at that time, that the man does not live who can continue to keep off a fighting cobra from striking home; but Skag learned in that short interval. He faced not only the fastest thing he had ever seen move, but it was also the *stillest*. It would come to a dead stop before him—stillness compared to which a post or a wall is mere squat inertia. This lifted head and hood was sustained, elate—having the moveless calm one might imagine at the centre of a solar system. Its outline was mysteriously clear. Often the background was Carlin's own self. The action took place in the period of the Indian afterglow, in which one can see better than in brilliant sunlight, a light that breathes soft and delicate effulgences. The cobra at the point of stillness was like dark dulled jewels against it—dulled so that the raying of the jewels would not obscure the contour.

And once toward the last, as he fought (the inside of his head feeling like a smear of opened arteries), Skag had seen Carlin over the hood of the cobra. She had seemed utterly tall, utterly enfolding; his relation to her, one of the inevitables of creation. Nothing could ever happen to take her away for long. Matters which men call life and death were mere exigencies of his scheme and hers *together*.

In a word, it was a breath of the thing he had been yearning for, from the moment he first saw her in the monkey glen; the need was the core of the anguish he had known in the long pursuit of the thief elephant; the thing that must come to a man and a maid who have found each other, if there is to be any equity in the romantic plan at all, unless the two are altogether asleep and content in the tight dimensions of three-score-and-ten.

Skag had seen that he could not win; but he had also seen that Carlin was *there*—there to stay! . . . Something in her—that no fever or poison or death could take away—something for him! The thing was vivid to him for moments afterward; it lingered in dimmer outlines for hours; but as the days passed, he could only hold the vital essence of what he had learned that hour.

Carlin was more to him every day—more dear and intimate in a hundred ways; yet always she held the quest of her before him; a constant suggestion of marvels of reserve; mysteries always unfolding, of no will or design of hers. It seemed to the two that they were treading the paths of a larger design than they could imagine; and Skag was sure it was only the dullness of his faculty and the slowness of his taking, not Carlin's resources of magic, that limited the joy.

Ian Deal took up his quarters across the river with the cavalry. He did not come to the bungalow.

"He has always been strange," Carlin said. "In some ways he has been closer to me than any of the others. Always strange—doing things one time that showed the tenderest feeling for me and again the harshest resentment. You could not know what he suffered—remaining away when we were married. He has always hoped I would stay single. The idea was like a passion in him. Some of the others have it, but not to the same degree. . . . You know we have all felt the tragedy over us. We are different. The English feel it and the natives, too; yet we hold the respect of both, as no other half-caste line in India. It is because of the austerity of our views on one subject—to keep the lineage above reproach as it began. . . . No, Ian will not come here. He has seen his sister. He will make that do—"

"Why don't you go to him?" Skag asked.

She turned her head softly.

"You Americans are amazing."

"Why?" he laughed.

"An Englishman or any of my brothers in your place, wouldn't think India could contain Ian Deal and himself."

"It wouldn't do any good to fight that sort of feeling," Skag said.

"Only a man whose courage is proven would dare to say that."

"If I were on the right side, it would not be my part to leave India."

Carlin liked this so well that she decided Skag deserved to hear of a certain matter.

". . . Ian has something on his side. You see I had almost decided not to marry—almost promised him. He always said he would never marry if I didn't; that our people would do better forgotten—so much hid sorrow in the heart of us. . . . Something always kept me from making the covenant with him; yet I have been closer and closer up the years to the point of giving my life to the natives altogether. . . . That day in the monkey glen, after the work was done . . . I looked into your face! . . . You went away and came again. I had heard your voice. The old tiger down by the river had made *you* forget everything—but your power"—

Carlin laughed. The last phrases had been spoken low and rapidly.

"I didn't forget everything, dear," she went on. "I didn't forget anything! Everything meant *you*—all else tentative and preparatory. I knew then that the plan was for joy, as soon as we knew enough to take it—"

On the third morning of the pig-sticking Ian Deal rode by the elephant stockades in Hurda just as the American passed. The hands were long that held the bridle-rein, the narrowest Skag had ever seen on a man. The boots were narrow like a poster drawing. It was plainly an advantage for this man to ship his own horse from the south for the few days of sport. The black Arab, Kala Khan, seemed built on the same frame as its rider—speed and power done into delicacy, utter balance of show and stamina. When the Arab is black, he is a keener black than a man could think. His eyes were fierce, but it was the fierceness of fidelity; of that darkness which intimates light; no red burning of violence within.

Ian's face was darker from the saddle; the body superb in its high tension and slender grace. Was this the brother that Roderick Deal, the eldest, had spoken of as being darker than the average native? Yet the caste-mark was not apparent; the two bloods perfectly blent.

The depth of Skag's feeling was called to pity as well as admiration. The rift in this Deal's nature was emotional not physical—some mad poetic thing, forever struggling in the tight matrices of a hard-set world. India was rising clearer to Skag; even certain of her profound complexities. He knew that instant how the fertilising pollen of the West was needed here, and how the West needed the enfolding spiritual culture which is the breath within the breath of the East. This swift realisation had something to do with his own real work. It was filmy, yet memorable—like the first glimpse of one's sealed orders, carried long, to be opened at maturity. Also Skag had the dim impulse of a thought that he had something for Ian Deal. He meant to speak to Carlin of this at the right time.

"Pig-sticking no-end," the cavalry officers had promised and they were making good.

That third afternoon Carlin and Skag took Nels out toward the open jungle, which thrust a narrow triangular strip in toward the town. At intervals they heard shouts, far deeper in. The Great Dane was in his highest form, after weeks of care and training by Bhanah. He could well carry his poise in a walk like this; having his full exercise night and morning. A marvel thing, like nothing else—this dignity of Nels. . . . The two neared their own magic place—not the monkey glen; that was deeper in the jungle—the place where they had really found each other as belonging, in the moment of afterglow.

"It was wonderful then," he said, "but I think—it is even more wonderful now."

That was about as much as Sanford Hantee had ever put into a sentence. Carlin looked at him steadily. They were getting past the need of words. She saw that he was fulfilling her dream. Their story loomed higher and more gleaming to him with the days. He had touched the secret of all—that love is Quest; that love means on and on, means not to stay; love from the first moment, but always lovelier, range on range. It could only burn continually with higher power and whiter light, through steady giving to others.

A woman knows this first, but she must bide her time until the man catches up; until he enters into the working knowledge that the farther vistas of perfection only open as two pull together with all their art and power; that the intimate and ineffable between man and woman is only accomplished by their united bestowal to the world.

They walked long in silence and deeper into the jungle before halting again. Nels brushed the man's thigh and stood close. Skag's hand dropped and he felt the rising hackles, before his eyes left Carlin's. They heard the Dane's rumble and the world came back to them—the shouting nearer.

For a moment they stood, a sense of languor stealing between them. Without a word, their thoughts formed the same possibility, as two who have a child that is vaguely threatened. They were deeper in the jungle than they thought. . . . The cordon of native beaters was still a mile away in its nearest arc, but there is never any telling what a pig will do. . . . They turned back, walking together without haste, Nels behind. They heard the thudding of a mount that runs and swerves and runs again. It was nearer. . . . Their hands touched, but they did not hasten.

When Carlin turned to him, Skag saw what he had seen on the cobra day—weariness, but courage perfect. A kind of vague revolt rose in him, that it should ever be called again to her eyes—more, that it should come so soon. *He* was ready, but not for Carlin to enter the vortex again.

This foreboding they knew, together. Love made them sentient. Not merely a possibility, but almost a glimpse had come—as if an ominous presence had stolen in with the languor.

"Let's hurry, Carlin—"

She was smiling in a child's delicate way, as their steps quickened. The thrash of the chase was nearer; the jungle was clearing as they made their way to the border near Hurda. The low rumbling was from Nels. He would stand, turning back an instant, then trot to overtake them. . . . No question now. One pig at least, was clear of the beaters, coming this way, someone in chase.

The great trees were far apart. They were near *their* place, after many minutes. They had caught a glimpse of a mounted man through the trees—playing his game alone—the pig, but a crash in the undergrowth. . . . There was silence, as if the hunter were listening—then a cutting squeal, a laugh from the absorbed horseman, and it was all before their eyes!

The tusker halted at the border of their little clearing. He had just seen them and the dog—more enemies. . . . Hideous bone-rack—long as a pony, tapering to the absurd piggy haunches—head as long as a pony's head, with a look of decay round the yellow tusks—dripping gash from a lance-wound under one ear—standing stock just now, at the end of all flight!

Nels seemed to slide forward two feet, like a shoved statue. It was a penetrating silence before the voice of Ian Deal:

"You two—what in God's name—"

That was all of words.

His black Arab, Kala Khan, had come to halt twice a lance-length from the tusker. Carlin and Skag and Nels stood half the circle away from the man and mount, a little farther from the still beast, the red right eye of which made the central point of the whole tableau.

Ian looked hunched. He seemed suddenly ungainly—as if all sport like this were mockery and he had merely been carried on in these lower currents for a price. His lance wobbled across his bridle-arm which was too rigid, the curb checking the perfect spring of the Arab's action.

The tusker was bone-still, with that cocked look which means anything but flight. Skag moved a step forward. His knees touched Nels; his left hand was stretched back to hold Carlin in her place. There was no word, no sound—and that was the last second of the tableau.

The tusker broke the picture. Flick of the head, a snort—and he wasn't there. He wasn't on the lance! His side-charge, with no turn which the eye could follow, carried him under the point of Ian's thrust in direct drive at the black Arab's belly.

Kala Khan was standing straight up, yet they heard his scream. The boar's head seemed on a swivel as he passed beneath. Ian Deal standing in the stirrups swung forward, one arm round his mount's neck, but badly out of the saddle. . . . The tusker turned to do it again.

Skag spoke. That was the instant Nels charged. In the same second, the Arab, still on his hind legs, made a teetering plunge back, to dodge the second drive of the beast, and Ian Deal fell, head-long on the far side, his narrow boot locked in the steel stirrup.

Skag spoke again. It was to Kala Khan this time. Nels' smashing drive at the throat had carried the tusker from under the Arab's feet. His rumbling challenge had seemed to take up the scream of the horse; it ended in the piercing squeal of the throated boar.

Skag still talked to Kala Khan, as he moved forward. The Arab stood braced, facing him now—the tumbled head-down thing to the left, arms sprawled, face turned away. A thousand to one, among the best mounts, would have broken before the second charge and thrashed the hanging head against the ground.

Skag's tones were continuous, his empty hand held out. There was never a glance of his eye to the battle of the Dane and the beast. Four feet from his hand was the hanging rein, his eyes to the eyes of the black, his tones steadily lower, never rising, never ceasing. His loose fingers closed upon the bridle rein; his free hand pressed the Arab's cheek.

He felt Carlin beside him and turned—one of the tremendous moments of life to find her there. (It was like the last instant of the cobra fight, when he had seen her over the hood—utterly white, utterly tall.) She took the rein from his hand. Her face turned to Nels' struggle—but her eyes pressed shut.

Skag stepped to Kala Khan's side, lifted the leather fender, slipped the cinch, and let the light hunting saddle slide over, releasing Ian Deal. Then he sprang to Nels, calling as he caught up the fallen lance:

"Coming, old man—coming to you!"

Nels on his feet was bent to the task—the tusker sprawling, the piggy haunches settling flat.

". . . So, it's all done, son," the man said softly. "You're the best of them all to-day."

He laughed. Nels looked up at him in a bored way, but he still held. Skag went back to Carlin. Ian Deal had partly risen. The American did not catch his eye, and now Kala Khan stood between them, Carlin still holding the rein. Skag's hand rested upon the wet trembling withers, where the saddle had covered. There was a blue glisten to the moisture. Skag loved the Arab very hard that moment, and no less afterward. Kala Khan needed care at once. His wound was long and deep, from the hock on the inside, up to the stifle-joint.

Ian Deal was on his feet, the Arab still between him and Skag's eyes. But now her brother drew off, back turned, walking away, his arms and hands fumbling queerly about his head, as he staggered a little.

"He will come back!" Carlin whispered.

Nels loosed now, but sat by his game—sat upon his haunches, bringing first-aid cleansing to his shoulders and chest, where the pinned tusker had worn against him in the battle. . . . All in astonishingly few seconds—the blue beast still with an isolated kick or two.

It was as Carlin said. They had scarcely started toward Hurda before they saw Ian Deal following. His pace quickened as he neared—his first words queerly shocking:

"Is he hurt—oh, I say—is the Arab hurt?"

Skag answered: "A bad cut, but he'll be sound in a week or two."

"One might ask first, you know. He's rather a fine thing—"

Carlin seemed paler, as she held her brother with curious eyes. Ian didn't see her. He was slowly taking in Skag, full-length.

"One might ask, you know," he repeated presently. "One couldn't make a gift of a damaged thing. Oh, yes, you're to have him, Hantee. Things of Kala Khan's quality gravitate to you—I was thinking of the dog, you know—"

Skag shook his head.

"Don't make it harder for me!" Ian said fiercely. "He belongs to you—Carlin, too, of course—no resistance of mine left. A man sees differently—toes up."

Carlin pressed Skag's arm.

The American bowed. Ian Deal straightened.

"That's better," he breathed. "You'll see to the mount? I'd do it for you, but I need an hour—in here among the trees, you know, alone. . . . If it isn't quite clear to me, I'll cock one foot up in the crotch of a tree—until it's straight again. . . . But it's clear, Hantee," he added. "I'm seeing now—the man she sees—or something like!"

Ian turned toward the deeper growths. . . . They walked in silence. The untellable thing—for Skag alone—lingered in Carlin's eyes, in the pallor of her face. She was the one who spoke:

"It is terrible—terribly dear, like a blending of two souls in a white heat together—those moments at the play-house and now—as you held Kala Khan—"

"It was not one alone," he answered strangely. "Something from you was with me—half, with mine."

CHAPTER XIII

NEELA DEO, KING OF ALL ELEPHANTS

This is the story of Neela Deo, King of all elephants! Protector of the Innocent! Defender of Defenders! Equitable King!

For his sake, knowledge of the place where he was known and of those who looked upon his person, shall go down from generation to generation into the future and shall be continued forever, under the illumination of his name.

How he preserved the great judge and how he fought that mightiest of all battles, for the honour of his kind and for the preservation of his liege-son, must be told in order.

The fortune of the season, the features of the town, and the chief names must be established.

See that nothing shall be added. See that no part be left unspoken. It is the law.

The great rains had passed on their way north; and they had been good to the Central Provinces country. The water-courses were even yet but a line below flood; the tanks were full, the wells abrim. The earth was clothed with new garmenture. Jungle creatures were all in their annual high-carnival. Life-forces were driving to full speed.

The town of Hurda, on the great triple Highway-of-all-India, clung to the side of her little river leaning against the massive buttressed walls of her old grey stone terraces, where—on their wide step-landings—at all seasons, she burned her human dead by the tide's margin.

The great Highway spanned the river on a broad low stone bridge and turned—just south of the burning ghats—with a majestic sweep northward, between its four lines of sacred, flowering, perfumed and shade trees. Remember, those trees were planted by the forgotten peoples of dead kings, for each within his own realm; they were all nourished under the unfailing rivalry that the highway of each king should be more excellent in beneficence and in beauty than the highway of his neighbour kings.

But from High Himalaya to the beaches of Madras, from sea to sea, the triple Highway-of-all-India was nowhere more august than here, where Neela Deo lived. The exalted splendours of those so ancient and imperial trees rendered distinction to the town, in passing through it, like a procession of the radiant gods.

Beyond the hill and well outside the town—which would be called a city if it were walled, which would be walled if a wall would not separate it from the great Highway—was the station Oval, where railway people lived in European bungalows of many colours, round about the *gymkhana*—a building made to contain music and strange games; but from the arches of all its verandahs the railway people saw.

On the other side from the Oval and toward Hurda, was the little old bungalow where Margaret Annesley—of the tender heart—out of her lonely garden, looked that day and saw.

Across the great Highway from the temple of Manu, the bungalow of Dickson Sahib sheltered under the mighty sweep of full bearing mango trees. His small son stood between two teachers in the deep verandah and beat his hands together while he saw.

At the top of the hill, the bare bungalow of the old missionary Sahib made protest against the perfume-drunken orient and the colour-mad European world of India with its carbolic-acid whitewash and chaste lines. Down the driveway his children ran away from their teachers and saw.

But in sight of the town—as should be—and beside the courts—as should be—stood the austere home of the Chief Commissioner, most high civil judge of Hurda and all surrounding villages. One of his deputies leaned from an upper balcony and saw.

Back of his park, more than three quarters of a mile away, were the stockades of the Chief Commissioner's elephants. A round parade ground spread its almost level disk straight away front of the stockade buildings. Perfectly rimmed by a variety of low jungle growths, nesting thick at the feet of a circle of tall tamarisk trees, its effect was satisfying to the eye beyond anything seen about the homes of men. Nay, the avenues which led up to the palaces of ancient kings were not so good!

Now all is established concerning the time and the place and those who saw; and it will not be questioned by any save the very ignorant—who are not considered in the telling of tales.

So in the day of Neela Deo, most exalted King of all elephants, came a runner at the end of his last strength. Stripped naked, but for his meagre loincloth, the oils of his body ran thick down all his limbs and his splitting veins shed blood from his nostrils and from his mouth. In the market-place he fell and with his last breaths coughed out a broken message.

Many gathered to discover his meaning. Spread a swift excitement. The shops were emptied, the doorways and alleys opened, and streams of people poured out into a common tide.

Perfume dealers brought copper flasks of priceless oils. Flower merchants gathered up their entire stock of freshly prepared garlands of marigold and tuberose and jasmine and champak blooms—banked masses of garlands were hung on scores of scores of reaching arms, lifted to carry them. Sixty full pieces of white turban-cloth were caught from the shelves of cloth sellers.

Companies and companies of nautch-girls, with their men-servants and instruments to accompany them—even the most costly of these, who were also singing women—poured out of the districts where the towns-women lived and blended in their groups as individual units, in the increasing surge that flowed out along the great Highway, like a river which had broken its dam.

The multitude followed the great highway past the station oval and turned aside into the open jungle—deepening, thickening, swelling, teeming forward. Twenty thousand voices, lifted in all pitches of the human compass, were caught by tom-toms and the impelling cadence of the singing nautch-girls—like drift-wood in a swift current—and driven into rhythmic pulsation.

So the people of Hurda went out to meet Neela Deo, King of all elephants.

When the front of the throng went by his place, Hand-of-a-God enquired of running men from his own gateway. By his side the Gul Moti stood with Son of Power. When they understood, she pushed her chosen of all men through the vine-made arch and he sprang away and ran with the people.

They shared their garlands with him, that he should not come into Neela Deo's presence with empty hands; and they exulted because he ran with them, for the fame of Son-of-Power was already established.

At the margins of the true jungle, a high-tenor voice came out to meet them. The feeling in it chained Skag's ear; it was like a strong man contending bravely with his tongue, but calling on the gods for help, with his heart. Listening intently, the

American began to get the words:

"What are we before thee—oh thou most Exalted! Children of men, our generations pass before thee as the seasons. But thou, oh mighty King—thou Destroyer of the devastator, thou Protector of our wise judge, blessed among men is he for whom thou hast spilled thy blood! We will send his name down from generation to generation under the light of thy name! Thou most Glorious!"

The next words were more difficult to catch:

"Nay, nay! but my beloved, it is a little hurt! Do I not know, who serve thee? I whose father served thee before me—whose father served thee before him? I whose son shall serve thee after me? As my small son lives, he shall serve thee—being come a man—in his day, even as I serve thee in this my day!"

This was evidently enticing the great creature to live. But the voice winged away again:

"Ah, thou heart of my heart, thou life of my life! Hear me, the milk of a thousand goats shall cool thee. The petals of a thousand blooms shall comfort thee. Tuberose and jasmine and champak shall comfort thee, thou Lover of rare things! Nay, it is not enough, but the offerings of the heart's core of love shall satisfy thee—the blood of a million-million blooms shall anoint thee, to thy refreshment!"

The words were lost for a moment, before they rang again:

"Are not the coverings of our heads upon thy wounds? Thou, most excellent in majesty! Have we not laid the symbols of our honour upon thy wounds? Thou, with the wisdom of all ages in thy head and the tenderness of all women in thy heart! We have seen thee suffer, that he who is worthy might live! Thou Discerner of men! We have seen thee destroy the killer, without hurt to him who is kind! Thou Equitable King!"

And slowly out of the shadows of forest trees, came the Chief Commissioner's elephant caravan, trailing in very dejected formation, behind Neela Deo, who showed naked as to his back—for his housings had been stripped off him; and as to his neck, for Kudrat Sharif was not on it but on the ground—walking backward step by step, enticing him with the adoration and sympathy of his voice.

Sanford Hantee saw Neela Deo stop to receive the first garlands on his trunk. From there on, the great elephant paused deliberately after every step to take the offerings of homage from hundreds of reaching hands.

When the American had laid his garlands over Neela Deo's trunk and was about to make his turn in the press, he saw the Chief Commissioner himself, walking behind the wounded elephant with uncovered head. After a keen glance, the great judge motioned Skag to close in by his side. His strong face was shadowed by deep concern; and for some time he did not speak. This was the man of whom Skag had heard that his name was one to conjure with. His fame was for unfailing equity, which—together with strange powers of discernment and bewildering kindness—had won for him the profound devotion of the people. Skag's thoughts were on these matters when he heard, on a low explosive breath:

"Most extraordinary thing I've ever seen!"

The Englishman's eye scarcely left the huge figure swaying before him and the distress in his face was obvious.

"I see you're greatly concerned," Skag said gently.

"Well, you understand, I've jolly good right to be—he saved my life! And he's got a hole in his neck you can put your head into—only it's filled up and covered up with twenty dirty turbans! And by the way, you may not know, but it's unwritten law—past touching—the man in this country never uncovers his head excepting in the presence of his own women.

It's more than a man's life is worth to knock another's turban off, even by accident. But look, yonder are the turbans of my caravan—deputies, law-clerks and servants together—on Neela Deo's neck! Their heads are bare before this multitude and without shame. What's one to make of it? There's no knowing these people!"

Skag's eye quite unconsciously dropped to the white helmet, carried ceremonially in the hand; and glancing away quickly, he caught a mounting flush on the stern countenance.

Presently the Chief Commissioner spoke again:

"We were coming in on the best trail through a steady bit of really old tree-jungle—Neela Deo leading, as always. We've been out nine weeks from home, among the villages. It's not supposed to be spoken, but a stretch like that is rather a grind. The elephants wanted their own stockades; they were tired of pickets. You understand, they're all thoroughly trained. They answer their individual mahouts like a man's own fingers. Neela Deo is the only elephant I've heard of who has been known to run; I mean, to really run—and then only when he's coming in from too many weeks out.

"Few European men have ever seen an elephant run. Nothing alive can pass him on the ground but the great snake. I stayed on top of Neela Deo once when he ran home. It was not good sitting. I've never cared for the experience again.

"As the jungle began to open toward Hurda, he was nervous. Of course I should have been more alive to his behaviour—should have made out what was disturbing him. If we lose him, I shall feel very much responsible. But his mahout was easing him with low chants—made of a thousand love-words. They're not bad to think by. I was clear away off in an adjustment of old Hindu and British law—you know we have to use both together; and sometimes they're hard to fit.

"I know no more about how it happened than you do. I was

knocked well up out of my abstraction by a most unmerciful jolt. Kudrat Sharif had been raked off Neela Deo's neck and was scrambling to his feet on the ground. In one glimpse I saw his *dothi* was torn and a long dripping cut on one thigh. He shouted, but I couldn't make it out, because all the elephants were trumpeting to the universe.

"There are always four hunting pieces in the howdah and I reached for the heaviest automatically, leaning over to see whatever it was. There was nothing intelligible in the hell of noise and nothing in sight. I tell you, I could not see a hair of any creature under me—but Neela Deo. And don't fancy Neela Deo was quiet this while. My howdah was pitching me to the four quarters of heaven—with no one to tell which next. Six of the hunters had rifles trained on us, but I knew they dared not fire for the fear of hitting me or him. And I'm confident they would be as ready to do the one as the other.

"Then he began swaying from side to side with me. It was a frightful jog at first, but he went more and more evenly, further and further every swing, till I kept myself from spilling out by the sheer grip of my hands. The rifles were knocking about loose.

"At last I was up-ended cornerwise and I thought, on my word, I thought my elephant had turned upside down. A shriek fairly split my head open and Neela Deo was dancing straight up and down on one spot. It was a thorough churning, but it was a change.

"I should say his dance had lasted sixty seconds or more, before he himself spoke; then he put up his trunk and uttered a long strong blast. I've never heard anything like it; in eighteen years among elephants, I've never heard anything like it.

"After that he slowed down and they closed in on him, with weeping and laughter and pandemonium of demonstrations, mostly without meaning to me, till I climbed down and saw the remains of what must have been a prime Bengali tiger—under his feet.

"It had charged his neck and gotten a hold and eaten in for the big blood-drink. It had gripped and clung with its four feet—there are ghastly enough wounds—but the hole it chewed in his neck is hideous.

"He poured blood in a shocking stream till they checked it with some kind of jungle leaves and their turbans. And you see—he's groggy. He's quite liable to stagger to his knees any moment. If he gets in to his own stockades, there may be a chance for him; but he doesn't look it just now. Still, I fancy they're keeping him up rather. Eh? Oh yes, quite so."

The Chief Commissioner wiped his forehead patiently, before he went on:

"You're an extraordinary young man, Sir. I've heard about you; the people call you Son-of-Power. You haven't interrupted me once—not one in twenty could have done it. I'm glad to know you."

This was spoken very rapidly and Skag smiled:

"I'm interested."

The Chief Commissioner's eyes bored into Skag with almost impersonal penetration, till the young American knew why this big Englishman's name was one to conjure with. Then he went on:

"Yes, we'll have much in common. You see, I'm working it out in my own mind. . . . The curious part of it all is, they say an elephant has never been known to behave in this manner before. The mahouts seem to understand; I don't. This I do know: When a tiger charges an elephant's neck, the elephant's way is—if the tiger has gotten in past the thrust of his head—to plunge dead weight against a big tree, an upstanding rock, or lacking these—the ground. In that case he always rolls. You see where I would have been very much mixed with the tiger.

"In this case, Neela Deo measured his balance on a swing and when he found how far he dare go, he took his chance and struck the cat off with his own front leg. It's past belief if you know an elephant's anatomy."

The Chief Commissioner broke off. Neela Deo had lurched and was wavering, as if about to go down. The sense of tears was in Kudrat Sharif's voice; but it loomed into courage, as it chanted the superior excellence of Neela Deo's attributes.

Then Neela Deo braced himself and went on, but more slowly. The big Englishman smiled tenderly:

"He's a white-wizard, is Kudrat Sharif—that mahout! He does beautiful magic, with his passion and with his pain. It's practically worship, you understand; but the point is, it works!

"The mahouts say Neela Deo did the thing for me; stood up and took it, till he could kill the beast without killing me. Oh, you'll never convince them otherwise. They'll make much of it. They're already pledged to establish it in tradition—which means more than one would think. These mahouts come of lines that know the elephant from before our ancestors were named. They know him as entirely as men can. All his customs are common knowledge to them—in all ordinary and in all extraordinary circumstances. They say that once in many generations an elephant appears who is superior to his fellows—he's the one who sometimes surprises them."

The Chief Commissioner stopped, looking into Skag's eyes for a minute, before he finished:

"I'm a Briton, you understand; stubborn to a degree—positively require demonstration. I'm not qualified to open the elephant-cult to you—it's as sealed as anything—but I've had bits; and I recommend you—if you'll permit me—to give courtesy to whatever the mahouts may choose to tell you.

You'll find it more than interesting."

"I'm very grateful to you," Skag answered. "I've had a promise of something and I mean to know more about the mahouts and about elephants."

It was well on in the night when the elephants turned down out of the great highway into their own stockades. Neela Deo staggered and swayed ever so slowly forward, with his head low and his trunk resting heavy and inert on Kudrat Sharif's shoulder; but he got in.

After that no man saw him for sixteen weeks—save the mahouts of his own stockades. But every morning the flower merchants sent huge mounds of flower garlands to comfort him.

Then a proclamation was shouted in the marketplace—in the name of the Chief Commissioner—calling all to come and sit in seats which had been prepared around the parade ground before his elephant stockades—to witness the celebration of Neela Deo's recovery. Great was the rejoicing.

Many Europeans of distinction answered the Chief Commissioner's invitation—from as far as Bombay. But all the Europeans together looked very few; for from the surrounding villages and towns and cities, a vast multitude had been flooding in for days. Sixty-two thousand people found places in good sight of the arena, in prepared seats. That number had been reckoned for; but half as many more thronged the roofs of the stockade buildings and hung—multicoloured density—from their parapets. And above all, a few tall tamarisk trees drooped long branches under hundreds of small boys.

Famous nautch-girls had come from distant cities and trained with those of Hurda for an important part in the celebration. They were all staged on twelve Persian-carpeted platforms, ranged on the ground within the outer edge of the arena and close against the foot of the circular tier of seats. Artists of the world had wrought to clothe these women. Artists in fabric-weaving, in living singing dyes; in cloths of gold, in pure wrought-gold and in the setting of gems.

People were looking to find the concealed lights which revealed this scene of amazing splendour, when thirty-nine of the Chief Commissioner's elephants came out through the stockade gates, single file. Many drums of different kinds, together with a thousand voices, beat a slow double pulse. The elephants, setting their feet precisely to the steady rhythm of it, marched around the entire arena three times. Those elephants were perfect enough—and they knew it! They were freshly bathed and groomed. Their ears showed rose-tinted linings, when they flapped. Their ivories were smooth and pure. Their howdahs—new-lacquered—gleamed rose and orange and blue, with crimson and green silk curtains. Their caparisons of rich velvets, hung heavy with new gold fringes.

Every elephant turned toward the centre of the arena, coming to pause at his own appointed station, evenly spaced around the circle. Then every mahout straightened, freezing to a fixed position that did not differ by a line from the position of his neighbour on either side. Now the people saw that this celebration for Neela Deo, King of all elephants, was to show as much pomp as is prepared for kings of men—and they were deeply content.

The strings of one sitar began to breathe delicate tones. Other sitars came in illusively, till they snared the current of human blood in a golden mesh and measured its flow to the time of mounting emotion. Then Neela Deo himself—Neela Deo, the Blue God!—appeared at the stockade gates alone, with Kudrat Sharif on his neck. His caparison was of crimson velvet, all over-wrought with gold thread. The gold fringes were a yard deep. The howdah was lacquered in raw gold—its curtains were imperial blue. Kudrat Sharif was clothed in pure thin white—like the son of a prince—but he was very frail; and ninety-odd thousand people sent his name, with the name of Neela Deo, up into the Indian night—for the Indian gods to hear.

Neela Deo was barely in on the sanded disk, when the elephants lifted their heads as one and saluted him with an earth-rocking blast; again and yet again. Then he thrust his head forward, reached his trumpet-tip—quivering before him—and made speed till he came close to the Chief Commissioner's place, where he rendered one soft salute and wheeled into position by the stand. This was a movement no one had anticipated. Nothing like it was in the plan; the Chief Commissioner had not intended to ride! But Neela Deo demanded him and there was nothing for it but to go; so with a very white face, he stepped into the howdah.

Waves upon waves of enthusiasm swept the multitude. They shouted to heaven—for all time it was established. No man could ever deny it—Neela Deo himself had made his meaning perfectly plain, that he had done the marvel thing sixteen weeks before, to save the life of his friend—their friend! They stood up and flung their flower-garlands on both of them—as Neela Deo, with a stately tread, carried the Chief Commissioner around the circle. The nautch-girls sprang from their platforms into the middle of the arena and danced their most wonderful dances—tossing the fallen garlands, like forest fairies at play.

Then a thousand voices lifted upon the great chorus of laudation, which had been prepared in high-processional time; the drums and the sitars furnishing a dim background for the volume of sound. The elephants turned out of their stations as Neela Deo passed them and came into their accustomed formation behind him. The tread of four times forty such ponderous feet, in perfect time with the music, shook the earth.

The chorus told the story of the incredible manner of their Chief Commissioner's deliverance; it exalted his record and his character; it pledged the preservation of his fame. Then a master-mahout from High Himalaya went alone to the centre of the disk and in incomparable tones—such as master-mahouts use—having no accompaniment at all, told the story of Neela Deo's birthright. The people were utterly hushed; but the elephants kept their even pace—as if listening. Then the great chorus came back, rendering the acknowledgment of a human race.

At last the multitude rose up and loosed its strangling exultation in mighty shouts. The elephants raised their big heads, threw high their trumpets and rent the leagues of outer night—as if calling to their brothers in the Vindha Hills.

The next part of the celebration was to happen suddenly. The mahouts had planned it in sheer boyishness; and to their mountain hearts it meant something like the clown-play in a western circus. Its success depended on whether Neela Deo had enough foolishness in him—to play the game. So now they wheeled the elephants into their stations again, just in time before one section of the enclosure folded down flat on the ground. This left that part open to the outside world; for the shrubs that used to grow thick at the feet of the tamarisk trees had been rooted up and green tenting-cloth stretched in their place. One shrub still grew in the midst of that opening.

Neela Deo stopped short one moment—frozen so still that he looked like a granite image—then, feeling toward the shrub with his trumpet tip an instant only, flung up his head with a joyous squeal and was upon it before a man could think. The shrub melted to pulp under his tramping feet. Then they saw the black and yellow stripes of the tiger he had killed in this same way—tramping, tramping. He was doing it over again, for them.

The mahouts laughed, calling their strange mountain calls; and the people went quite mad. Even the English taxidermist who had taken the trouble to sew and roughly stuff that mangled tiger-skin for the mahouts—even he shouted with them. Every time Neela Deo put that little quirk into his trunk and slanted his head in that absurd angle—Neela Deo, whose smooth dignity had never shown a wrinkle before—they broke out afresh.

This clown-play certainly brought the people back to earth; but it did something queer to the elephants. Having learned to know human voices, they had already felt the mounting excitement; they had already been tamping the ground with hard driving strokes, as if making speed on the open highway—for some time. But in this abandonment to amusement, this joyous unrestraint, they must have found some reminder. They did not have Neela Deo's sense of humour. But they must have remembered the unwalled distances of their own Hills—the hedge of shrubs had been taken away; the tall slender tamarisk trees still standing, made no obstruction. Beyond the waning torches they must have looked and seen the quenchless glory of the same old Indian stars.

It was Nut Kut, the great black elephant not long down from his own wilds among the Vindha Hills, who left his station first and moved on out into the night. Gunpat Rao followed him. . . . One by one they filed away. Indeed, there was not one shrub left to bar their path. But in this falling of calamity upon their so successful foolish plan, the mahouts were stricken—desperate. There was something grotesque about their hands, as they disappeared. With wild gestures and twisted-back faces many of them went out of sight. The elephants were surely their masters, in that hour.

They all passed quite close to where the Chief Commissioner sat in Neela Deo's howdah. Neela Deo had regained his dignity; he was gravely driving fragments of black and yellow stripes into the sand—patiently finishing his job. But Kudrat Sharif's voice had no effect upon the others; and the Chief Commissioner was entirely helpless. No one could prevent their going. Then it appeared that one had not gone—one other, beside Neela Deo.

Mitha Baba, the greatest female of the caravan, under her pale rose caparison and gold lacquered howdah with its curtains of frost-green, was beating the ground with angry feet and thrusting her head aside impatiently. Something was holding her. When he saw, the Chief Commissioner made haste to reach her—leaving Kudrat Sharif, who was confident of keeping Neela Deo.

Mitha Baba's station in the circle was close to where the Gul Moti sat; her new housings had been specially designed to recognise her devotion to the Gul Moti, whose low 'cello tones were now soothing the great creature and restraining her. But when the Chief Commissioner approached, Mitha Baba started, flinging herself forward—and the Gul Moti was suddenly at the edge of the stand. Just as the elephant lunged out to take her stride, the colourful voice that she had never refused to obey said:

"Come near, Mitha Baba, come near!"

Mitha Baba was not sure about it; she struck the voice aside with her head. But the voice was saying:

"Mitha Baba, you may take me with you!"

Then Son-of-Power was on his feet, but it was too late—Mitha Baba decided quickly and she acted soon—he could not reach the edge in time to go himself, but on an impulse he threw his great-coat into the Gul Moti's hands and she laughed as she caught it from the howdah.

In swerving suddenly to pass close by the stand, the elephant had unbalanced her boy-mahout from her neck; but his father—the very old mahout—was coming as fast as he could across the space before them, calling to her—like the lover of wild creatures that he was.

Carlin bent from her howdah and spoke joyously:

"Put him up, Mitha Baba, put him up!"

And Mitha Baba scarcely broke her stride, which was lengthening every step, as she obediently circled the old man with her trunk and carelessly flung him on her neck.

"We'll fetch them all home!" the Gul Moti's voice floated back, as they melted away into the night.

The Chief Commissioner gave Son-of-Power his hand—being without words, for the moment.

"Is she safe?" Skag asked.

"Absolutely safe!" the Chief Commissioner assured him. "The caparisons may be doused in the Nerbudda, but the howdahs will not be in the least wet."

"What did she mean—that she'd fetch them all back?"

"She meant that Mitha Baba has been used in the High Hills—for years before she was sent down—to decoy wild elephants into the trap-stockades. She's entirely competent, is Mitha Baba; she's the leader of my caravan—next to Neela Deo. Of course Neela Deo is our only hope of overtaking them; he's fast enough, but this is rather soon after his injury, and he'll have to rest a bit. In the meantime, come away up to the house; we'll talk there."

CHAPTER XIV

NEELA DEO, KING OF ALL ELEPHANTS (CONTINUED)

To possess one white elephant is calamity. But if Evil—the nameless one—could possess a pair, he would breed an army able to break down the very walls of Equity.

Indra—supreme hypocrite—fathered the first two, who were brother and sister. Kali—wife of Shiva, the great destroyer—Kali—goddess of plague and famine and fear and death—was their mother.

Beware the white elephant—who is never white. The stain of Indra is on his skin; the shadow of Kali on his hair. Honour is not in him!

The Gul Moti had always loved adventures; and she had been in the throat of several. But this was no lark; it was more serious than funny. Thirty-eight of the most valuable elephants in India were rolling away before her toward the Vindha Hills. If they once arrived there, no man could say how many of them, or if any of them, would ever be recovered. The Nerbudda River crossed their path mid-way—almost at flood. If they entered that tide—deep and wide and muddy—state-housings of great value would be hopelessly damaged.

Mitha Baba was beginning to show that she did not like the old mahout's urging—but Mitha Baba was always willful.

Indeed, the Gul Moti was depending much on this same willfulness. The splendid female was still young, but she had been for years a celebrated toiler of wild elephants; and it was well known she had loved the game. Had she forgotten it? Could she be reminded? First, it was supremely important to overtake all the others this side the Nerbudda.

The old mahout gasped a broken cry, as Mitha Baba lifted him and set him not too gently on the ground; she was in a hurry herself and she was making speed on her own account—she objected to being urged. The Gul Moti, understanding in a flash, cried quickly:

"No, no! Mitha Baba, I want him! Put him up to me—put him up to me—soon!"

Mitha Baba wavered in her long stride.

"Mitha Baba, I want him—I want him!"

And the elephant turned on a circle and caught him up, throwing him far enough back, so the Gul Moti could help him into the howdah.

"My day is done!" he said bitterly.

"Nay, father!" the girl physician answered him. "She knew you were not safe there."

"Is it so?" the old man marvelled. "Indeed, she always loved me! Now I am satisfied!"

Then, in the white fire of what men call genius, the Gul Moti stood up to meet this new emergency—leaning toward Mitha Baba's head—and called in ringing tones:

"Now come, Mitha Baba, we're away! We're going out to fetch them in! Away, away, awa-a-ay!"

So long as he lived, the old mahout told of the intoxicating splendour of that young voice—the golden beauty of those tones; of how Mitha Baba reached out further and further every stride, to its rhythm, till the earth rose up and the stars began to swing.

"We'll fetch them in, Mitha Baba, we'll fetch them in! . . . Away, away, awa-a-ay!"

But the toiler of wild elephants had remembered the game she loved.

As they topped the crest of a low hill, the Gul Moti scanned the country declining before her toward the Nerbudda. A string of jewels appeared—incredibly gorgeous in mid-day light. It was thirty-eight full-caparisoned elephants—going fast. Mitha Baba called on them to wait for her; but they remained in sight only a few minutes. The Gul Moti's high courage sank; the caravan was too near the river to be delayed by Mitha Baba's calls—the river too far ahead.

"Do they ever obey her, Laka Din?" the Gul Moti asked.

"They always used to," the old man replied dubiously.

Finally Mitha Baba came out into the straight descent toward the river. No elephants were in sight, but a blotch of colour showed on the bank.

"Well done for those mahouts!" the Gul Moti cried out in relief. "The caparisons at least are safe. How did they do it?"

"It was well done, Hakima-ji," the old man exulted. "The masters were listening to Mitha Baba, delaying between her and the river—space of six breaths; then those men became like monkeys! It is no easiness—unfastening everything from top of an elephant. (I who am old have done it!) Also, some went down to loosen underneath buckles. You shall see."

They found four very disconsolate mahouts on the bank of the river beside the great pile of nicely arranged stuff.

"I want the smallest howdah you have!" called the Gul Moti, as the men sprang in front of Mitha Baba.

"But, Hakima-ji," they protested, "by getting down—we were left behind!"

"I must not be left—and yet you must take these clothes from her!" the Gul Moti said, while they helped the old man to the ground.

"Then go to her neck—oh, Thou Healer-without-fear! She will not wait long—she follows Nut Kut, the demon! and Gunpat Rao, who both got away with everything on!"

Still hoping, the Gul Moti slipped over the edge of the big howdah and climbed toward Mitha Baba's neck. The mahouts worked fast stripping her. Then Mitha Baba flung her head, striding away from their puny fingers, and plunged into the river. Sinking at first enough to wet the Gul Moti a little, she rose beautifully as she found her swimming stroke.

Day went by—and no elephants in sight. Night came on—and no elephants in sight. Mitha Baba rolled across the Nerbudda valley, as confident of her way as if she travelled the great Highway-of-all-India. She began to climb into the rising country beyond, as certain of her steps as if she were coming in to her own stockades. The Gul Moti took up her call again—thinking of the caravan they were following. But Mitha Baba was not thinking of the caravan. It had happened that the Gul Moti's tones had fallen upon those intonations used in High Himalaya, to send the toilers out to toil wild elephants in.

It was night-time, before the moon came up, when a strange elephant crashed past them—lunging in the opposite direction. It reeled as it ran and went down on its knees; evidently having been done to death in a fight. But the outline of it, in the shadows, appeared too lean to be one of her own.

Soon after that, Mitha Baba trumpeted in a new tone of voice—one the Gul Moti had never heard before. It sounded very wild, very desolate.

"In the name of all the gods, Mitha Baba, what's the meaning of that?" the Gul Moti enquired with a little tension—it being one of those moments when one gains assurance by speech.

But Mitha Baba's reply was in the very oldest language of India—one even the mahouts know only a very little of. It rose in wild, wistful tones—higher and higher. It was repeated from time to time; the sense of it strangely thrilling to the girl on her neck.

. . . They were well up in the mountains, so far that the trees had become massive of body and heavy and dense of top—the moon only just showing through—when they heard the trumpeting of elephants, off toward the east. Mitha Baba answered at once, turning abruptly toward the east.

"Mitha Baba!" the Gul Moti protested, "our people have never gone off in this direction—where are we, anyway?"

Mitha Baba's calling was just as wild as before; but it had become wild exultation.

. . . They were coming up into what reminded the Gul Moti of something she had heard—that the really old jungle is always dark; that the light of day never touches earth there. This was almost dark, the moon glinting through black shadows—only at intervals.

The sense of this place was strange. It might be on another planet. And that thought touched the root of the difference—this was not on, this was in. Everything felt in—deep in.

Here Mitha Baba changed her voice again. (Nothing had ever

happened to the Gul Moti like it.) It was still wild, still wistful—quite as much so as before. But there was a cooing roll in it—away and away the most enticing thing human ears ever listened to. It sounded like Nature—weaving all spells of all glamour, in tone; soft-flaming gold, in tone; soft-flaming rose, in tone; and on and on—the very softest, deepest magics of life-perpetual!

. . . The trumpeting ahead was fuller and nearer, distinctly nearer; almost as if they were coming into it. Then, without warning, the mighty mountain trees cut off the moon-lit sky. It had been dark before—now it was utterly dark!

Suddenly the Gul Moti was aware of a strong earth-smell. There was no stench about. It had a quality of incense made of tree-gums and sandalwood and perfume-barks, all together. Then a dull thudding caught her ear—almost rhythmic.

. . . The earth-smells deepened and the thudding thickened. Mitha Baba was not climbing any more; moving smoothly, on what felt like firm soil, she seemed to turn and turn again. It was fathoms deep in rayless night—the place that never knew the light of day!

Carlin clung tight to Mitha Baba's neck and remembered everything actual, everything definite, everything sound and sensible she knew. The earth-smells filled her nostrils, her lungs, her blood; tree-gums, sandal-wood, perfume-bark, body-warmth—charging the air.

And over all—wild, and wistful, and pulsing-tender—the weaving of Mitha Baba's enchantment through the dark.

The thudding all about her on the ground—must be the sound of many wild feet! This must be—the "toiling in."

. . . A rending, tearing noise broke in on Mitha Baba's voice; and at once a great crash among the trees, high up. (Someone had torn a sapling from its place and flung it far.)

. . . The keen squeal of a very little elephant—right near—and the angry protest of a strange voice. (Some mother's baby had been pinched, in the crowd!)

. . . It must be imagination—this strong nearness! The Gul Moti, putting out her hand, touched—skin! And within the same breath, on both sides of Mitha Baba—first this side and then that side—two great elephants challenged each other. They were both long, rocking blasts, a little above and almost against the Gul Moti's quickened ears. She shivered under the shock.

Mitha Baba, without breaking her step, backed away from between them; and the impact of frightful blow meeting frightful blow, bruised through the outbreak of much trumpeting.

As Mitha Baba went further and further from the fighters, the Gul Moti was amazed at the sounds of their meeting—like explosions. She remembered their tonnage; and recalled having heard that an elephant fight is not the sort of thing civilised men call sport.

. . . A soft, *feeling* thing crept from the Gul Moti's shoulder along down her back! With convulsive fingers she clung tighter to Mitha Baba's neck. Instantly Mitha Baba turned a bit, driving sidewise at the stranger with her head. The Gul Moti's confidence in the great female's intention to protect her, was established!

At last, lifting her head sharply to utter a different call, Mitha Baba developed a peculiar drive in her motion; a queer drive in the whole huge body that had something to do with a wide swinging of the head. It made them both touch the strange elephants, every few minutes; and always there was a storm of trumpeting all about. Gradually these outbreaks began to sound toward one side; but the direction kept changing—so the Gul Moti made out that Mitha Baba was moving round and round on the outside of the mass.

After a while they came again into the vicinity where the big males were still fighting. Mitha Baba rocked on her feet a moment, calling a curious low call—a question, softly spoken. At once there was the sound of rapid movement in front. Then Mitha Baba literally whirled—plunging away at incredible speed—almost exactly in the opposite direction from the one she had been facing.

Doctor Carlin Deal Hantee tried to remember Skag—tried to remember her own name. She locked herself about that neck with her strength—she clung with her might. She flattened her body and gripped with her fingers and with her toes—long since having kicked off her low shoes. Away and away they went, coming out into the moonlight—long enough to see a mass of dun shadows rising and falling, lurching and rolling, on all sides. Surely the Gul Moti had known that this was a wild elephant herd—these hours. Surely the Gul Moti had heard the "toiling" of them in! But what was Mitha Baba going to do with them—now that she had them?

Down the long slopes and up the steep inclines—the two big elephants close on either side of Mitha Baba—plunging into khuds and out again—most of the time up-ended, one way or the other, at astounding angles—the wild herd raced with Mitha Baba toward whatever destination she might choose.

Dawn broke upon them while they were still in the very rugged hills; and as the mountain outlines cleared of mist, the Gul Moti saw that Mitha Baba was leading her catch straight away back to Hurda. True to her training—there being no trap-stockades near—the toiler was taking them home! The situation was absurd; but it roused the Gul Moti—like one out of a dream—to actual joy.

Through grey avenues of forest trees—rolling down khuds, ringing up crags—the voice of Nut Kut went on out beyond the mountain peaks, to meet approaching day. Nut Kut, the great black elephant who had been trapped in these same Vindha Hills only a few years ago, was rejoicing in freedom again. Nut Kut, who had already made his reputation as the most deadly fighter known to the mahouts, was exulting in strength. It was his joy-song. It came from straight ahead. Mitha Baba answered with a rollicking squeal. But the wild herd voices were savage—chaotic. Now Nut Kut's challenge came back—looming. The situation was no longer absurd.

It meant a fight—an open fight—between the wild herd and the caravan. The wild herd would never give Mitha Baba over to her own—they would surely fight to keep her. Everything tightened in the Gul Moti and locked—hard. She had known most of the caravan elephants all her life—what would happen to them? They had lived among men these many and many years—never permitted to fight—they could not be equally fighting-fit. The herd would be much leaner—it must be much tougher. So she bruised her head and her heart between the things that were due to happen to her caravan—horrible punishments and almost certain deaths.

When the caravan appeared, the males were leading; the four females well in the rear. Nut Kut's flaming orange and imperial-blue trappings covered and cumbered him; and young Gunpat Rao's gorgeous saffron and old-rose burned through the Gul Moti's eyes to the hard lump in her throat—it was the one time in their lives when they should be free.

At once the wild females gathered their youngsters—and some who seemed almost mature—cutting them out from the herd and driving them back. This revealed the wild fighters—many more in number than those of the caravan. The approaching challenges, from both sides, were thundering thick and fast now. The two bodies of elephants were plunging down the opposite sides of a deep khud and would meet in the broad bottom. Mitha Baba—the big males on each side of her—was setting the pace for this side, as if everything depended on time. But when they were quite close, she rushed ahead—straight through the caravan and beyond.

Mitha Baba had been leading her catch to her own stockades—being in no wise responsible that they were not trap-stockades! Now, the home elephants having come to receive it, she had rushed it in—exactly as she would have rushed it into a trap. But Mitha Baba was not satisfied. With a curious little call she wheeled, coming back to face the wild herd from her own side.

It was a turmoil that looked and sounded like nothing imaginable. The fighting pairs were choosing each other and taking place. They had plenty of room. When it was settled between them, Nut Kut was facing the most powerful-looking of the wild fighters; and Gunpat Rao, another who looked almost as dangerous. The extra males of the wild herd—every one formidable—were skirmishing about, watching for a chance to interfere. It looked bad for the caravan.

The mahouts—the Gul Moti had scarcely remembered them till now—were calling back and forth about a bad one, a "tricky elephant." Following their gestures, she saw a pale shape moving around in the open. They left no doubt that he represented the worst of all danger. They were charging each other to watch him—never mind what.

. . . The fight was on. Plainly—in every tone, every action—the wild went in with wild enthusiasm, the tame with grave determination. Mitha Baba, having come in closer than any of the other females, did not move,—save for a constant turning of her head under the Gul Moti's icy fingers—seeming to keep an eye on all the separate fights at once.

Her fear for the caravan elephants was anguish, her fatigue extreme; but excitement held the Gul Moti in a vise. She saw the fighters meet, skull to skull. (Those were the frightful blows she had heard in the dark, through the trumpeting of a whole herd!) How could any living thing endure the impact of such weight? She looked to see the skin break away and fall apart at once. She expected to see an elephant's head split open. It was nerve-wrecking—an arena of giant violence.

"Pray the gods to send Neela Deo!" one of the mahouts shouted.

"Pray the gods to send Neela Deo!" others called back.

The Gul Moti knew that Neela Deo did not fight; that it was his leadership they needed. Soon she heard a muffled cry from the same mahout:

"Men of the Hills, mourn with me!"

(A low wind of tone replied.)

His elephant seemed slower than the one against him; slower in getting back—in coming on. . . . Now he was wavering—shaken through his whole bulk by every meeting. . . . He was not running—he was dazed—he was down! Staring wide-eyed at the horror—the way a barbarian elephant kills—the Gul Moti was glad Skag did not see! . . . The mahout had managed to reach a tree in time to save his own life and was crouching on a branch, with his head buried in his arms.

Nut Kut was finishing with the leader of the wild herd—more mercifully than the wild was of doing it—when two of the extras charged him together. Ram Yaksahn, his mahout—whose voice had not been heard before—cried out; and Mitha Baba went in like a thunder-bolt. How it happened no one could tell, but one of the wild elephants—before Mitha Baba's rush, or in the instant when she reached him—caught his tusk under Nut Kut's side-bands. They were made of heavy canvas, with chains on top. As Mitha Baba drove at him and Nut Kut turned—his tusk ripped out sidewise. With a frantic scream he got away, running up into the jungle—still screaming so far as they could hear.

The Gul Moti, numb with weariness, had held on with her last ounce of strength. Now she sat amazed at her escape—while a tumult of trumpeting shattered the air about her. There was disturbance among the fighting pairs; some staying with each other, some changing—running to and fro—charging at odd angles. But when the confusion cleared—more fresh ones had come in!

Now Nut Kut was a whirl-wind—he was unbelievable. One broke away from him and ran—demoralised. One died—fairly defeated. Still others came to meet him; yet his challenges were triumphant to the point of frenzy.

"Call on the gods! The devil is in!" rang out.

Gunpat Rao was now fighting for his life. The "tricky elephant" had charged him from the open. This was the bad one whom the mahouts had recognised on sight—had feared from the beginning. Gunpat Rao was one of the finest young elephants in captivity; one of the swiftest in the caravan; but the mahouts knew he could not think a trick! The sense of his danger swept them.

The Gul Moti knew that "white elephants" are always feared—being almost always bad. This one was not white; nor grey, nor yellow. He was whitish-grey—dull-tawny overcast—unclean looking. He was larger in frame than Gunpat Rao; but very lean—long, loose-jointed. He moved like a suckling trying to caper. But there was a rakish look about him.

In spite of all their own stress—every one of their elephants being in some degree of jeopardy—the mahouts gave as much attention to Gunpat Rao as they could. It was foregone conclusion—he was doomed. Bracing themselves to witness his defeat, expecting to see his bitter death in the end, yet the bad one's method at the start maddened them beyond control.

"He was bred in the Pit!" one mahout called.

"His father was Depravity!" another called back.

And they cursed him with the curses of the Hills.

Chakkra, who was Gunpat Rao's mahout, was a plucky little man; but his face had gone old.

The pale one's behaviour was entirely different from any the Gul Moti had seen. He was doing nothing regular—not using the common methods at all. He was giving Gunpat Rao no chance to get back—to put his body-weight into his drive. He was staying too close. He was circling—starting to rush in and veering away—round and round, in and out. Then the Gul Moti saw! He was manoeuvring to strike Gunpat Rao back of his ear! He was trying to "hit below the belt!"

So Gunpat Rao was kept pivoting in his own tracks to face the danger, with scant room to meet a rush when it came. And always it came when least suggested by the other's manner. Then the pale one squealed—a succession of thin, cutting tones—and Gunpat Rao answered with a charge. The pale one raced away from him, wheeling suddenly and coming in behind his head. (An instant before, it looked as if they would meet fairly.) But Gunpat Rao, being in full drive and not on guard against such a manoeuvre, could not stop quickly; yet he swerved just enough to clear that yellow tusk—with a long slash in his flank! . . . Gunpat Rao began to show that he was baffled. His trunk came around—feeling of Chakkra!

"He wants Neela Deo! His heart is alone!" Chakkra cried out.

"Pray the gods to send Neela Deo!" the mahouts answered together.

And from the khud-wall behind them, a thundering challenge rolled down. It was like an avalanche of dynamic power.

Now the elephants of the Chief Commissioner's stockades gave account of themselves. Youth had returned to them—courage had been restored. They clamoured to heaven that they were doing well. They shouted to the universe that they belonged to him—to Neela Deo, their King!

Sanford Hantee scarcely saw—an impossible thing—Carlin on Mitha Baba's neck! Her face was actually strange—the awful pallor—the fire. It left his brain a blank to other impressions, for minutes.

The Gul Moti only glimpsed the stone-white face of her American, beside the Chief Commissioner, as Neela Deo charged past, on his way to take over the fight that was taxing Gunpat Rao to the last breath before defeat. Neela Deo had seen at once where he was needed most. He went in with a charging challenge that was intoxication to those who heard—all the assurance of ancient mastership in it.

No one had ever seen Neela Deo fight before. Kudrat Sharif was so astonished that he barely got back from his neck in time to be out of the way. The mahouts were amazed—Neela Deo did not fight! Neela Deo was the Lord of peaceful rule!

Many of the fighting pairs broke away from each other, when they heard Neela Deo's charging challenge, as if agreeing that the destiny of all hung on the issue of his contest. This left most of the mahouts free to watch. With passionate distress they saw the King—wounded almost to death less than four months since—carrying a heavy howdah and three men—going in to fight with a bad elephant who was all but fresh. They cursed the wild elephant with every inward breath, seeing as little hope for Neela Deo as they had seen for Gunpat Rao.

The Gul Moti watched—appalled. It seemed to her that the pale one had been playing—before he engaged with Neela Deo. But he did not play any more. He manoeuvred so fast that his body appeared to glance in and out. But Neela Deo foiled him with still greater speed. Her eye could not follow all—the maze, the glamour, the incredible spectacle.

Neela Deo's first blow had shaken the pale one, carrying a different dimension of force from any in himself. He gave way—backing from it with an angry scream, showing surprise and rage in every movement. When he circled round, trying to get in on Neela Deo's side, the King was too quick for him—forcing him out, forcing him further out; not permitting him to follow his chosen course, whatever direction he took. He came in with his peculiar art of approaches—the jarring blow was there! He played all his lightning feints—the shock that rocked him was a flash quicker! Neela Deo met him squarely, whatever curve he made—whatever tangent he turned upon. This, every time, in spite of himself; for he always meant to avoid that crash!

He tried his falsetto squeals—all aggravation in them. But Neela Deo refused to accept taunts. This caused an instant's pause—the pale one seeming to consider. Then he raced away and came back on a full drive, as if meaning to meet the King in a legitimate encounter—after all. But Neela Deo only lowered his head a fraction, leaning a bit forward; and the pale one, instead of finishing straight, or passing alongside close enough to strike—swerved out. This was the moment when Neela Deo charged him and he ran, dodging—far beyond the range of the fighting arena—down the khud valley. Everyone followed; the wild elephants running by themselves—screaming in harsh tones; the caravan—trumpeting in clear, full tones; the mahouts, calling the name of the King—beside themselves with delight.

But Neela Deo was at the pale one's heels—his tusks not dangerous, having been shortened and banded. Yet they were sharp enough to make the pale one turn and defend himself. And desperately he fought, using every faculty of his nature—every value of his wild fitness. Still the crook in him showed. It was all faster now than in the beginning, but he was not exhausted, he was not broken; only a bit less certain, a breath less quick, when he tried the same old trick—to get in back of Neela Deo's ear. And it was on that false turn that Neela Deo caught him fairly in the throat—caught him and finished him in one thrust—with the blunt point of a banded tusk. (That was the miracle of it all—the banded tusk!)

Then Neela Deo stood back, put up his trunk and uttered a

long, strong blast. They were ringing tones—mounting clarion tones, with tremendous volume at the top. They were the King's proclamation of victory.

The mahouts answered him in High Himalayan voices—full of unleashed devotion. The caravan made announcement of that allegiance the heart of an elephant gives—sometimes. But the wild herd broke away and ran shrieking up into the Vindha Hills.

Coming down from Mitha Baba's neck between Skag's hands, the Gul Moti smiled into his anguished eyes.

"Carlin! Are you—safe?" he asked.

"Safe—now!" she answered.

The tone of that low "now" startled him.

"Where have you been?" he breathed.

"Far—" she said, "very far!"

"But where?" he questioned.

"It was not in *our* world, Skag," she said. "It was—dark!"

The Chief Commissioner had come close, to hear; was stroking her shoulder, in fact—in an absent-minded way—shaking his head.

"You can't mean—*the dark*?" he broke in.

"I mean it was utterly dark, sir," she said. "It was absolutely dark!"

"But—I'm not able to understand!" her old friend protested.

"It was there Mitha Baba found them," the Gul Moti

explained. "It was there she did the '*toiling in.*' Then, she was leading them home to Hurda, when we met the caravan—at dawn."

Some of the mahouts had gathered about. The Chief Commissioner spoke to them in their speech and they answered him—calling others. Soon the men of High Himalaya drew near with grave deference, slowly stooping to touch the ground at her feet.

"No human has ever been in *that* before," said Kudrat Sharif. "We will prepare rest for her—Chosen-of-Vishnu, the Great Preserver!"

It was after they had cared for the Gul Moti with the best they had—water from a mountain stream and food Neela Deo had carried, in a shelter made of tender deodar tips, where she now slept on a bed made of the same—that the mahouts told the Chief Commissioner and Skag, all they themselves had seen.

By this time concern had spread from Hurda throughout the country. Neela Deo had gone out to find the Gul Moti, carrying the Chief Commissioner and Son of Power. No one had come back. Calamity must have fallen. Men went out on horses to trace them. But it was certain priests of Hanuman who found the caravan first. (The Gul Moti having saved the life of a monkey king once, her safety was their concern also.) Without being seen or heard themselves, they went close enough to learn that she was making recovery from great exhaustion; and that the mahouts were caring for an elephant unable to travel by reason of a bad wound. They overheard talk of strange happenings; but more about Neela Deo's undreamed-of achievement.

Before any of the searchers from Hurda reached the caravan, mysterious gifts of provisions—much needed—were found by the mahouts, with a crude writing beside them: "For the Healer-without-fear." And those same priests of Hanuman—preparing a signal-system as they came—brought the good word back to the anxious people, who became joyous at once. Their Gul Moti was safe! Neela Deo was safe—everyone was safe. (But that was a strange saying—that Neela Deo had fought!)

Bonfires blazed up in every village within sight of the caravan's way home—from so far away as watchers on Hurda's highest hill could see—burning night and day. At last the one furthest from Hurda went out. The watchers raced in—Neela Deo's caravan was coming! One by one, the bonfires went out—till it was this side the Nerbudda. Then the people made ready.

They thronged out the great Highway-of-all-India, meeting the caravan where the slow-moving elephants turned in from open jungle. Eagerly striving to see the Gul Moti's face, eagerly pointing at Neela Deo, yet it was a stranger silent multitude. Only many tears on many tears showed their feeling.

The Gul Moti sat in Neela Deo's howdah, with the Chief Commissioner and Son-of-Power. Two men came close, carrying a long slender shape covered with pure white cloth—dripping wet.

"We be poor men," one said, "but our hands bring to thee, oh Healer—from the people of Hurda, oh Healer—" and breaking off, because his lips could speak no more, he stooped reverently to lay aside the covering.

A great folded leaf appeared; a long heavy stalk; then the flawless splendour of one bloom—immaculate! a sacred lotus, brought from far lakes. The Gul Moti received its ineffable loveliness and rose to stretch her fingers toward the multitude. Then their shouts swept the horizon.

Still, their concept of Neela Deo's character must be either shattered or restored—and soon; they would not wait. Ominously quiet questions went up to the mahouts; and the mahouts were full-ready to answer! In the end, it sounded like a wild Himalayan chant about Neela Deo's great fight to save

Gunpat Rao. The people listened patiently, till an inward meaning enlightened them. Then they exulted:

"Neela Deo, Neela Deo, King of all elephants!"

"Exalted in majesty, Defender of honour, protecting his own with strength! We will remember him!"

"Neela Deo, Neela Deo, King of all elephants!"

"He with the wisdom of ages. Destroyer of devastators, preserving his friend with blood! Our children shall not forget!"

"He the Discerner of men, Equitable King! He the Discerner of evil, Invincible King! All generations after us shall hear of him; but we have looked upon his face!"

"Neela Deo, Neela Deo, King of all elephants!"

CHAPTER XV

THE LAIR

Carlin appeared to get right again in a few days of quiet after her terrific experience on Mitha Baba. There were a few more wonderful weeks for Skag and herself in the Malcolm M'Cord bungalow in Hurda—weeks always remembered. Then Skag undertook a little adventure of his own that had to do with Tiger. He was away seven days in all and made no report of the thing he had done to his department. He came back with a deeper quiet in his eyes and told no one but Carlin what the days had shown him. Skag never was at his best in trying to make words work. He was slow to explain. He had been hurt two or three times in earlier days, trying to tell something of peculiar interest to his work and finding incredulity and uncertain comment afterward. This made the animal trainer more wary than ever about talk.

But Carlin required few words. Carlin always understood. She didn't praise or fall into excesses of admiration, but she understood, and the older one gets the dearer that becomes. Carlin didn't advise with Skag whether she should speak of the matter. She merely decided that her old friend, Malcolm M'Cord, Hand-of-a-God, deserved to be told. The silent Scot knew much about animals and this was an affair that would stand high in his collection of musings and memories. M'Cord observed, in a Scotch that had suffered no thinning in thirty years of India, that if he hadn't known Hantee Sahib he would be forced to pass by Carlin's report as an invention, though a "fertile" one. It was M'Cord who decided that Government should get at least a private account of the affair.

A remarkable tiger pair had operated for several years in the broken cliff country stretching away toward the valley of the Nerbudda beyond the open jungle round Hurda. As mates they had pulled together so efficiently that the natives had started the interminable process of making a tradition concerning them. These were superb young individuals and not man-eaters, for which reason Hand-of-a-God had not been called out to deliver the natives; also on this account Skag had been interested from the beginning.

Their lair had never been found, but they had been seen together and singly over a ranging ground that covered seventy miles and contained several dejected villages. Once, hard pressed for game, the male tiger had entered a village grazing ground and made a quick kill—on the run—of one of the little sacred cows—a tan heifer much loved by the people. The point of comment was that the tiger had spared the boy; in fact, the young herder had been unable to run so rapidly as his little drove, which was lost in a dust cloud ahead of him. The tiger had actually passed him by, entered the drove, knocked the heifer down and stood over it as the boy circled past.

There were no firearms in the village, so that the natives did not venture close in the falling darkness. It was evident next day, however, that the tiger had not fed on the spot of the kill. It was supposed that the female had come to help him carry away the game.

Also, this was the same tiger pair that had leaped an eight-foot wall surrounding another village, made their choice of a sizable bullock in a herd of ordinary cattle, and actually helped each other drag the carcass over the wall and away—a daylight raid, this, witnessed from the shadows of several village huts.

So the stories went, but nothing monotonous about them. Often for months at a time no villager would sight the tiger mates. It was positively stated that there were no other mature tigers within the vicinity: that is, within the seventy-miles range. The pair had been known to bring up at least three litters; but the young had been driven at the approach of maturity to outlying hunting grounds, as had been all the weaker tigers of the vicinity.

Now the report came into Hurda that an English hunter had wounded the big female. Another report followed that the Englishman had killed the male and wounded the female. The hunter himself did not appear in Hurda; nor was a trophy hide recorded anywhere. Skag heard the two stories. Thinking over the affair, he called Nels for a stroll in the open jungle toward the Monkey Glen.

To the American there was a pang about the hunter's story. He was altogether unsentimental, but wild animals had to do with his reason for being and there was his fixed partiality for tigers. The uncertainty about the story troubled him. This was the time of year for kittens and it was seldom far from his mind that these parents were not man-eaters. The stories of the hunter were indefinite. The thing worked upon Skag as he walked. The thought of finding the motherless lair and bringing in a hamper of starving young occurred to him as a sane performance, but not one to speak about. Also his servant, Bhanah, reported Nels superbly fit for travel and adventure.

The animal trainer rode the elephant, Nut Kut, into one of the villages in the tiger-ranging grounds and left him in charge of the mahout, saying that he might be gone two or three days and that he was out for a ramble among the waste places of the valley. Skag took merely a haversack, a canteen, light blanket and a hunting belt, carrying a knife and a six-shooter but no rifle. Nels actually lost his dignity in enthusiasm for the excursion, and they were miles away from a village and hours deep in an apparently leisurely journey before he subsided into that observant calm which was his notable characteristic.

This light travelling, with none other than the great hunting dog, brought him back a keen zest of appreciation and memories of early days among the circus animals, and his first adventures in India with Cadman. Moreover, there was a fresh mystery that had to do with Carlin after Skag's first supper fire afield. He had always resented the fact that it was straight out-and-out pain for him to be away from the place she had made in Hurda. Suffering of any kind to Skag was a sign of weakness. He had dwelt long on the subject.

The mystery of that first night out had to do with the fact that Carlin seemed to be near. He had known something of this before, a flash at least, but nothing like this. There wasn't the pain about separation he had known aforetime. It was as if the miracle he had longed for had come—some awakening of life within himself that was quick to her presence even at a distance and cognisant that absence was illusion. Carlin's uncle, the mystic of the Vindhas, had told him that there were mysteries of romance that had to do with separation as well as with together, and that real mates learn this mystery through the years. To-night Skag found to his wonder that the mystic had spoken the truth.

He cooked the supper joyously and shared it with Nels, talking to him often and answering himself for the Dane. The camp was in the open and the night was presently lustrous with stars. There was a sense of well-being, together with his fresh delight in the unfolding secret of Carlin's nearness, that made him enjoy staying awake. Nels was wakeful also—as if these moments were altogether too keen with life to waste in sleep.

"It's just a ramble, old man. We'll be about it early," Skag said toward the last. "We may find what we're after and we may not. In any case we'll live on the way."

That was Skag's old picture of the Now; making the most of the ever-moving point named the Present.

"And I'm expecting great things from you, my son—an altogether new brand of self-control—if we find what we're out after. I don't mind telling you that it's Tiger, Nels—tiger babies possibly—little orphans just grown enough to be demons and just knowing enough not to behave."

Nels woofed.

"Half-grown tiger cubs are apt to be a whole lot meaner than their parents," Skag went on. "Wild—that's the word. They haven't sense enough to be careful or mind enough to be appealed to. I think that's something of what I mean to say."

Skag was taking more pains to explain than he would to a man. Nels didn't get it—didn't even make a pretense. He knew what Tiger meant, but so far as he was concerned that subject had been dropped some moments since. He had listened intently to the point in which Tiger ceased to be the topic—sitting on his haunches. Then he dropped to his front elbows, and as Skag's voice trailed away he rolled quietly to his side, keeping himself courteously awake.

There was silence. Skag's eyes were far off among the blazing Indian stars.

"We'll manage 'em together," he added sleepily. The next day they wandered—rough desolate country in burning sunlight. It gave the impression that the whole surface crust of earth had been burned to a white heat ages ago. Low hills with clifflike faces; shallow nullahs used only a month or two a year to carry the monsoon deluges to the Nerbudda; the stones of the river bottoms bone-white—everywhere sparse and scrubby foliage with dust-covered leaves. There was no turf in this stony world except the sand of the hollows and the wind eddied most of these spaces like water, quickly covering all tracks. It was toward the end of the afternoon that Nels first intimated a scent.

Tiger of course—that was Nels' orders—but it wasn't fresh. Skag gave the Dane word to do the best he could and followed leisurely. The big fellow worked with painful care for more than an hour before he became sure of himself; then his speed quickened, following a dry nullah at last, for several miles. The dark was creeping in before they came to a deep fissure among the rocks where the empty waterway sunk into a pool which was not yet dry. Skag and the Dane drank deep; then the man filled his canteen, with the remark:

"We'll camp a little back, not to obstruct the water hole. All trails end here. To-morrow morning we'll get fresh tiger scent if we're in luck. But I wonder what we're trailing?"

It was a fact of long establishment among the villages that only the one mated pair worked this section of the country. According to one of the stories of the English hunter, the male tiger had been killed and the female wounded—in which case what was this? Certainly there was nothing to indicate that the scent was left by a wounded tiger. Others might have doubted Nels' discrimination, but Skag scouted that in his own mind. The Dane knew Tiger. It was as distinct and individual to him from the other big cats as the voices of friends one from another.

Nels was said to have met Tiger in battle before he came to Skag, but it was no purpose of his present master to give him a chance now. It was established that several of the great Indian hunting dogs had survived such meetings. Malcolm M'Cord declared that a veteran in the cheetah game would show himself master in any ordinary tiger affair.

They were tired and sun drained. Skag laid down his blankets in the early dusk and there were hours of sleep before he was awakened by the different activities at the water hole. Nels apparently had been awake for some time, studying the separate noises in a moveless calm. Skag touched his chest affectionately. A panther or some smaller cat had just made a kill among the rocks above the pool, yet Nels' hackles had not lifted in answer to the bawl of the stricken beast.

"Spotted deer possibly," Skag muttered. Then he added to

the Dane:

"You're an all-right chap to camp with, son. You'd sit it out alone until they brought the fracas to our doorstep rather than disturb a friend's sleep. That's what I call being a white man."

Skag always thought of Cadman as the unparallelled comrade for field work. In fact, he had learned many of the little niceties of the open from the much-travelled American artist and writer—finished performances of comradeship, a regard for the unwritten things, reverence for those rights which never could be brought to the point of words, but which give delicacy and delectation to hours together between men. Skag never ceased to delight in the silence and self-control of the Dane. The dog rippled and thrilled with all the fundamental elements of friendship and fidelity, but his big body seemed able to contain them with a dignity that endeared him to the one who understood. Bhanah's work in the training of this fellow was nothing short of consummate art.

Breakfasting together, Skag refreshed Nels' mind with the work of the day—that it meant Tiger, that all lesser affairs might come and go. The big fellow was up and eager to be off, before Skag finished strapping his blanket roll. There was rather a memorable moment of sentiency just there. Skag was on one knee as he glanced into Nels' face. His own powers were highly awake that minute, so that he actually sensed what was in the dog's mind—that they must go down to the pool for a look before moving on. The thing was verified a moment later when Nels led the way down into the dim ravine to the margin of the water.

Tiger tracks—full four feet on the soft black margin of the pool—a huge beast, unmarked by any toe scar or eccentricity. Long body, heavy, a perfect thing of his kind. It was as if the tiger had stood some moments listening. Yet the natives declared that only the mated pair operated in this range and the hunter was said to have killed the male. If these were the tracks of the tigress she certainly was not badly hurt. There wasn't the overpressure of a single pad to indicate her favouring a muscle anywhere. And this couldn't have been the track of anything but a mature beast—the finished print of a perfect specimen.

"That hunter didn't tell it all, Nels, or else he didn't do it all," Skag remarked. "We started out to find a sick tigress and a hamper of neglected babies. I'm not saying we won't find that much. The thing is, we may find more."

Nels was already five yards away across the pebbly hollow, waiting for Skag to follow along the ravine. Not a sign of a track that human eye could detect after that—straight, dry, stony nullah bed, deeply shadowed from the narrow walls and stretching ahead apparently for miles. At least it was cool work; the sun would not touch the floor of the fissure for hours yet. Nels never faltered. His pace gradually quickened until Skag softly called. The Dane would remember for fifteen or twenty minutes, when Skag, again finding that he had to step uncomfortably fast to keep up, would laughingly call a check. The man was watching the walls and the coverts of broken rock, and Nels' speed, if left alone, altogether occupied his outer faculties.

It was eleven in the forenoon and Skag reckoned they must be close to the Nerbudda when Nels halted—even bristled a bit, his broad black muzzle quivering and held aloft. Skag came up softly and stood close. He touched his finger to his tongue and drew a moist line under his nostrils, trying to get the message that Nels was working with so obviously. Presently an almost noiseless chuckle came from the man, and he touched Nels' shoulder as if to say that he had it too. The thing had come unexpectedly—the faintest possible taint of a lair.

They would have passed it a hundred times if it had not been for the scent. The silence was absolute and the walls of the fissure apparently as unbroken as usual. No human eyes would have noted the wear of pads upon the stones, and one had to pass and look back to see the cleft in the walls of the ravine, far above the high-water mark, which formed the door of significant meaning for the man. Nels hadn't seen this much, but he couldn't miss now. He nosed the pebbles again and made an abrupt turn to the right. They climbed to the rocks near the entrance. The taint was unmistakable now—past doubt a bone pile of some kind in there—and Nels had followed Tiger to the door.

Skag sat down upon a stone a little below and mopped his forehead, with a smile at the Dane. For ten minutes he sat there. He thought of the first time he had ever entered a tiger cage as a mere boy, way back in the Middle West of the States, travelling with the circus. A bored show tiger in that cage, and he had blinked unconcernedly at the boy. Years of circus life had atrophied that tiger's organs of resentment. Miles and miles of the public stream had passed his cage with awe, speculating upon the great cat's ferocity. Skag had merely to learn after that, the trick of it all—that one's perfect self-control not only soothes but disarms most normal beasts. Skag had cultivated such self-control in recent years to a degree that made him the astonishment of many Hindu minds. India had shown him that the attainment of this sort of poise is a stage of the same mastery that the mystics are out after—to gain complete command of the menagerie in one's own insides. Hundreds of times after that, night and day, in storm, in sultry weather, Skag had entered the cages of all kinds of animals in all their moods.

His first adventure in India came back, when with his friend Cadman he had fallen into the pit trap and the grand young male tiger had tumbled after them. Skag had prevailed upon the nervy Cadman to sit tight and not to shoot, against all that the writer man knew; also he had appeared to prevail upon the tiger to keep his side of the pit until they were rescued. And now Skag recalled the big tiger that had lain on the river margin near the Monkey Glen while he had told Carlin that he had never really seen what a woman was like before. The presence of the big sleepy cat down among the wet foliage had nerved him and called out all his strength for that romantic crisis.

He thought of the moment under the poised head of the great serpent in the place of fear in the grass jungle; and of the coming of Nut Kut, the incomparable black elephant, whom he had forced to listen in spite of the red hell in the untamable eyes. Always between and in and round, his thoughts were of Carlin—her voice, her presence, the curious art of her ministration and the utterly wise lure of her heart. Even now he couldn't quite be calm under the whip of memory of the afternoon of the cobra fight. The whole panorama might have been named Carlin so far as Skag was concerned.

He didn't think of his own danger now. It wasn't that he ignored it; rather that he had entered upon a new dimension of his power. He had no thought of failure. No thought came to him that Carlin would have prevented his entering had she been near. This was different from anything he had ever been called to do, but his power was different. The thing that engaged his mind was utterly clear from every angle. He couldn't have missed the novelty from the unusual stress of Nels' manner. The big Dane was actually burning with excitement. His eyes were filled with firelight and back of the smoky burning was a dumb appeal turned to his chief. Hyenas alone had been able to break Nels' nerve for himself, but he was frightened now for the man. The big bony jowl was steadily pressed like a knuckled hand against Skag's knee, the body only half lifted from the dry stones and cramped with tension.

Skag's eyes were turned up toward the mouth of the lair and his left hand fell to the Dane's head. The beast actually shook because his eyes were covered a second.

"Of course you're to stay outside, Nels," he said softly as he rose.

The dog lowered his breast to the stones. It was like a blow to him—the one thing he had feared most.

"Don't, Nels!" the man muttered. "You're to stand at the mouth of the lair and watch there. I need you there—outside, of course."

The dog followed him heavily up the slope past the high-water mark. Skag turned with a cheering whisper, shielding his eyes from the light for a moment before peering in. There was a sound like blown paper across a marble floor and then another sound—low, soft, prolonged, like the hiss of escaping steam.

Skag shoved himself into the narrow, rocky aperture. He could see nothing for the moment. The taint was oppressive at the first breath of the still air. There were kittens—no doubt of that. He heard their scurrying; he felt their eyes and the sort of melting panic in the place that would have utterly unstrung any but a perfectly keyed set of nerves.

It was a cave, the mouth higher than the floor. The way down was jagged and precipitous. Skag, advancing softly, had to feel for each step and yet give no distracting attention to keep his footing, for the full energy of his faculties was directed ahead.

The sound of blown paper was from the kittens—that was clear enough. Yet the hissing continued and this was the mystery of it all—that there appeared to be no movement besides. If this sound came from the tigress, at least, she had not stirred to meet him.

The hiss sunk to a low guttural grating. No cub had a cavernous profundity of sound such as that. Still there was not the stir of a muscle, so far as his senses had detected.

Skag was puzzled. Big game before him, possibly nerved to spring, and yet the tensity was not like that. The man stood still, waiting for his eyes to adjust to the darkness—waiting for the mystery to clear. Then to the right, like a little constellation suddenly pricking through the twilight, Skag saw a cluster of young stars. His heart warmed—kittens hunched there in a bundle and watching him. Their pricked ears presently shadowed somewhat from the blacker background; then he saw the little party suddenly swept and overturned, as if a long thin arm had brushed them back out of reach of the intruder.

Now his eyes turned slightly to the left and began to get the rest—the great levelled creature upon the darkened floor. Skag kept his imagination down until his optic nerves actually brought him the picture. The long thin sweep was the mother's tail, yet she was not crouched. Skag saw her sprawled paws extended toward him. She lay upon her side.

Thus it was that he was rounded back to the original proposition. He had found the lair of the wounded tigress and her young. For fully two minutes Skag stood quiet before her, working softly—her hiss changing at slow intervals to the cavernous growl. The kittens were too young to organise attack—the tigress was too maimed for resistance, even though at bay in lair with her kittens to defend.

Now the man saw the gleam of her eyes. She had followed his movements and was holding him now, but half vacantly. The pity of it all touched him; the rest of the story cleared. Her tongue was like a blown bag, the blackness of it apparent even in the dark. She was dying of thirst, the bullet wound in the shoulder turned up to him. The little ones were still active, for the tigress had fed them until her whole body was drained. He saw how her breast had been torn by the thirsty little ones—the open sores against the soft grey of her nether parts. Skag backed out. Nels pressed him—half lifted his great body in silent welcome.

"Oh, yes," Skag was saying, "we got the call, all right, my son. Four little duds in there eating their mother alive, and she full of fever from a wound—no water for days. I'm just after the canteen, Nels."

Skag entered again. His movements were deliberate, but not stealthy. He spoke softly to the creature on the floor—his voice lower than the usual pitch, yet sinking often deeper still. The words were mere nothings, but they carried the man's purpose of kindness—carried it steadily, tirelessly. The great beast tried to rise as he stepped closer. Skag waited, still talking. He had uncorked the canteen and held it forward—his idea being not only that she would smell the water but become accustomed to the thing in his hand. Each time he pressed a bit nearer she struggled to rise toward him—Skag standing just out of reach, tirelessly working with his mind and voice. He keenly registered her pain and helplessness in his own consciousness and was unwilling to prolong it, yet at the same time he had a very clear understanding of the patience required to bring help to her.

It was fully a quarter of an hour before he bent close, without starting a convulsion of fear and revolt in the huge fevered body upon the rocky floor. Skag poured a gurgle of water upon the swollen tongue, watching the single baleful tortured eye that held his face. The water was not wasted, though not drunk, for it washed away some of the poison formed of the fever and the thirst. Skag poured again and for a second the great holding eye was lost to him and the tongue moved.

Thus he worked, permitting her fear and rage to rouse no answer in kind from himself; talking to her softly, luring her out of fury into the enveloping madness of her own great need.

He waited a moment and her tongue stretched thickly to draw to itself the water on the rock; then he turned toward the cubs. They scurried back deeper into the cave. He poured a gill or two of water into a hollow of the rock and returned to the mother. Presently as he moistened her tongue again, one of the little ones crept forward and began to lap the puddle on the rock.

Skag smiled in the gloom. The others were presently beside the baby leader. A few moments later Skag interrupted his ministrations to the mother to fill the hollow for the kittens again. All this with less than three pints of water—the work of a full half hour as he found when he emerged to Nels and the light.

"It's only a beginning, old man. We've got to get more water. It's five hours' march back to the pool where we camped. I'm gambling that we're a lot nearer than that to the Nerbudda."

Nels' jubilation was stayed by the unfolding of fresh plans that were not slow to dawn upon his eager mind. They hastened along the river bed, continuing in the direction they had come. Skag was in a queer elation, dropping a sentence from time to time. Suddenly he halted. It had occurred to him to recall something his mind had merely noted during the work in the cave. There was fresh meat there. He had not looked close, but at least two partly devoured carcasses had lain in the shadows.

"They were mighty thirsty, Nels," he muttered. "The mother dying of thirst, but the little ones were only sultry compared. Yes, they're old enough to tear at fresh meat. They weren't so bad off and there was plenty of meat there. Only thirsty," he added thoughtfully.

It was clear to his mind that the tigress had been helpless at least three days, possibly four. She could not have brought the game. There was one conclusive reason—that the meat was in an altogether too fresh condition to have been brought by the mother before she gave up. Skag walked rapidly. They did not reach the Nerbudda, but sighted a village back Horn the river bed after nearly two hours' walk.

They refilled the canteens and procured two water skins besides; also a broad deep gourd which Skag carried empty. The man's difficulty was to escape without assistance. A white man in his position was not supposed to carry goatskin water bags over his shoulders. The boys of the village followed him after the elders had given up, and Skag halted at last to explain that this was an affair that would interest them very much—when a teller came back to tell the story; but that this was the doing part of the story and must be carried to its conclusion alone.

A little later in the nullah bed he fastened the canteen and the gourd to Nels' collar, but continued to pack the two skins himself—a rather arduous journey in full Indian daylight with between forty and fifty pounds of water on his shoulders. It was four in the afternoon when they neared the mouth of the lair and Nels was drooping again.

"Buck up, old man!" Skag said. "I'll go in for a while with the thirsty ones. Then we'll make a camp and have some supper together."

Skag heard the hiss again as he entered the darkness, and the kittens were not so still as before. Only a trifle less leisurely he approached the mother. He knew that any strength that had come would only feed her hostility so far; that a man was not to win the confidence of a great mammal thing like this in a day. His first impulse was to silence the kittens with a gourd of water, but he could not bear to make the mother wait.

She raised her head against him as before, but the smell of the water caught and altered her fury more swiftly this time. Skag saw the glare go out from the great eye as the tortured mouth was cooled; and now the hope grew within him that the tigress might actually be saved. He talked softly to her as he poured drop by drop upon her tongue from the side—the little ones pressing closer and closer. Even in the convulsive trembling that took her body from time to time there was an inflowing rather than the ebb of strength.

Presently he left her long enough partly to fill the big gourd for the babies. He had scarcely drawn back before the first was at the edge. Lapping was not enough for this infant. He wanted to cover himself; apparently to overturn the dish upon himself. The others helped to balance the gourd for a moment or two, but the massed effort became too furious and over it went among them. Skag laughed. Only a portion was wasted, for the kittens followed the little streams on the rock, tonguing them as they moved and filled. He tried them again, only covering the bottom of the gourd, but it was as swiftly overturned. Still the young had drunk enough presently and went to tearing at the meat in the deeper shadows.

Skag went back to the mother, still using the canteen for her. Alternately now he dropped the water upon the wound in her shoulder. There were hours of work here to soften the fever crust and establish drainage. Some time afterward this work was stopped abruptly by the warning of Nels at the door. Skag stood his canteen against a rock and hurried forth. Nels stood at the mouth of the lair, his head turned up the river bed. His eyes did not alter from their look of fixity as the man emerged. The shoulder nearest Skag merely twitched a trifle, the left paw lifting to the toes. Skag followed the Dane's eyes.

The great male himself stood stock-still in the centre of the river bed, the carcass of a lamb having dropped from his mouth. So strange, so vast and still, the picture, that it seemed dreamlike; the great, round, sunny eyes unwinking—serious rather than savage—a dark-banded thing of gold in the ruddy gold of late afternoon.

Skag was silent, the magic of the moment flowing into him. Nels had not moved. Skag had been forced to walk round him to find room to stand. They faced the big Bengali together for an instant, the man's hand dropping softly to the dog's shoulder.

"The king himself, son," Skag whispered raptly. "He's the loveliest thing in stripes. We'll have to look out for this fellow, Nels. There's no fear in him. We're on his premises and the missus is sick and needs quiet. He's apt to charge, and I can see his point of view. We'll back down, son, and not obstruct the gentleman's door."

They couldn't have been three seconds clambering down the rocks to the nullah bed, yet the male tiger was twenty feet nearer when they looked up. Moreover, he had brought the lamb with him, and this time he kept it in his mouth as he watched.

"We mustn't let him see our dark side again, Nels," Skag muttered. "See if we can't stare as straight as he does. God, what a picture! Yet I'm rather glad he's got that lamb. He must have brought it far. Carrying out her orders doubtless. Only a great male would do that. Oh, it's not that he cares for the babies, Nels. It's to please her that he does it! And she's down and done, but running the lair!"

So Skag talked, hardly knowing what he said, keeping in touch with Nels with his hand and holding the eyes of the royal beast that seemed to be made of patience and poise and gilded beauty. Skag didn't step back, but presently to the side, away from the mouth of the lair. The tiger's counter movement was not to lessen the distance between them this time, but to drop to his haunches, still holding his game. He rocked a little on his hind feet, that ominous undulation which portends the charge. Not more than ten seconds passed and no outward change was apparent, yet there was a relief of tension in Skag's voice.

"It's the little lamb that saved us that time, Nels. I think we've passed it—passed the crisis, my boy. We'll just stand by now and measure patience with him."

It was two minutes before Skag ventured a further movement to the right. The tiger made absolutely no counter this time. Skag now spoke to Nels:

"You're doing beautifully, son."

The dog had stood by like part of himself. The droop and the quiver that he had known twice that day when the man disappeared into the lair had given way in the real test to unbreakable nerve and defiant heart. Yet it was less the courage than his absolute obedience that entered the man with a charge of feeling that instant. A minute later Skag took another ten steps to the right.

In the deeper shadows, less than an hour afterward, he struck a match to the little supper fire a hundred yards up the slope from the mouth of the lair. Skag then loosened his hunting belt, dropping the weight from him to the blanket with a sigh of content. The hardware had chafed him all day and had only been really forgotten in the stresses of action.

"I didn't pack that gun for tiger," he said softly. "Why, I would as soon have shot our good Arab, Kala Khan, or put a bullet between Nut Kut's eyes, as to stop that big fellow bringing young mutton home—to please her! Won't Carlin love to hear that! Oh, yes, it's been a day, son, one more day! I've loved it minute by minute, and you've been—well, I can't think in words, when it comes to that."

The big fellow drowsed in the firelight, his four paws stretched evenly toward the man.

In the morning and afternoon of the next two days Skag brought water to the tigress and bathed her shoulder long. On the third day he could not be sure that the male had left the lair until late afternoon, and when he finally ventured to the mouth and his eyes grew accustomed to the darkness within he saw that the tigress was watching him from the deeper shadows—not prone, but on three feet.

He filled the gourd and weighted it with stones; then backed out.

"We're starting for Hurda to-night, son," he said to Nels. "I've left her a drink or two, and by the time she needs more, she'll be able to get to the river herself."

Carlin must have caught the reality of that moment of crisis from Skag's telling—the moment when the male tiger might have charged but didn't, because she succeeded in making Malcolm M'Cord see it, too.

"And you say there was no sign from the tiger, but that Hantee Sahib knew when the instant was past?" the famous marksman repeated curiously.

Carlin nodded.

"But how did he know?"

"Ask him," she said.

"Huh," he muttered. "I might as well enquire of the Dane beastie."

CHAPTER XVI

FEVER BIRDS

Carlin had been listless for a day or two. This was several weeks after her forty-two hours on Mitha Baba. They were still living in Malcolm M'Cord's bungalow. Skag woke in the night, not with a dream, but rather with a memory. He was broad awake and recalled an incident that had entirely escaped his day-thoughts for a long time. It had to do with that hard-testing period, just after his meeting with Carlin, when he had journeyed to Poona to confer with the eldest brother, Roderick Deal, and had been forced to wait more than a month. In that interval he had learned about hyenas at first hand, through the plight of Beatrice Hichens and the children; also his servant Bhanah had come to him, and the Great Dane, Nels; still it had been a vague stretch of days, in retrospect.

It was during the return-trip to Hurda that the thing happened which held him now as he lay broad awake. Toward twilight, as the train halted at one of the civil stations, a white-covered cot was lifted aboard. There was a kind of silence about that station. The mountains were near on the left hand which was to the West. The white glare of Indian day had softened into delicate rose. A haze of orange and bronze lay upon the lower slopes of the mountains, magically enriching the greens; and the blue against which the mountains were contoured, was pure and immense and still. It was difficult to remember the fret and pain and discolouration of a world bathed in so vast a peace. . . .

At first he thought that the body on the cot was in its shroud. The hush about it and from the mountains touched him with a feeling that he had not quite known before, the depth of it having to do with Carlin. Then he saw, back of the natives who had lifted the cot, yet not too near, the figure of an Englishman of the Military—standing quietly by, as if casually ordering a platoon of soldiers in the duty of loading the train. Now Skag looked at the man's face. It had nothing to do with the lax grace of the officer's figure. This was the face of a man who could endure anything without a cry—a narrow face, tanned and a bit hard possibly from years of self-repression—a silent man, doubtless loved for the *feeling* around him, rather than because of what he was accustomed to say or do—a face stricken now to the verge of chaos—unchanging anguish of fear and loneliness and sorrow imprinted from within. A strange white glow, that had nothing to do with the tan, shone forth from the skin—etheric disruption, subtler than the breakdown of mere cells. This man would put a bullet in his brain if pressed too far, but he would not cry out. Just now he was close to his limit.

Skag knew something of what passed in the English officer's heart, because he himself was learning what love means. Before his hour with Carlin in the afterglow, on their way back from the monkey glen, he would never have dreamed that there was such feeling in the world; in fact, he would have been unable to read the vivid story of it in the officer's face. . . . So much in a second or two.

The cot had been partly lifted into the coach. The face now was uncovered—the white wasted face of a lovely woman, a woman still living; an utterly delicate face, telling the story of one who had never met a rough impact from the world. It was as if there had always been a strong hand between her and the grit and the grind of world-affairs—first her father's and then the lover's. In the great silence, the eyelids opened. It seemed that night and chill had suddenly come in. The lips moved. The most mournful and hopeless voice spoke straight into Skag's eyes:

"Oh, won't you please stop those fever birds!"

Skag supposed it an isolated sentence of delirium. He didn't understand. There was a drive of drama or tragedy back of it, but his mind did not give him details. He did not see the English officer again. He did not know if he entered the train. One thing Skag knew: Deep under that narrow masculine face there was a capacity for feeling that this officer's men never saw; that his closest associates never saw. The American reverenced the secret. . . . Sometimes during the hushes of the night, when the train stopped for a moment, Skag lying awake, heard the voice of the woman. There was a feeling from it utterly strange to him. It carried him out of himself, as if he shared something of her delirium and something of the man's agony.

The next day was one of the hardest that Skag ever lived, for Carlin was not at Hurda to meet him. She had gone with a strange elephant into the country. That was the day of the chase on the great young elephant Gunpat Rao, the day in which the story of the monster Kabuli unfolded. The face of the man at the mountain station and the sentence of the woman were completely erased from his surface consciousness, as the memory of an illness.

That was months away, and life had been very full in between. . . .

Carlin said she was just tired, when he went to her room in the morning. She looked at him long. It suddenly came to him vaguely, that she wasn't thinking; rather that her eyes were merely turned to his face. A queer breathlessness came to him a little later, as her head rolled to one side—such a sinking of weakness in the movement. It reminded him with a shock that she had never seemed quite tireless since that long ride on Mitha Baba's neck. But never before had her face turned away from him.

And now he saw a certain inimitable loveliness of her. There were no words to describe the last—only that it was Spirit made of all the dusks and all the white fires. There was something little about her that called an undreamed-of tenderness; and something superb and mysterious, so vast that he could be held in it like a toy in the hands.

Burning Indian day was walled and curtained and barred from the place where she lay. White of the walls, white of her face, white of the pallet—the rest a breathless, ungleaming shadow that held a heat not from the sun, as it seemed, but from the centre of the earth.

. . . Skag was away in timelessness and an unfamiliar space. This space was not fixed to one dimension, but moved back and forth. As Bhanah came to him, he saw more than Bhanah animate upon the features—like someone who had belonged always, whom he had known for ages, whom Carlin had always known. So many things struck him differently now; as if they belonged not just to this crisis, but to a crisis of eons.

Yet externals in the main were so trifling. Carlin didn't eat; people seemed to take that as significant. Malcolm M'Cord came. Margaret Annesley came. Horace Dickson's father came. Skag went to the bazaars and back again. He went to the monkey glen. It was all a blur. Once he caught himself walking on the great Highway-of-all-India; and once deep in the jungle. He passed the civil surgeon of Hurda on his own verandah; and someone said that the old "family doctor" was to come from Poona. . . . Now he was in Carlin's room and Carlin was looking at him. He saw her face the moment he entered the room, and the fact that he had come in from the fierce daylight into the shadows did, not seem to blur his eyes, even for a second.

Her people in the room—Bhanah, the ayah, the civil surgeon, Ian Deal and someone else—but the line from her eyes to Skag was not crossed. The heart of the man leaped from what he saw—the transcendent understanding which needed no words;

the look of all looks that meant *herself*—a little lingering smile on the lips, the endless lure of her wise eyes.

But all that was whipped away as he came three steps nearer her couch. The wonder of it was not taken, but the old pain returned; rather, the pain had been there all the time, but he had forgotten for a space. He saw the ashen and frail face again and the inexpressible weariness of her eyes, too tired to tell of it, too tired to stay! Then the face of the English officer appeared for his eyes—hovering back of the people, in a background of mountains. . . .

Carlin seemed listening. What she heard came out of a grey intolerable monotony; but still her eyes held his. They seemed concentrated upon some weakness of his nature—some dementia that had been before her for years, that had confronted her in every highway of life, frightened away every opportunity and spoiled every day. Her hand lifted just slightly, the palm turned toward him:

"Oh, won't you please stop those fever birds?"

. . . Then one day Skag, standing in the darkened library, heard Margaret Annesley and one of her friends speaking together in the verandah.

"But does she really hear anything?" the friend asked.

"Oh, yes; though you never hear them unless you are ill with the fever."

"How strange and terrible, and is it a particular fever?"

"Jungle fever, dear. It comes to us sometimes of itself, but more often after a shock. . . . Carlin's night in the dark—"

Skag's arm lifted in a curve to cover his face as if from a blow. . . .

Yet Margaret Annesley was not quite right; for he had learned to hear what Carlin heard:

From far away very faint, curiously thin tones came to him; always repeating one word, with an upward inflection, like a question. Every repetition sounded the fraction of a degree higher than the last, till they were far above the compass of any human voice:

"Fee-vur? fee-vur? fee-vur? fee-vur? —" and on and on.

When it began, quite low, he heard infinite patience in it; gradually, it grew full of fear; then it climbed into a veritable panic of terror.

When it stopped at last, on a long distracted "u-u-u-r-r-r-r?"— he heard the male bird's answer, sounding nearer, in deep tones of utter hopelessness, with a prolonged descending inflection:

"Bhoo-kha-a-a-r-r-r! bhoo-kha-a-a-r-r-r! bhoo-kha-a-a-r-r-r!"— the Indian word for fever, repeated only three times. Then the female began again; so, day and night—night and day.

After he had once heard it, he could always hear it. So he learned that they never rest. Always, by listening, he could hear it at some point of its maddening scale—its insane assurance of the hopelessness of jungle fever.

Skag faced the ultimatum. This was different. It had nothing to do with his world of animal dangers. This was a slow devouring which he could not touch nor stay. *Carlin was melting before his eyes. . . .* The brothers had come in, one by one, from over India. (Margaret Annesley had attended to that.) Skag met them, moved quietly about, yet could not remember their faces one from another. He answered when spoken to, but retained no registration as to whom he had spoken, or what had been said. Sometimes he was alone for a few moments with Carlin; and when her eyes were open he was appalled by the growing sense of distance in them. Then before she spoke, he would hear what she heard:

"Bhoo-kha-a-a-r-r-r! bhoo-kha-a-a-r-r-r! bhoo-kha-a-a-r-r-r!"

There were queer rifts of light in his mind, instants when he realized that all the hard moments of the past had prepared him for this. He saw clearly that he could not have endured, even to the present hour, without every experience life had shown him—especially without the difficult ones. He lived again the great moments—all the Indian afterglows that were identified with Carlin—perfect lessons of mercy she had taught him, through the very yearning of his own heart in her presence to be worthy of days with her. Never useless words from Carlin, but always the vivid meaning. He had been slow at first to see how much more magic were their days together, because she paid for them with a night-and-day readiness to go forth to the call of service to others.

Yet through all, he was utterly, changelessly desolate. Not only bitterness, but an icy bitterness, was upon all meaning and movement of life. It was almost like a conspiracy that no part in ministration was demanded of him by those who were now in his house. The doctors talked to Miss Annesley or to the servants; the brothers came and went with their fear and fidelity—but spoke to Skag of other things than the illness. Still, in his heart a concept slowly formed—that he had something which Carlin needed now; that this something had to do, though it was different, with the power he used to change animals. It seemed absurd even to think of this—with all these wise ones around him, not perceiving it. They formed a barrier of their thoughts which kept him from expression. He stood apart for hours as the days passed, thinking of his part; and yet the icy bitterness held him from action.

Sometimes his heart seemed dying; chill already upon it. Again he seemed filled with a strange vitality, other than his own. This phenomenon frightened him more than the first, so that he would hurry to look at Carlin lest the strength had come from her. He tried to *think* the strength back to her; to think all his own besides; but there was no drive to his mind-work because he did not have faith in himself.

At length came the night when the fever birds ceased for Carlin. Out of a great soft depth of tone which no one but Skag had heard before (which he had thought no other would hear until there was a baby in her arms), her words came with unforgettable intensity:

"Oh, the jungle shadows! The jungle shadows!"

After that he did not know whether it was night or day, until he heard the end of a sentence from the doctor from Poona:

". . . only four hours left to break the fever."

The room was in great still heat—heat of a burning night, a smothering heat to the couch from a distant lamp—the fire of the day coming up from the ground like flashes of anger. . . .

A strange stillness was settling on everything; the silence before had not been so heavy. The old family doctor from Poona came into it; and Margaret Annesley stood by him near the bed.

"Carlin has not spoken for more than an hour," Skag heard her tell him.

It seemed long before he answered:

"She has passed too far down into the shadows. She will not speak again."

The words came to Skag as if through limitless space; but the last ones penetrated deep and laid hold.

Margaret went out swiftly and the doctor followed. He looked a very, very old man—with his head bent, like that.

. . . She will not speak again!

The universe was falling into disruption.

It was all white where she lay. Only the heavy masses of her dark hair, spread on the pillows and across one shoulder, showed any colour—shadowed gold, shadowed red.

. . . She will not speak again!

Seven tall men filed into the room before Skag's eyes, and ranged on either side of her. These were her own brothers. Skag felt the vague pang again, of being alien to them.

Roderick Deal, the eldest—the one with the inscrutable blackness of eyes—leaned and kissed the white, white forehead; and a fold of the splendid hair.

One figure had gone down at the lower end of the bed—long arms stretched over her feet—slender dark hands clenching and unclenching. The detail of it cut into Skag, like a spear of keen pain through chaos. Returned away—it was intolerable.

. . . An arm fell about Skag's shoulders.

"Brother?" Roderick Deal's fathomless eyes drew Skag's and held them while he spoke: "We are leaving you to be alone with her—at the last!"

The arm gripped as he added:

"You are to know this—we will not fail you, now!" and he was gone. They were all gone.

Faint tones of the fever bird, ascending, came from far out. Other tones, descending, came from greater distances within . . . . She will not speak again!

Bhanah touched his sleeve.

"My Master!" The man's nearness of spirit, as he spoke, vibrated into Skag and roused him to something different, something clearer. "A mystic from the Vindha mountains has but just reached this place. They are very powerful, having great knowledge. This man is blood-kin to her. Give me permission and I will call him."

Skag looked into Bhanah's eyes, finding the ancient friendship there; then he said only one word:

"Hurry!"

Bhanah leaped away across the lawn and Skag turned to stand by Carlin's side.

The silence seemed absolute now; the whiteness absolute. He remembered that she had gone down into shadows. He bent his head toward her breast and looked down.

. . . Sense of time was gone—even the endlessness of it. Sense of whiteness was gone. His vision wakened, as he groped through deepening shadows, on and on—till they turned to utter blackness. In that utter blackness appeared a thread of pure blue; he traced it back up till it entered Carlin's body. There, it was not blue any more, but a faint glow of high white light centred in her breast and shed—like moonlight—through all her person.

The heart of his heart called to her. . . . There was no answer.

. . . He became aware that a tall slender man stood at his side; but it did not disturb him. The man wore long straight robes of camel's hair. The sense of him was strength. At last he spoke:

"Son, why do you call to her? She cannot come back—of herself. You cannot fetch her back."

"Why?" breathed Skag. "I ought to be able to."

"No," the man said kindly, "you are not able to—I am not able to—no created being is able to."

The man emphasised the word created.

"What can?" Skag asked.

"First you must learn not to depend on yourself; then you must know something of the law."

The man was holding one hand out, above Carlin's head—quite still, but not close, while he spoke. Skag felt his strength more than at first.

"Do you want her for yourself?" he asked.

Skag looked into his kind dark eyes—his own eyes speaking for him.

"Do you want her for her own sake—because she loves you? Is it that you have knowledge what will be best for her? Did you create her—did you prepare her ultimate destiny, do you even know it?"

"I know that I am in it!"

Skag answered very low, but with conviction. His eyes were agonised; but the man bored into them, without relenting.

"Do you want her to come back from the margin of departure, for the sake of others—for the sake of her ministry to their need?"

The answer to this last question came up in Skag—waves on waves, rolling into engulfing billows.

"That answer may avail!" the man said conclusively. "If it is accepted—if your love for her is perfect enough to forget itself—if you are able to make your mind altogether inactive—"

"Then how shall I work—if not with my mind?" Skag interrupted.

"First know that you yourself can do nothing." The man spoke with soft, slow emphasis. "No created being has power to do that kind of work."

"What has?" Skag asked.

"A Power that we are not worthy to name," the man answered, with reverence. "If it accepts your reason why she should stay—if your love is found to be without tarnish of self—it will work her restoration; not otherwise.

"Make yourself still. Give your mind to the apprehension of her nature—till your mind has come to be *as if it were not.* . . . Peace!"

The man dropped his head a moment, before he moved to stand at the food of her bed. With his eyes on her face he leaned, laying his palms over her feet; then, seeming to float backward to the wall, he sank slowly—to sit as the Hindus do.

The sense of his strength seemed to fill the whole room. It was the last outward thing Skag was aware of.

. . . It was as if Skag had passed through eons of ages trying to put away all the tender yearning anguish of his love for Carlin. He came to know her as a beneficent entity of high voltage—needed in more than one place.

It must be that he should make it possible for her to serve here, more potently than there—else she could not be held back. With all his strength, he would try.

"Son," the mystic's voice rang out, "now give yourself to your love for her—with your strength!"

Presently a warm glow flowed up into Skag's feet, filling his person and extending his physical sentiency into her body. That body was utterly bound in a strange vise—very heavy; as if every particle of every part were separately frozen.

. . . It seemed to Skag as if he could not breathe.

"Breathe!" the mystic said, as he rose from the floor to stand on his own feet.

That instant an impact of force from him struck Skag like a blow; and the next moment his sense of strength had become like that of twenty men—it was hard to bear.

"Steady—slow!" It was a soft, but imperative order.

Gradually the warmth increased; not in degree, but in the rate of its flow. At last it was a surge, so intense that Skag could feel his own blood-pulse—a different kind of pulse.

The need of help was very great. There was a faintness—surely more terrible than any death!

"Fear not!" the mystic called tenderly. "The Supreme Power cares for her—more than you can!"

As he heard these words, a great tide rose up into Skag, penetrating his body and his mind and the uttermost deeps of his consciousness. A vast sweeping tide—it descended below all depths, it ascended above all heights, it compassed all reaches. It was ineffable love—transcendent. It was for her! But it was for him—too! Nay—it was for every living thing in this mortal condition and in all other conditions!

. . . Carlin turned her head a little, lifted one hand a little and sighed deeply. Then she moved till she lay easily on one side, just murmuring:

"I think I'll sleep."

Carlin had spoken again!

"Son" (the mystic spoke very softly, while he drew Skag to a large couch in the same room), "it is finished. She is altogether safe now. You should be this far away; stretch yourself here and give yourself to sleep also—it will be best for her if you do.

"Be at perfect rest—there is no fear. (I will give Bhanah directions.) Now—Peace be on thee; and on thy house, forever!"

His words permitted no answer. He went and smiled down on Carlin. He touched her forehead with his finger-tips—he even kissed her curling hair.

"Child of my brother's love!" he said softly, as he turned away.

Then Skag also slept.

Friedrich Kerst
Friedrich Nietzsche
Fyodor Dostoyevsky
G.A. Henty
G.K. Chesterton
Gabrielle E. Jackson
Garrett P. Serviss
Gaston Leroux
George A. Warren
George Ade
Geroge Bernard Shaw
George Cary Eggleston
George Durston
George Ebers
George Eliot
George Gissing
George MacDonald
George Meredith
George Orwell
George Sylvester Viereck
George Tucker
George W. Cable
George Wharton James
Gertrude Atherton
Gordon Casserly
Grace E. King
Grace Gallatin
Grace Greenwood
Grant Allen
Guillermo A. Sherwell
Gulielma Zollinger
Gustav Flaubert
H. A. Cody
H. B. Irving
H.C. Bailey
H. G. Wells
H. H. Munro
H. Irving Hancock
H. R. Naylor
H. Rider Haggard
H. W. C. Davis
Haldeman Julius
Hall Caine
Hamilton Wright Mabie
Hans Christian Andersen
Harold Avery
Harold McGrath
Harriet Beecher Stowe
Harry Castlemon
Harry Coghill
Harry Houidini

Hayden Carruth
Helent Hunt Jackson
Helen Nicolay
Hendrik Conscience
Hendy David Thoreau
Henri Barbusse
Henrik Ibsen
Henry Adams
Henry Ford
Henry Frost
Henry James
Henry Jones Ford
Henry Seton Merriman
Henry W Longfellow
Herbert A. Giles
Herbert Carter
Herbert N. Casson
Herman Hesse
Hildegard G. Frey
Homer
Honore De Balzac
Horace B. Day
Horace Walpole
Horatio Alger Jr.
Howard Pyle
Howard R. Garis
Hugh Lofting
Hugh Walpole
Humphry Ward
Ian Maclaren
Inez Haynes Gillmore
Irving Bacheller
Isabel Cecilia Williams
Isabel Hornibrook
Israel Abrahams
Ivan Turgenev
J.G.Austin
J. Henri Fabre
J. M. Barrie
J. M. Walsh
J. Macdonald Oxley
J. R. Miller
J. S. Fletcher
J. S. Knowles
J. Storer Clouston
J. W. Duffield
Jack London
Jacob Abbott
James Allen
James Andrews
James Baldwin

James Branch Cabell
James DeMille
James Joyce
James Lane Allen
James Lane Allen
James Oliver Curwood
James Oppenheim
James Otis
James R. Driscoll
Jane Abbott
Jane Austen
Jane L. Stewart
Janet Aldridge
Jens Peter Jacobsen
Jerome K. Jerome
Jessie Graham Flower
John Buchan
John Burroughs
John Cournos
John F. Kennedy
John Gay
John Glasworthy
John Habberton
John Joy Bell
John Kendrick Bangs
John Milton
John Philip Sousa
John Taintor Foote
Jonas Lauritz Idemil Lie
Jonathan Swift
Joseph A. Altsheler
Joseph Carey
Joseph Conrad
Joseph E. Badger Jr
Joseph Hergesheimer
Joseph Jacobs
Jules Vernes
Julian Hawthrone
Julie A Lippmann
Justin Huntly McCarthy
Kakuzo Okakura
Karle Wilson Baker
Kate Chopin
Kenneth Grahame
Kenneth McGaffey
Kate Langley Bosher
Kate Langley Bosher
Katherine Cecil Thurston
Katherine Stokes
L. A. Abbot
L. T. Meade

L. Frank Baum
Latta Griswold
Laura Dent Crane
Laura Lee Hope
Laurence Housman
Lawrence Beasley
Leo Tolstoy
Leonid Andreyev
Lewis Carroll
Lewis Sperry Chafer
Lilian Bell
Lloyd Osbourne
Louis Hughes
Louis Joseph Vance
Louis Tracy
Louisa May Alcott
Lucy Fitch Perkins
Lucy Maud Montgomery
Luther Benson
Lydia Miller Middleton
Lyndon Orr
M. Corvus
M. H. Adams
Margaret E. Sangster
Margret Howth
Margaret Vandercook
Margaret W. Hungerford
Margret Penrose
Maria Edgeworth
Maria Thompson Daviess
Mariano Azuela
Marion Polk Angellotti
Mark Overton
Mark Twain
Mary Austin
Mary Catherine Crowley
Mary Cole
Mary Hastings Bradley
Mary Roberts Rinehart
Mary Rowlandson
M. Wollstonecraft Shelley
Maud Lindsay
Max Beerbohm
Myra Kelly
Nathaniel Hawthrone
Nicolo Machiavelli
O. F. Walton
Oscar Wilde
Owen Johnson
P.G. Wodehouse
Paul and Mabel Thorne
Paul G. Tomlinson
Paul Severing
Percy Brebner
Percy Keese Fitzhugh
Peter B. Kyne
Plato
Quincy Allen
R. Derby Holmes
R. L. Stevenson
R. S. Ball
Rabindranath Tagore
Rahul Alvares
Ralph Bonehill
Ralph Henry Barbour
Ralph Victor
Ralph Waldo Emmerson
Rene Descartes
Ray Cummings
Rex Beach
Rex E. Beach
Richard Harding Davis
Richard Jefferies
Richard Le Gallienne
Robert Barr
Robert Frost
Robert Gordon Anderson
Robert L. Drake
Robert Lansing
Robert Lynd
Robert Michael Ballantyne
Robert W. Chambers
Rosa Nouchette Carey
Rudyard Kipling
Saint Augustine
Samuel B. Allison
Samuel Hopkins Adams
Sarah Bernhardt
Sarah C. Hallowell
Selma Lagerlof
Sherwood Anderson
Sigmund Freud
Standish O'Grady
Stanley Weyman
Stella Benson
Stella M. Francis
Stephen Crane
Stewart Edward White
Stijn Streuvels
Swami Abhedananda
Swami Parmananda
T. S. Ackland
T. S. Arthur
The Princess Der Ling
Thomas A. Janvier
Thomas A Kempis
Thomas Anderton
Thomas Bailey Aldrich
Thomas Bulfinch
Thomas De Quincey
Thomas Dixon
Thomas H. Huxley
Thomas Hardy
Thomas More
Thornton W. Burgess
U. S. Grant
Upton Sinclair
Valentine Williams
Various Authors
Vaughan Kester
Victor Appleton
Victor G. Durham
Victoria Cross
Virginia Woolf
Wadsworth Camp
Walter Camp
Walter Scott
Washington Irving
Wilbur Lawton
Wilkie Collins
Willa Cather
Willard F. Baker
William Dean Howells
William le Queux
W. Makepeace Thackeray
William W. Walter
William Shakespeare
Winston Churchill
Yei Theodora Ozaki
Yogi Ramacharaka
Young E. Allison
Zane Grey

www.ingramcontent.com/pod-product-compliance
Lightning Source LLC
Chambersburg PA
CBHW020554310726
48979CB00008B/1208/J

* 9 7 8 1 4 2 1 8 3 9 1 9 6 *